My Son's Girlfriend

LIBRARY OF KOREAN LITERATURE

4

My Son's Girlfriend

Jung Mi-kyung

Translated by
Yu Young-nan

DALKEY ARCHIVE PRESS
CHAMPAIGN / LONDON / DUBLIN

Originally published in Korean as *Nae adŭl ŭi yŏnin* by Munhak Tongne, Paju, 2008

Library of Congress Cataloging-in-Publication Data

Chong, Mi-gyong, 1960- author.
[Nae adul ui yonin. English]
My Son's Girlfriend / Jung Mi-kyung ; translated by Yu Young-nan. -- First edition.
pages cm
ISBN 978-1-56478-910-5 (acid-free paper)
1. Short stories, Korean. I. Yu, Yong-nan, translator. II. Title.
PL994.2.M54A2 2013
895.7'35--dc23
2013027220

Partially funded by a grant from the Illinois Arts Council, a state agency

Library of Korean Literature
Published in collaboration with the Literature Translation Institute of Korea

LTI Korea
Literature Translation Institute of Korea

www.dalkeyarchive.com

Cover: design and composition by Mikhail Iliatov

Thanks to Wei-Ling Woo of Epigram Books (Singapore)
for helping with the editing of this book.

Printed on permanent/durable acid-free paper

Table of Contents

I Love You

Images on the television screen sway like a pendulum.

People in summer clothes dart off like surprised fish, their faces taut with fear. But no one screams. A wooden building sways to and fro and collapses. A cloud of dust rises in its place. A road twists and cars fly off the tarmac. A raised highway has collapsed into neat pieces, heightening the drama. The image on the screen stops wavering and comes into focus. The camera settles on an old man's face.

"My house . . . it's gone." His voice is calm, as if he had known it would happen. Words appear at the bottom of the screen: Earthquake Site, Niigata Prefecture, July 16.

I would have been calmer if I'd been at the earthquake site. If I had other people to share the experience with, even fear would be tolerable, wouldn't it? This was what I thought, my eyes glued to the images of catastrophe. Having spent days fretting all by myself and feeling anxious, I felt envious. Still, I had to finish what I had been saying to Y.

"Just six months. Till the end of the year. You'd be surprised how time flies."

"You're crazy!" Despite the force of her words, her voice was calm.

Neither high- nor low-pitched, her voice was like that of the old man in Niigata Prefecture: *My house . . . it's gone.* Besides, she

7

didn't roll her eyes at me, revealing the whites. Did she think I was joking? A long time ago, I had told her she looked cute when she gave me dirty looks. And I'd meant it. Since then, I'd gotten countless glares from her. Women remember the most pointless things for the longest time. Now, she didn't seem to realize that the only thing that hadn't changed in the past seven years were the whites of her eyes.

At any rate, I sensed some glimmer of hope in her voice and expression. Though she had spat out the word "crazy," her brain was kicking into gear, deliberating and calculating. Seven years is long enough to see through a person's words.

"He's going on seventy," I said. (He was actually sixty-three.) "You'll be like his youngest daughter."

"Youngest daughter?" she repeated after me, as if picking up her part in a musical round. She dug out a long octopus tentacle from the soup, put it in her mouth, and chewed energetically.

"So, see him once a month or so. Go eat at a fancy restaurant and talk about the meaning of life or, you know, something like that. I'm not asking you because there are no other women out there. He says he likes brainy women."

"Then tell him to look for someone at the Judicial Research and Training Institute." Her voice took on a tinge of arrogance.

So, what? No one's got you beat in the brains department? I thought to myself. She spooned up some of the broth that had simmered down, poured it over her rice, mixed it methodically, and polished it off. Had I wanted her to explode in anger? Was seven years really long enough to understand a person, clearly and objectively? Whenever I saw her finish her food—whether she was happy or sad, mad or joyous, healthy or sick—I couldn't help but think, I'd better not mess with this woman.

She poured herself some water from the carafe, its chilly surface studded with drops of water, and knocked it back. She set down the glass as if signaling the end to a long dinner. I swallowed my saliva. If she said she wouldn't do it, then that was it. Even if all I could do was await death, I would never, ever lower myself by trying pathetically to persuade her.

If marriage had been in the picture, we would have gotten married five years ago when Y got pregnant by accident. We came to the easy conclusion that we'd be better off starting our life together after we had a stable income, but little had changed since. She had yet to find a full-time position; as for me, everything had gotten worse. To be frank, my life was teetering on the edge. Our love, once gorgeous and vivid like summer flowers, had hardened like a tree stump with the passage of time. If not completely calcified, at the very least, it had turned colorless. I liked to think of us as a 21st century family.

We'd gone through difficult patches, discussed each other's paths in life, our weight and health, economic situations, problems with our families, and dispensed disinterested advice. When a person of the opposite sex caused mild ripples in our hearts, we'd confide in each other before mentioning it to anyone else. Then we'd both critically assessed the person in question. "You think she's cute now, don't you? But you'll be supporting her for the rest of your life." Or, "A vagabond? Have fun washing his sweaty cargo pants the rest of your life. Are you ready for that?" Hearing such advice, we'd usually nod in agreement. "Yeah, you're right." You couldn't say those things to each other if you didn't feel like family. For better or worse, these nondescript figures appeared and faded away like comets. It was probably because we hadn't met anyone who was attractive enough to abandon the easy companionship we had, but more than that, our solidarity was firm. Truth was, whatever the case, when we gave each other advice, the other's happiness was our top priority.

My suggestion today, however, was a pretty tricky one. I had talked to the old man about it last week, but I swear I'd never linked Y with it. At least until a few minutes ago, when the live octopi had been in the throes of dying, their tentacles writhing desperately.

Was that the butterfly effect of live octopus?

Whatever the case, it was good we ordered the live octopi. When Y and I walked into the restaurant, the dinner crowd had just ebbed. Strewn about on the tables were pots stained with dried red sauce. Y looked around in dismay and took a seat at a table where the dishes had at least been cleared away. When we ordered octopus stew, the waitress asked, "Do you want them alive or dead?" It was a tricky question. This was not a matter of the octopi's life or death, but a question of what was fresh and what was going bad. To take it a step further, it was tantamount to a challenge, to declare whether your dinner companion was important to you or not. The word "dead," no matter how it is used in conversation, tends to dampen the mood. Dead octopus, octopus that's almost dead, octopus that has been dead for a few seconds, octopus that desires to be dead. That's right. People immediately project themselves onto the octopus. The octopus that is alive, but not really living.

That was all good. But the problem was that live octopus cost almost double. I looked at the waitress and gave her an ambiguous response: "I guess it's going to die eventually, right?" The look on her face said, "I know your type," and she shouted toward the kitchen, "Dead ones for two!" Y jerked her head up and quickly corrected her. "Miss, give us live ones." Before the waitress could shout to the kitchen again, Y addressed me in a clear voice, "Looks like you're pinching pennies after losing big money."

An intense hatred bubbled up in me, but I realized at once how absurd that was. She wouldn't have said that if she'd known how desperate I was. I couldn't blame her because I hadn't told her lately how financially hard up I was.

The waitress brought out a pot—several live octopi were resting on top of vegetables and mushrooms—and placed it on the burner. Under the glass lid, the octopi began to investigate their unfamiliar surroundings, cautiously stretching their legs on the bed of shredded cabbage. "How's it going?" Y asked absent-mindedly. "So-so." The more dire the situation, the less inclined I was to whine. Y didn't probe. Rather than spoiling the mood, we tacitly agreed to enjoy the live octopi. Their legs and heads quickly turned red and splotchy. They seemed to be in real pain, judging by the way each of their tentacles squirmed frenetically. Gazing at the way they moved, Y mumbled sadly, "Life is tough for you guys, too." Her expression spoke volumes. "What, did something happen?" I asked. The waitress came over with a pair of scissors and haphazardly chopped up the octopi into bite-sized pieces, then roughly mixed them in with the vegetables. She went away.

"It's all over." Despite the calm in her voice, her face was shadowed with deep regret—there was something unfinished, or something she couldn't give up. The spicy red broth bubbled over vigorously. After scooping up a generous amount of watercress, Y's favorite, and with the now-dead octopus into her bowl, I urged her to tell me. A string of words rolled off her tongue, and what I heard was far from "it's all over."

Up until two years ago, Y had been looking for a position at a university, having set Metropolitan Seoul University as her final line of defense. Since last year, however, she had vowed she was ready to rent a moving van the moment a job offer came in and rush off to any hick town, but she'd stopped bringing up the subject for some time now. It looked like she was hurt, her pride bruised. I didn't ask unless she mentioned it herself. Now she confessed that it was a university in South Chungcheong Province, far inland at that, and that she'd made the list of finalists. She'd given an open lecture and had been interviewed afterward. "How were you able to keep the news to yourself? Weren't you itching to tell me? When did this happen?" I asked a stream of questions. "The day before yesterday," she replied. I demanded, "Why didn't you tell me?" She pouted and said, "The people there asked me, as if it was nothing, 'Can you contribute around 200 million won to our development fund?'"

Then, as if she'd seen and heard everything, she said disdainfully, "They're not even in North Chungcheong Province!"

I swallowed my comeback: Would you have the money if the school were in North Chungcheong Province? Instead, I asked, "So, what did you say?" She slowly chewed on an octopus tentacle. If she'd flatly refused the school administration, I'd have heard about it almost in real-time as she rode the bus back to Seoul. She'd probably left the school after giving a vague answer. But it would have been much better if she'd said no unequivocally. I thought, 200 million won? It was all because of me. She'd heard the comment I'd dropped about the hundreds of millions that I moved daily, and now it looked like she'd completely lost her sense of proportion, how much hundreds of millions meant. For her benefit, I started ranting.

"Development fund? Who's it for? Are they even a university? I've never even heard of the name. If they have the nerve to demand 200 million, how much do the real schools demand? Two billion won?" Y gazed at me, her eyes letting me know I was making a fool of myself. She retorted, "You really don't know what's going on in academia? If you drew a graph, the reputation of a school would be inversely related to the size of its development fund. What matters," she paused here to ladle some broth and bring it up to her mouth, "is if you can get a position anywhere that way, you'll be poised for the next move to your dream job."

Contrary to what I'd thought, seven years was not long enough to understand someone clearly and objectively. I had no idea she was tormenting herself over 200 million won just to get somewhere in life. I don't know exactly when I started nodding in earnest. Both of us had fallen, simultaneously, into the same hellish inferno. Then I had an epiphany. We could be pulled out of the quagmire, like the good brother and sister in the fairytale who are rescued by the hemp ropes tied around their waists. With my eyes clamped shut, ready to be slapped on the cheek but in a tone that suggested it was no big deal, just as we'd changed to the live octopi when we didn't care for the dead ones, I threw out the topic of "just six months."

I said, "How long will the old man live, anyway?" This was too much of an exaggeration when describing a sixty-three-year-old man who was healthy except for his prostate. In fact, he was in good health. I went on, "He's been flailing over the futility of life recently, like he's suffering from apathy. He has a wife, but she makes him lonelier than he would be without one, and he's lost his zest for life. He's in his twilight years, and he won't be scrimping if someone, whoever she is, should become a beacon for him and light up what's left of his life. Just tell him you'd like to borrow it. Hey, for him 200 million is like a scoop of water from the Han River. What I mean is that I want you to act like you're his friend, his youngest daughter, say, for six months."

I grew verbose, as if I'd rehearsed this speech before coming to see her. I sounded like a nun who was trying to talk people into a hospice volunteer program for the terminally ill. But when all is said and done, don't all negotiations boil down to just that?

Y was well aware of the old man's wealth. She knew a lot of other things about him, too. The old man's thirty-year-old daughter, who was mentally retarded, had a crush on me; she would steal behind me, sneak her hand into my shirt, and caress my chest, giggling in delight. His son had been a constant headache as he was addicted to computer games and always glued to the screen, but now the old man had given up on him completely. His wife had seventeen fur coats, all of different colors and lengths, hanging in her closet, and was quite irritated by global warming. He'd recently collected 7.5 billion won from the government for a piece of land that had been absorbed into the new municipal development project, but that was a small sum for him. He'd hired three experts to manage his assets, but he couldn't trust any of us, so his daily work consisted of keeping an eye on us and constantly suspecting the worst. Y might have let these details go in one ear and out the other because they didn't concern her.

Of course, there were things she didn't know yet. The old man had no inkling of the losses I'd incurred; I had to recover the principal somehow before the next financial audit, but there was no way I could do so with the remaining funds in my account; I could trade again only after the old man could be persuaded to shell out another investment; if not, my personal assets, meager as they were, would be wiped out in a flash, and to boot, I would find myself sitting on a mountain of debt; so, to win him over, and to divert his attention, I had volunteered to play royal emissary in search of a beautiful damsel.

"Six months?" Y mumbled, after taking a sip of the rice punch served for dessert.

"Yeah. So until the end of this year, at most."

From *You are crazy!* to *Six months*, I felt as if I'd shut my eyes tight and leapt over a gulf, its bottom far down in the dizzying distance. Y spun her punch bowl round and round. I couldn't explain how I was feeling. "Six months?" she had asked, and I worried that my explanation hadn't been clear enough. What were these tangled emotions flitting through my heart? Did I want Y to snap at me in anger, glare fiercely, and widen her eyes in disbelief, even if it meant finding myself listening for the bell that would at any moment announce the end of my life, even if I were to die a miserable death in the office tomorrow? We left and got into my car. I had been planning to go to bed after dropping her off, but when I saw Y's pensive profile, with her pouting lips and eyes fixed outside the window, I was suddenly aroused.

"You want to stop by my place?"

"Your place?"

Was this some kind of personal pronoun game? Come to think of it, her diction had been a little off tonight. Before, she had lisped *Six months?* like a child learning to speak, her eyes blinking, and now what kind of game was she playing, answering my question with a question when she knew full well we were talking about the same old place. What she seemed to mean was, *You're the one who brought it up, not me. I don't know anything. Is it okay for us to do it? Since I know nothing, you're responsible for the consequences.*

At the sound of her voice, my insides wriggled with displeasure, but they burned with lust all the same.

As soon as we stepped inside, Y went to the bathroom. She came out grumbling. "Look at your bathroom! Will you please clean it sometime? A bathroom is the face of your home. It advertises what your home is like, what kind of person you are."

She sounded like a showroom hostess for a new condominium project. When we first started going out, we used to rendezvous in upscale motels as a matter of course, partly because we were in better financial shape, and also because we still cared to save face with each other. Since the beginning of this year, however, her nagging had increased dramatically. She didn't wash dishes for me, but she made faces at the dishes piled up in my sink—acting no differently from a wife.

After entering the bedroom, we took off our own clothes. I turned on the air conditioning, and she turned off the light. Her breasts glowed white in the light coming from outside. They still looked good, though the effects of seven years of gravity were fully evident. "Put some music on, will you?" she grumbled, as if by rote. "There's a lot of music in the world, but your groans and moans are the best music to my ears," I said. I pushed my tongue into her mouth. A pungent sting, whether from my tongue or hers, spread from the tips of our tongues. I got on top first, then she rode me. Right before she came, she called out my name, as she always did. Stroking her hot, wet back with my palms, I said, "I love you, I love you."

Other than my whispering a few times that I loved her, our sex was no different from any other day.

It all began because of the prostate.

Since the beginning of the year, the old man's trips to the bathroom had grown noticeably more frequent. After he came out, he would have a deeply dissatisfied look on his face, and he would sigh heavily, as if he had nothing to live for anymore. That's not fair, I thought. If even the old man could frown, what about the multitudes who led truly tough lives?

When I bumped into him at the bathroom door, I asked, just to be polite, "Sir, is everything all right with you?" "Uh, the problem is, my prosate is giving me trouble . . ." The old man pronounced prostate as *prosate*. When he enunciated it that way, it somehow had a ring of affluence. From the look on his face, the prostate problems were worse than cancer. I felt I needed to deliver some sincere, comforting words.

"About that, um, I heard the best remedy for prostate problems is a healthy sex life."

I'd heard that by chance. Everything in my own life was a mess except for my prostate.

"That so?"

"Yes. However busy you are, your health comes first. Let me think about what I can do for you."

The old man, as wary as an old female cat, blinked a few times.

I observed the back of the old man's head as he sipped tea and looked out at the well-manicured garden. I'd always thought he had it all. What did "all" refer to here? The huge, beautiful house, the underlings who would die if he so wished, the tonics for longevity crammed in his refrigerator, the money that spawned interest by the minute, by the day, even while he was sleeping, a man who didn't have the vaguest idea what an overdrawn bank account meant. What was tangible happiness to him, the man buried deep in the armchair upholstered in buffalo leather? The back of his head struck me as unexpectedly forlorn. His face projected an image of arrogance, fastidiousness, self-sufficiency, of a man who was accustomed to playing king in his self-made kingdom, but the back of his head exuded a sense of emptiness, as though his vitality were seeping out through some invisible hole. I recalled a story in which a man who can make a sad princess smile is promised heirship to the kingdom. A path seemed to reveal itself.

The following scene played out exactly a week ago.

"Sir, do you have a girlfriend?" I asked lightly, as if tossing out a joke. I had approached him when Miss Jang had stepped out briefly.

The old man looked up from sipping his green tea. The look on his face said, Where is this coming from? Though I had asked the question, I wasn't totally in the dark. I spent six days a week with him. Men, as a rule, never hide their personal lives; if anything, they exaggerate them. He'd given up intimacy with his wife long ago and paid for women from time to time. He never asked for the same woman twice, however. I was well aware that he didn't even have male friends, let alone a girlfriend.

I ventured, "When it comes to friendship, age is not so important. I looked around because I thought it would be great if you had someone to see from time to time, to share a meal or go on a trip with. Once your prostate problem is solved, life will be smooth sailing, won't it? It isn't easy. If a woman is too beautiful, she'll attract too much attention. That would be inconvenient. And if she's too young, that gets tiresome. Thin women look good, but in practice . . . well, surely you know. The best is a woman who can hold a conversation . . . And it turns out there's someone who fits the bill. She's a friend of my sister's. She's over thirty, still single because of her studies, but she doesn't look her age. She's an intelligent woman who lectures at some universities. In my opinion, she's perfect. So I was thinking of introducing her to you."

The old man was sitting with his back against the light, so I couldn't read his expression, but he didn't say yes or no. He grabbed three grapes from his plate and handed them to me.

"Have some."

Good thing he wasn't giving me a piece of meat. I'd have felt like his loyal dog. With the grapes lightly clenched in my fist, I shut the door behind me. Suddenly I got confused. Had I told him that she was a friend of my sister's or my friend's sister? You have to be smart to make up a good lie. I grew impatient. Time was running out.

"Professor, what's your opinion on the sudden summit meeting?" the old man asked seriously, his eyes fixed on Y, as soon as the formal introduction was over.

I almost spat out my orange juice. I managed to swallow it, but it went down the wrong way. A series of small coughs ensued. Why was he bringing up the North-South summit here, and as the first topic of conversation at that? He must have prepared for this meeting in his own way, working off the information I'd given him that Y specialized in political science. In reality, she was practically allergic to politics. I lied so the old man, who had studied political science in college, would feel more at ease, but I had no idea he'd go along with it to this degree. Y majored in zoology, but she usually said her major was biology. Since human beings were animals, too, I didn't think I'd told a whopping lie; zoology isn't such a departure from political science, is it?

Don't be late. I had called her before we left the office, and she said she was at the hairdresser's and was almost done. I thought, Hey, aren't you going overboard? As I hung up, I felt a little annoyed. Now, with her shoulder-length hair neatly blown out and curled, she certainly looked prettier than when she carelessly tied it back with a black rubber band, which was her usual style. She had made her entrance five minutes after the appointed time; first, she bowed without saying anything to the old man, then she turned to me and politely nodded as she said, "It's been a long time." The old man's eyes traveled to her face first, dropped down to her chest, and darted back up. She had amazing tits, if nothing else. Though a little saggy, the size alone made it a shame to always keep them under wraps.

Ha! Though his mind was on her breasts, chatter about the summit talks rolled off his tongue. This gathering was indeed a political occasion. I tensed up, thinking I'd better help her out if she stumbled. Gazing into the old man's eyes, however, she let out a flurry of words.

"Well, I don't think it was sudden at all. Everyone was expecting the summit talks to come before the presidential election. If the current president wants to turn the tables, then it's the best card for him to hold. But his timing is rather predictable. Or should we call it exquisite? Everyone was caught unprepared, because none of us thought he would hold the meeting at such an obvious time."

In spite of myself, I turned my head to stare at Y. It was the first time that she'd shown any interest in human, rather than animal, politics. The problem was that her opinion echoed the newspaper article I'd read that very morning. She'd repeated word-for-word an external contributor's op-ed column, with only a slight change in sequence. I thought: This is nothing to be surprised about. How many years has she been working as a part-time lecturer? It was easy for her to talk for an hour or two as long as she had a few threads. The old man listened to her, his head bobbing. As Y sipped wine, having stopped at "What's more comical," the old man's eyes were glued to her, without blinking. He's completely gone, I observed. I grumbled to myself: What is most comical is this very situation, so what could be *more* comical? C'mon, wrap it up now and move on to another topic; you're overextending yourself, you know that? She set her glass down gracefully and continued, the look in her eyes reminiscent of a guest on a TV news show.

"The government has proudly announced that this time around the talks have been arranged transparently through an official institution, not as a behind-the-scenes transaction. But the official institution in question is the National Intelligence Service, and the person who was running all over, pulling his weight to make it happen was none other than the NIS director. It's pretty comical, isn't it, that the government's spy organization runs around transparently for an official meeting with the counterpart that used to be called our 'main enemy.' So this is a very solemn comedy."

With the conclusion of her comment, the old man burst out laughing. Droplets of spit splattered on the pumpkin soup on the table.

"That's your NIS in the 21st century," he said. "How much impact do you think the talks will have on the presidential election?"

"It's clear it will affect the situation, but things have changed since the first summit. With public sentiment as it is, and with so many variables at play, I believe it's premature to hazard a prediction now."

Aha! The old man nodded like a toy dog with a spring in its neck. He read the papers with such diligence every morning, how come he didn't know she'd lifted her comments from there? By ending her remarks with questions of her own, Y completely took the wind out of the guy.

"Which side are you on, sir? What stance have you taken on the summit talks? What are your political views?"

The man grew flustered. No one in his circle had the nerve to fire one question after another like that while looking him straight in the eyes. The form of the questions was perplexing, and so was their substance. He was likely to have mixed feelings about his political leanings. Last year, when he heard about the bill for composite real estate tax, the first of its kind in the country, he practically coughed up blood, saying, "This is the world of the Reds, only capitalist on the surface." But his complaints disappeared after he collected the reward for land absorption, all 7.5 billion won, from the government this year, without having to pay a cent to a real estate broker. His circumstances had grown too complicated recently for him to declare whether he was conservative or progressive.

The old man flushed a little and stuttered, "So, about that, in principle, I think reunification must come at some point. What I mean is that it's good for people of the same nation, the heads of state, to meet, and there are many issues to be resolved, and they've got to discuss separated families, the nuclear issue, economic cooperation, and tourism to Mt. Paektu, and things like that, but I'd say all this is so abrupt. It's hard to catch my breath just watching it all, you know." He wrapped up vaguely, probably realizing that his words, which lacked even the tiniest bit of sincerity, were too stiff to be coaxed into some kind of coherence.

"What do you mean, it's so abrupt?" Y asked and then added, "Earlier this summer when hundreds of people departed from Torasan Station at the border, it was crystal clear that this much progress was on the horizon. It was all too natural to predict that the protagonists would make an appearance, ta-da, behind the gray-haired cheerleaders, though far from sexy, who were on that train."

This is really a comedy, I thought. I lowered my head and concentrated on finding and eating every piece of cheese in my salad. The woman who had been lisping, *Six months?* and *Your place?* was overly eager now.

Aha. The old man nodded, deeply impressed. Too impressed, perhaps, because as he picked up his wine glass to give a toast, he dropped it. The long-stemmed glass fell toward Y, spilling wine. The spreading pool of purple, which dyed the tablecloth, stopped just at the edge of the table. Y calmly took her napkin and firmly pressed the stained map. *Oops.* The old man was clearly remorseful, and asked whether her dress was okay. "It's okay," Y said with a fleeting smile. "I'm sorry, I'm sorry," the old man lamented, and, as if remorse weren't enough, he looked stricken with grief.

The steak had cooled from the breeze of the air conditioning, but the texture was superb. I polished it off, mopping up the bloody juices with a piece of bread. Contrary to her usual practice, Y left half of her steak untouched. Watching her put down her fork, the old man expressed concern. "How can a person devoted to her studies go on if she eats so little?" "I always eat small portions, I really do," she said. I couldn't vouch that she always ate small portions, but her mouth certainly looked smaller than usual. Throughout the long dinner, the old man hadn't gone to the bathroom even once. It was an encouraging sign for his prostate.

While we were waiting for the old man's car to be brought to the hotel entrance, he took out an envelope. When had he prepared it?

"Professor, I've been so rude during our first meeting. It looks like I've ruined your dress. I'm not sure if you can even find a similar one. And I think you'd feel very uncomfortable if I went with you, so . . ."

After this speech, he handed the envelope to me, saying, "She'd feel more comfortable if you escorted her home, right?" The old man was much slyer than I'd thought. If he'd given her the envelope, she'd have certainly refused to take it, but my position was different. It wasn't my clothes he'd almost spilled his wine on, so what right did I have to say whether it was all right? "You don't have to do this," Y said, but just a moment too late, after I'd already taken the envelope. We saw the old man's car off before going to the basement garage. Y, who had been smiling all evening, now had the wretched expression of Sim Cheong, the legendary filial daughter of a popular folktale, after parting with her blind father, and once inside the car she hurled herself against the seat. I somehow felt wronged, like Sim Cheong's father, who'd sold his own daughter. Y didn't say a word, probably drained from all the talking throughout the evening.

"Do you want to stop by my place?" I offered.

"Just take me home."

When the car stopped at the traffic light at the entrance to her apartment complex, I pulled out the envelope from my pocket and slipped it into the purse on her lap. The envelope was very thin. It had to contain a single check. Just as it was impossible to guess the number of zeros on the check, it was impossible to read Y's mind at that moment. As if she hadn't noticed, she absently gazed at the passing cars, her shoulders hunched forward, as if she were Sim Cheong just after she'd boarded the boat that would take her to her death.

By the time I returned home and took a shower, it was very late, but I couldn't fall asleep. I hadn't been able to sleep all summer. The accounts of independently hired traders, like me, were not disclosed, but there were no secrets in the trade. Whether winning big or losing big, news traveled at the speed of light. If I busted accounts and was sacked by the old man, no one would hire me. Like some people I knew, I might have to resort to selling coffee out of a truck to former colleagues. From time to time people committed suicide, probably thinking that they would never stoop to that level. When I checked the clock again, it was three o'clock.

I was holding Y. Her breasts were warm and soft. Her arms and legs, as slick as an Indian python, were wrapped tightly around me. The sensation of slipping into her was more than real. "Love you, love you, Y," I whispered, whimpering as I ejaculated, and opened my eyes, surprised by my own voice. It was still dark outside. When was the last time I had had a wet dream? As I stretched out my hand and fumbled for a tissue, I thought my dream had nothing to do with a desire for physical release. While thinking that what I wanted was the tactile sensation of stroking her back with my palm, our bare skin touching, that comforting feeling that I wasn't all alone, I fell back into a sleep as thick as molasses. Y was still lying next to me. She was deep asleep with one leg draped over my body. *I love you.*

In the office, the old man spent the morning no differently from other days. Sipping his green tea, he pored over the economic daily and the morning paper, each the top paper in circulation in its field, then took out a telephone bill from one of his drawers.

"I said no international calls from the office, didn't I? As I said, it's not an issue of money, but an issue of attitude. Why do you take care of personal business at work? This is my house and my office. Three telephone calls were made to Beijing on June 30. One for a minute, another for a minute, and one for seven minutes. Who did it?"

It was probably the new clerk who had joined the company in June. Neither Miss Jang nor I did things like that. A long-distance call was a target of dogged pursuit for the old man, so why would we brave it? Miss Jang lifted her chin and gave Cho, the clerk, a pointed look, as if urging him to fess up before things got ugly. But the guy had yet to catch on. He was probably thinking that the caller's name couldn't possibly be on the phone bill. In fact, the old man, too, would only feel the satisfaction of solving a mystery early in the day if Cho offered some resistance before being pinned down. Cho stood his ground. His expression was relaxed, and he was probably thinking, How much does an international call cost these days, anyway? He would learn soon enough that the old man lived each day for the fun of giving his staff a hard time. Before lunch, Cho confessed that he had talked to his friend who was studying in Beijing, that he couldn't get through the first two times, that he had to make a third call, and that he would pay for the calls himself.

At first glance, the old man's spending habits seemed to have no rules, standards, or patterns. When sending someone on an errand to a faraway place, he would fish out a small bill from his wallet and tell him to take a taxi, but when he felt like it, he would take us all to a Korean restaurant at a five-star hotel and treat us to kimchi stew priced at 70,000 won per person. It was disconcerting that he would splurge on a 670,000-won pair of summer slippers to wear in the office only to ferret out the person who made a long-distance call for 790 won, but he periodically did such things, to the bewilderment of employees.

When the old man was angry, he would stand next to the clerk and spew out orders as if crazed. He didn't care in the slightest how the market was doing and what the prices were, but he called out the items, numbers, buys, and sells like a fish auctioneer. Meanwhile, the clerk broke out in a cold sweat, failing to keep up with his speed. When the deal wasn't made at the price the old man quoted, he fired orders more rapidly, and the clerk, like a faint-hearted boy before a hysterical piano teacher with a stick in her hand, found his fingers flying to the wrong keys on the keyboard, making huge mistakes. The clerk would break down, shedding cold drops of sweat, begging forgiveness of the old man, who would give his underling hell over his mistake. When, however, a loss of 5 or 6 million won occurred in the blink of an eye as a result of the old man's instructions, it didn't annoy him as much. The clerk who had failed to handle orders was fired and replaced instantly by a new flunky. These separate incidents seemed contradictory, but witnessing them over and over led you to a clear-cut conclusion.

It all came down to power. The old man's money was a source of flexible, self-sufficient power. An absolute power which did not depend on voters to whom you were required to be solicitous, a power upon which even die-hard civic groups clamoring for transparency didn't dare encroach. To show that a thumbs-down from him meant immediate death, he used money, which was just a number for him, be it 790 won or 6 million won.

The old man returned from lunch and called me.

"She's smart and pretty. Why is she still single?" He blurted it out apropos of nothing. Of course he was referring to Y.

"For all I know, her hobby is studying. She devotes herself to scholarship day and night, so she has no interest in men. And she seems to be having some problems these days."

"What kind of problems?"

"I don't know the details, actually . . ."

"Why are you so indifferent to your sister's friend?"

"It would be different if she were a friend's sister, but when it comes to a friend of my sister's . . ."

"How come you're not married yet?"

He was like this about everything. *You suspicious old cat.* He was curious why we hadn't hit it off when we seemed to know each other well enough.

"Who doesn't want to get married? But I have no woman and no money."

"Son, with money, all you have to do is make it."

That's easy to say. Do you know who will marry first? The man with a woman but no money, or the man with a lot of money but no woman?

Come August, brief torrential rains fell frequently, as if we were in the tropics during the rainy season. After the abrupt end of a downpour, the persistent chanting of cicadas filled the void. Walking under the trees lining the streets, I noticed more cicada corpses strewn about than any other year. Day in and day out, I lay in bed and listened to the rain falling. The American stock market crisis, triggered by non-performing loans, reached Korea's shores in the first days of August. Circuit-breakers were activated in the stock market to halt trading and the biggest fall in history repeated itself. I wasn't in too bad a shape, because with no liquidity I had nothing more to lose, but every day I felt as if I were sitting on a cushion of thorns. If the downturn continued, the old man might liquidate all of his stocks and look for other investment options. As was the case with every early August, traffic in Seoul thinned as people went on vacation. Several incidents blew up almost simultaneously at home and abroad like a nuclear storm, sending tremors throughout the world. All the issues were tangled up in a tremendously shocking and complicated way.

The outcome of the Korean hostage crisis in Afghanistan was hard to foresee, as if obscured by a desert sandstorm. Tears and criticism rocked the entire country. Consternation was soon replaced by cold contempt. More news broke: when a young female professor was found to have forged her academic records, she reacted like a mental patient and flew to New York in business class. The consequences were mighty and lengthy. Rumors about her background and speculations about her parentage titillated those who were in still in Seoul and hadn't been able to go on vacation. Soon, exposures or confessions of celebrities who had lied about their academic credentials poured forth. More tears and criticism abounded. Meanwhile, a local sci-fi blockbuster opened in cinemas, stirring up box office fever. Both fans and haters of this movie fought ferociously, like enemies facing each other on a battlefield during the Crusades. Long queues were formed in the cinemas by patriotic moviegoers. The two presidential candidates shouted that they loved this nation until their voices grew hoarse but that their opponent could not and should not be loved. Even before the commencement of the North-South summit, endless questions were flying. All too heated and confusing.

The female professor who claimed that she'd return home with proof of her doctorate vanished in New York, and this was followed by a series of capitulations by heavyweights in the cultural sector, hit by the stray bullets of forged academic credentials, with performances and lines more impressive and memorable than any they'd delivered so far. "I said it was not true, not true, but they turned me into a college graduate," an actress wailed, shedding tears. She was an accomplished actress who had confidently stated at one point, "I am a graduate of none other than Ewha Womans University, whatever you may think of me." An English lecturer bowed her head, saying, "My parents' debts are to blame." An actress who only graduated from high school spat out that she didn't want to be interviewed by a press that regarded her as a mere high school graduate. Watching them, I realized afresh that no man was a match for the woman he was arguing with. Except for one man I read about in the paper that morning.

He kept his daughter hidden from view and directed the National Intelligence Service to keep an eye on her for fear she would hurt his prospects of winning a Nobel Peace Prize. One day, the daughter's mother was discovered dead in what looked like a suicide case. He had neither confirmed nor denied the existence of this daughter. The presumed daughter had lived a life of despair, going to her father's door to beg for living expenses as a child, and now volunteered an interview. In an exhausted voice, she said, "I don't think I'm his daughter." He was the one who had grabbed the Nobel Peace Prize for his work fighting for democracy and human rights. His wife commented that if the young lady had been her husband's daughter, she would have raised her well. The concerned parties in the affair, which could be clarified with one round of DNA testing, remained inactive; instead, a presidential hopeful quipped that he'd like to run a DNA test, if possible, on a plot of land whose ownership was in question. Real-life dramas, more eye-catching than any reality show, unfolded ceaselessly on the stage of this big city. Each one of these real-life dramas was shocking, so much so that neither background music nor lighting was necessary.

I phoned Y on a Friday afternoon. "Let's have dinner tonight," I said, but she said that she had plans. I didn't ask who she was seeing. On Saturday and Sunday, rain came and went intermittently. This thankfully made the weather not too sweltering for August. In the news, they said the rain was depriving the crops of sunlight. What a simple, calm life people were leading, worrying about sunlight-deficient plants!

I truly didn't want to tag along. As I was preparing to leave the office, the old man called me and said, "Let's have dinner together." I was trying to extricate myself, saying, "But I have a dinner date." Without even asking who my date was, he flatly said, "No buts." I had no choice but to come along. We sat down in a Japanese restaurant in a top hotel, and about five minutes later Y appeared, grinning, and said, "Oh, you're here, too!" I would have felt less miserable if she had asked outright why I'd come along again. I had no idea why the old man had dragged me along.

The old man poured sake, a special bottle that the restaurant kept for him, to the brim of a cup and handed it to Y.

"You're supposed to drink sake this way. It's made by a family who's been making sake for two hundred years. I don't know why we Koreans can't copy this flavor."

After a sip, Y nodded as if in appreciation. *Hah, what do you know about the taste of alcohol?* I said inwardly, with scorn. The old man poured a cup for me, too. Mine wasn't sloshing over the brim like hers. We were like a happy family. Over sashimi, the old man and Y began chatting earnestly about highbrow topics, as if they couldn't resist the urge to discuss social issues.

"It's a big problem because it isn't just one or two. What do you think will happen to the hostages?" the old man asked.

She didn't even know what was in the heart of the person she'd had sex with for seven years, so how could she understand the Taliban's motives? Scoffing to myself, I wrapped a slice of tuna belly sprinkled with gold flakes in a sheet of seaweed and tossed it into my mouth. The soft fat melted on my tongue like ice cream. The conjectured whereabouts of Korean hostages differed in the foreign media. The kidnappers kept changing their demands by the hour. One of the hostages had been brutally murdered, but domestic postings on the Internet had grown more merciless by the day.

Ask your God to save you. You even wrote wills before you left, so just die there. Don't ever use our bloodsucking taxes on useless things.

"They will eventually release the hostages after behind-the-scenes negotiations and a monetary reward, don't you think? It will be hard for them to hold onto the hostages, especially with so many women among them."

That was an exact echo of an editorial piece in the morning paper.

"That was what I was thinking. How much do you think they'll demand?"

"I heard that they'd internally set a sum for each country's citizens. On the Internet, people are fuming, arguing that our bloodsucking taxes should never be used to pay ransom. But I doubt any of the kids who post comments on the Internet have ever paid any taxes to speak of. People like you, who pay tremendous amounts of tax, never write such posts."

While saying "tremendous," Y drew a big heart in the air with her fingers. How lovely! I wanted to choke her or, if that wasn't possible, to hug her tightly. The old man laughed as if it were the best joke he'd ever heard and suddenly brought up the presidential election.

"What do people in academia think? The opposition party will win this time, don't you think?"

I put a slice of sea cucumber in my mouth and chewed it. Crunch, crunch. *You're trying to drive a shovel into concrete. Just go to a fortune teller's café and ask what the country's future will be. Why are you so interested in politics when you're not going to run for any office?*

"Until the December elections, no prospects are clear. It's harder to predict the path of a storm the farther away it is."

I grumbled to myself: *For us, what is urgent are not the summit talks and the storm of the presidential election, but how to survive in any way possible amid the storm that is about to knock me down. When will we approach the damn issue if we circle around the edges like this?* By the time dinner was over, it was almost ten o'clock. Outside, it was raining again. Unlike the anxiety I'd felt during dinner, a sudden pang of grief surged up when it was just the two of us sitting in my car, as if I were a boy abandoned by his mother.

"You were bending over backwards to give him a good impression. That affectation on your face, it was so funny that it made me sad."

"You treated me like bait. Do you know how I felt smiling like that? If your problem could be solved, you'd give me away as a freebie."

"Next time, see the old man by yourself. I'm a human being with feelings too."

"Exactly."

Y opened a container of chewing gum, tossed a piece into her mouth, and shut the lid without offering one to me.

She said, "Old man? I'd believe it if they said *you* were older. Who'd think he was in his sixties? Besides, I thought he'd be ultraconservative, but surprisingly, he's rather progressive. Even with the size of his assets, he's a Roh groupie. That's really refreshing."

I wanted to tell her why he had suddenly turned from someone who gritted his teeth at the mere mention of Roh Moohyun's name to a passionate supporter of the president.

But instead I said, "Give me a piece of gum, too, will you? I look older? If I had a personal trainer at the hotel's fitness center, I could tone up in a month."

"So you mean anyone could join a hotel fitness center if he wanted to?"

Seeing her refute every remark of mine with a mouthful of gum got me more worked up. I said, "He looks fine on the outside. It's just that he has nothing in his head."

"He graduated from your alma mater. Don't spit while you're lying down."

"Ha! You think that the old man was admitted to my university after passing an exam? Back in those lax days, he was admitted because his father donated money to build a dormitory. He's a pioneer of forged academic credentials."

"Getting lucky with the kind of parents you get—that's ability, too. Haven't you learned that yet? It might be the most important ability of all."

I squeezed my eyes shut. Where did this terrible, cold female reasoning come from? Right. How destructive emotions were! Why was I responding schizophrenically, after burning my own bridges in the name of survival to surmount the crisis we found ourselves in?

Universal tragedy purifies emotions, but when that tragedy becomes personal, people lose their reason. A surge of emotions made me think that if Y, even at this point, realized that this wasn't the right thing for her to do and said that she had been momentarily insane, I would understand what was unfolding before my eyes, but instead, I hardened my resolve, thinking, *What's the use of love after you're dead?* Didn't we, both Y and I, realize that this scheme was not a money-making project, but a purely emotional one?

I abruptly steered the wheel toward Mapo. "I'm tired," Y mumbled in an exhausted voice, shaking her head. *Of course you're tired, you just took part in the "100-Minute Debate."* I pretended not to hear her. Y burrowed deep into her seat, closing her eyes in resignation.

The body is simple and blind. These days, whenever I had the chance, I indulged myself in her body. As soon as I locked the front door, I led her by the hand to her bed. "Dark, I want it dark." Y sounded irritated. I stood my ground and did not turn off the light. "Just close your eyes," I said. When I shut my own eyes, I felt as if my entire self was being sucked into her body. At a certain moment, the inside of her body expanded into an infinite space. Y disappeared within herself. When I tried to go deeper to reach the farthest point, wherever it was, Y retreated farther, and my feet bounced up as if I were floating in zero gravity. Though inside her, I was far away from her. In the bright darkness, I whispered to Y, who was on the other side of the darkness, "I love you."

"I, I love Professor Yun. I've never felt this way before. My heart races and I can't erase her smile from my mind all day."

The gardener was mowing the lawn during a short interval between downpours. The noise from the mower was deafening, but the old man, absently gazing out the window with his hands wrapped around a cup of green tea, seemed oblivious. What could I say in response? The swath of grass that had been mowed was paler; the stalks lay down, revealing the undersides of the blades. In my heart, too, a machine seemed to be whirring. Something inside me was being mowed and overturned. *Did you say you loved her?*

"I don't have many expectations. I just hope there's some substantial progress. I don't know why I'm like this."

Was he playing a newspaper headline game or what? What did he think this was, a summit? Why did he say, "many expectations" and "some substantial progress"? And he had the perfect sense to add a line from a song popular in a bygone era. I gave a vague answer, "Ah, yes," and looked out to the garden where the wet trees and plants were dappled with sunlight. That a banal pop phrase struck a chord with him was clear proof he'd already fallen in love.

I had met a woman a while back, without Y's knowledge. I was infatuated with her. She looked and acted much younger than her age. The perkiness of her text messages, sent several times a day, made me think I'd also traveled back to my boyhood. But was it because Y had set a standard for me? After a few dates, it dawned on me that the back of the woman's perky head and the line of her shoulders just didn't look right. Besides, her frequent reliance on sentimental pop lyrics put me off. When I said, "Let's stop this war-like love," she replied, her eyes welling up with tears, "If it must be forgotten, I hope it can be forgotten." So I answered in a voice that sounded like a late-night radio DJ, "I hope you can 'say goodbye to the futile pain' as soon as possible." Perhaps because the appropriate phrase from Kim Gwang-seok's songs didn't pop into her head right away, she sobbed loudly. *Why did I ever get involved with a woman like this*, I wondered in self-pity. Now, looking at the old man as he snuck a line from the lyrics of a pop song into his political lexicon, I rather "missed that girl." Whose song was she wallowing in these days, that person who'd said meeting me when she already had a nice boyfriend felt as if she were committing a "beautiful sin"?

What had I overlooked?

At first, the scheme was very simple and clear. The only thing I'd overlooked was that people were not clear-cut, black and white like the stones on a Go board. Simmering desires, having come to the surface, were no different from molten lava. They melted rocks and charted their own course. While I was scheming, I'd failed to calculate the temperature and destructive power of desire. Only the illusions the beholder hoped to see shimmered over the mirage. While saying "just six months," I hadn't seen beyond that limited time span. I was focused only on the differences between "prostate" and "prosate," and turned a blind eye to the gap between "regular sex" and "love."

The gray eyes of the old man, professing his love with a peaceful gaze fixed on the garden washed in rain, were moist like the leaves. He was a teenager again. He carried his cell phone even when he went to the bathroom, anxiously awaiting text messages dashed off by Y, who was being charitable. His most important daily routine was opening and closing his phone. He no longer gave his staff a hard time or drove the clerk crazy. When I caught him laboriously pecking at the buttons to send a text, his back bent like an aged watch repairman, I had the urge to kick him on the back and snap, "Stop making a spectacle of yourself!" The old man's remark was not a simple confession, but a request for me to play go-between for him and Y. This was the very moment I'd been waiting for all along. The old man said he was going to meet Y and asked my advice about what gift he should buy her.

"Giving her a check and telling her to get a handbag would be the thing to do for a girl in the red light district. But she's in academia, and young, too."

What's the difference, the red light district or academia? She's the same age as your daughter, so their tastes should be similar. This was what I wanted to say. But the mountain summit was just over there, so I couldn't mess it up now.

"Let me think. What would be perfect for her? I've heard that men misunderstand female psychology. Men believe that women fantasize about receiving a hundred roses, but from the female's perspective, flowers are the most annoying gift."

Having said that, I felt I had beaten around the bush.

"What if you ask her directly?" he suggested.

"That's awkward. If she were a friend's sister, it would be different, but she's a friend of my sister's, you know."

The sunlight suddenly faded. The old man had been looking outside, tormenting himself about the gift, but now he turned to me, as if he'd just woken up.

He asked, "About the presidential election, what's it boiling down to? Who do you think will win?"

"I think it's too early to predict. The one who's more loved will win, I guess." My voice suddenly sounded grief-stricken. Why was I like this these days? Why this talk of love while weighing election prospects? I went on, "The people of this country will elect someone who's dead-on at their level and then when they are let down they will squeak again: Cut off the fingers. Croak. Cut off your fingers that voted for that crook. Croak, croak."

I pictured Y as a frog. I felt a little better.

The old man clucked his tongue. "Give me a realistic analysis, will you? We're not just talking about a fire on the other side of the river. I can try to be a step ahead of other people only when the prediction comes in regarding who will win. Do I go for real estate or invest in stocks? If the answer is neither, do I buy a commercial building in Dubai? Can't just keep it in the drawer forever . . ."

The thing that was kept in the drawer.

The source of power.

The source of this absurd romantic triangle.

"What's the use of this at this point?" Y lifted her left wrist and shoved it near my face.

I was in no mood for joking. *I see it well enough without you poking my eyes with it.* I knew the price of the diamond-encrusted watch. The old man and I had selected it together. The old man had paid for the watch in cash, an amount almost equivalent to the rental deposit for my studio apartment.

Both Y and I were aware that this was not simply a watch, but a proposal. For the old man, the university development fund would be a piece of cake. He hoped Y would show some sincerity first. But Y felt she couldn't wait forever with a watch like this strapped on her wrist. She wasn't a child, was she? It was not important whether the jewels were diamonds or crystals. Only when there was a clear, realistic proposal could she proceed to the next step. She couldn't bring herself to spell it out for me, but I saw through her, simply by the angle at which her head was cocked. I wasn't oblivious to why the old man had invited me to a threesome dinner from time to time. Both he and Y expected me to play a crucial role between them.

Outside, the window of the café was awash in waves of rain, as if suddenly submerged in water. With people coming in to escape the sudden downpour, there wasn't a single empty seat. Water dripped from their hair. From somewhere inside my heart, water dripped as well. Someone passing by carelessly splashed water on Y's dress with his umbrella.

"It's really pouring!" Y burst out in irritation.

Who should be the one to vent their anger here? I gulped down my glass of iced coffee as soon as the waitress set it on the table. In an instant, I could see the bottom of the glass. I crunched on the ice cubes, but my insides, burning like a grease fire, didn't cool. I caught the attention of a waitress who was passing by. "A refill, please." She replied, "We don't give refills on iced coffee, but I can get you an Americano." Y gave me an annoyed look and poured me more than half of the iced coffee she hadn't touched. Familiarity and detachment, the result of our shared ups and downs over so much time, manifested itself in her gesture. My heart was crushed.

"I heard you saw a movie with the old man. The one with the boa constrictor. That's exactly to your taste, huh?"

"You can say that again. Meanwhile, you saw the *Glorious Outing*, which you loved, and you came out crying, right? Do you think they're different? Neither is better than the other. This movie or that movie. You or me, we all think we're hurting the most. Just trying to elicit tears, just trying to appeal to a sense of justice. When everything is said and done, everyone wants to eat and live better than others. It all begins from there."

Her voice, trembling lightly, was so low that those at the surrounding tables couldn't catch what she was saying.

I had bullied her into accepting that I had no interest in knowing what happened between the two of them, and that she should never bring it up, but here I was, losing my calm first.

"So when you got pregnant five years ago, we should have gotten married, regardless of whether our marriage would have turned into a bowl of perfectly cooked rice or mush?"

"It certainly would have turned into mush."

"You're ruthless."

"I'm not ruthless. The world's toughened me up, that's all."

"I've told you all along we should have gotten married. You resisted, and now look what you have to show for it!"

"Do you think I acted the way I did because I wanted to? The world forces me to lead a single life. Other women can do it all, but I can't. I'll never accomplish anything with children hanging on me, carrying the kitchen on my back. You're not Superman and I'm no alpha female. I knew this well, so I wanted to get some decent armor to wear in this chilly, tempestuous world. Honestly, look at you. You're the type who'd sell your own wife. I feel faint just watching you. I don't even have a wife to sell, you know."

"Talk that kind of nonsense in your classroom, with your students."

"Then I'll talk about something else. He asked me to accompany him to Hokkaido next week to play golf. He says he has a membership and a villa there."

"I don't want to know, okay? Don't tell me anything from now on. Do it behind my back."

Y stared at me and asked in a sober tone, "How can I do it behind your back? You started it. Tell me. *Jagi.* What do you want me to do?"

I could see that the *jagi* she referred to was neither Goryeo celadon nor white porcelain from the Joseon Dynasty, she was using it as a term of endearment, but I was confused as to whether it referred to me or her. Right. The one who held the hilt of the sword was Y, not I.

"How can you do this to me?" This sounded absurd even in my own ears.

She nodded. "True. It's an unexpected turn of events, isn't it?"

I picked up her iced coffee, still untouched, drank it, and cracked the ice cubes between my teeth.

I was the one who had set up this absurd, sad, ridiculous and cruel board game, but I could no longer remain an observer. The dank, noisy café was an unexpectedly perfect place for a verbal sparring. Where else would a quarrel like this be conducted in such low voices, in such a non-violent manner? The waitress approached with a coffee pot, refilled my glass generously with weak Americano, and turned around. "Thank you," Y addressed her on my behalf.

The surface of the river glistened. The light splintered as it hit the water, blended into the waves, and flowed down together. River water, too hot and infinitely cold at the same time, undulated inside me as well.

This place, where the stream that had meandered through a gigantic apartment complex joined the river, was next to the one-way street I always went to after dropping Y off at her place.

The scenery viewed from the slow-moving car had been beautiful. Whenever I passed by I thought, I should come here with Y, but would soon forgot all about it. The big bridge that crossed the river, stretching from the multi-level freeways that created a harmonious loop, looked sturdy, like a backbone supporting this city. The blue decorative lights along the bridge's parapets gradually changed to green, as if a hand were brushing over it. Y hadn't answered my phone calls all evening. I had texted that I'd wait there for her and I had been waiting for two hours. "Where are you?" Y asked, when she returned the call at eleven o'clock.

"I said I'd be waiting for you."

Probably a bit alarmed, she simply said okay and hung up.

The scenery was different from when I had only driven by. The drain coming from the stream that had traversed the residential area gave off a rancid stench. The body of water that joined the river formed a gigantic foamy gray pool and was immobile like an art installation; even heavy rains failed to wash it away. On either bank, piled high with deposits of dark mud, tenacious weeds had sprouted up and looked offensive, their vivid green striking and incongruous. The overgrown weeds, with the lower half of their stalks beneath the water, rubbed against each other with each passing breeze. My sense of smell soon dulled from the incessant assault of the stench. *Where are the countless cars going at this hour?* I thought idly, looking at the headlights lining the bridge. It was tedious to spend two hours beside the stinking river at night. Rain poured down, so I took brief refuge in my car.

Turning to the news on my GPS, I listened with my eyes on the raindrops sliding down the window. Of the hostages, two men had been executed and two women released. No one had any idea what would happen to the rest. With a flood in North Korea, the summit talks slated for the end of August were postponed to October. The scandal of forged academic credentials had swept through the religious sector and spread into political circles, leaving more suspicion in its wake. With so many people owning up to their enhanced academic degrees, newspapers might need to create a space for "Today's Academic Record Forgers." What was Y saying to the old man at this moment? For all I knew, she would be analyzing whether the problem was the falsification of academic records itself or the social structure that had pushed people to do it, from the perspective of ontology and structural theory. No, such talk would be saved for when the three of us were together. When it was just the two of them, surely they talked about more personal things. Today, no different from seven years ago when we had met for the first time, the Meteorological Service forecast the weather, as always, despite its low rate of accuracy. The day was coming to an end, but the news was endless. There was no knowing when the eyes of these numerous storms would expand, wield enormous destructive power in their wake, and then die out, and also there was no knowing who would have the last laugh and who would drop to their knees in defeat. People responded hysterically to these extreme stimuli but turned their backs on them surprisingly fast. And by the following month, they would have completely forgotten about them all, as if everything had happened a hundred years ago.

A month had passed since we'd eaten the live octopi. A lot had happened in the span of one month, inside and outside of me. August would soon pass. When everything flowed away like that river water, what would remain of me? The end of the news coincided with the muted sound of raindrops. I pressed the button to turn off the screen and got out of the car. The persistent stench floated up. Misty rain was still falling. Just like a weak sob before violent weeping comes to a close, the sensation of being soaked by the misty rain was not bad, for it felt like someone was next to me. Thick clouds, low enough to be touched by an outstretched hand, rushed toward the upper stream.

If I had soared a little off the ground, if not as high as those clouds, and looked down at this city, at the people rushing about in the city, they would have looked like anaerobic bacteria. The beings in the mud who writhed, tangled up, divided themselves, ran amok, and died, all buried in the fetid air, in the dead water, and in the noise as loud as a drilling lathe.

I didn't realize Y was standing next to me.

"Why did you come here? Nobody ever comes out here," she said. She looked around, as if in disbelief all over again.

She smelled faintly of alcohol. I called her name. Without answering, she gazed at the river.

"This isn't right. It's all my fault, from beginning to end."

Y smiled. "You and me, there was no distinction from the start. We're a team. Do you think I started it for fun? You still don't know? I'm desperate. You can't survive here if you're not desperate."

"I love you. I'm telling you that I love you."

Y smiled again. It was a peculiar smile. Not mocking, not bitter or sour, it was a bit apologetic, as if she had learned a little about life and human beings, as if telling me not to get too worked up.

"July is gone. We've come a long way. If we turn around, you and I will turn into pillars of salt. Look how the rain doesn't stop. In the end we'll just melt away. We can't turn around now. The place we could return to has collapsed, and we have to keep walking with our eyes fixed ahead."

Y stopped talking. Her face was serene, except for a single tear sliding down her cheek.

The Bison

Should I go?

Today?

These questions had obsessed him for several days, yielding a different answer each time. What's the use of seeing her now, he'd think, but then he'd change his mind, thinking, I should see her at least once. All day long, he was pulled in two directions. He finally decided to go. Otherwise, he supposed, he'd never be able to do anything while the exhibition was being held. Today? A few days later? Myeong-jo bit his nails. It wasn't that he was still haunted by her remark: *You mean nothing to me.* What he hadn't been able to erase from his mind were her eyes. That anxious yet resolute gleam in her eyes might as well have come from a total stranger. Those eyes disconcerted him. A person often has a ready answer to a seeming conundrum. Despite his wavering, Myeong-jo glanced at his watch and stood up as if he had been waiting for that very moment.

As he stepped out of the cool lobby, he was hit by a blast of heat from outdoors. Smog was floating like metallic rain in the slanting sunlight. The gallery was less than a ten-minute walk away. During the short span of time from when he traversed the crosswalk until he reached the mouth of Insa-dong, all the nerves in his body sagged like overcooked vegetables. His footsteps were irregular, hindered by the rectangular stones dotting either side of the road to separate pedestrians from vehicular traffic. Who in the world had come up with the idea of putting these huge stones on the road? People swerved in and out to avoid the black stones that resembled sealed caskets, looking like inauspicious omens.

Insa-dong on a Wednesday evening was a republic of its own, if only for a limited span of time. An overwhelming fervor and a singular smell were palpable in the air, like ingredients that refused to melt or blend even when brought to a boil in an enormous cauldron. There was excitement on people's faces as though they were about to attend a secret, exclusive gathering. Six o'clock in the evening. This was the time when all the galleries, having installed new sculptures, paintings, and photos, held their openings, as if lifting their skirts all at once, revealing their underwear. *Look closely, this is me.* This was a time when all inhibitions were shed, in the desire to prove one's existence. The passersby, with the day's brochures in hand, milled about, bare arms and legs brushing against each other.

Myeong-jo didn't like Insa-dong on Wednesdays. When he was forced to come here to get information or see people, he would choose Thursdays or Fridays; he was more comfortable in the hours when desires had ebbed away. He neither had the curiosity to get too close to strangers, nor did he feel the need to expose himself. Su-hye hadn't sent him a brochure. But the reviews, both big and small, had appeared in newspapers the week before. He studied the photos of Su-hye, printed next to her work, for a long time. The woman in the pictures, whether beaming or expressionless, hadn't changed a bit. What had changed was her art. Completely, at that. The one year he hadn't seen her seemed like eons, or just a few weeks. Now he returned to his original conundrum.

Should I just walk all the way down to Jongno? Should I stop by and see her?

Toot, toot.

A short, shrill whistle rang twice. Deep in thought, Myeong-jo nearly banged his knee on one of the black stone caskets. As he swerved to dodge its sharp edge, a girl standing in front of him collapsed in a heap. Like a robot whose batteries had run out, her joints seemed to fold in on themselves all at once. He thought she was just sitting down, but she crumpled to the ground. Myeong-jo almost knelt down to shake her. The crowd around him suddenly thinned. Myeong-jo was the only one left standing. The people who had fallen didn't budge, their eyes closed. Some lay on their sides, others on their backs. The sunlight bounced off their taut skin. Their glowing faces testified to the fact that this was not death, but a staged performance. Goose bumps sprouted on his back, which was drenched in sweat. The pedestrians on the other side of the street came to an abrupt halt, like oglers before a collapsed bridge, and stared at Myeong-jo, their eyes wide open in astonishment.

Tooooot.

This time, the whistle lasted longer. The person with the whistle was nowhere in sight. Those lying on the road scrambled to get up. A yellowed leaf from a tree arced to the ground. The people who had picked themselves up from the ground mingled with the spectators. These had to be kids who believed that wearing red shoes and clicking their heels three times would bring them luck. As if fate didn't knock people down already, they bent their knees and collapsed of their own volition! The back of the girl who had sunk to the ground disappeared as if sucked into the crowd. It dawned on him that he was no longer young. *Should I go or not?* Those youngsters wouldn't have spent ten days agonizing over this question. The gallery was right in front of him.

A beast gazed at the space ahead, its four hooves planted on the ground.

Myeong-jo observed the shape of the animal he came across at the entrance before scanning the hall, which was unexpectedly spacious. A herd of bison stood at irregular intervals. Their facial features looked indistinct, as if they had been weathered while alive, their sharp edges slightly flattened out.

Su-hye was speaking to a man holding a video camera. "No close-ups, please, and shoot from a distance, if you have room." Of all the murmurings from the crowd, her voice alone reached his ears. The collection of sculptures in the hall was quite a departure from the single bison featured in the newspaper photo. The bison, sporting big spiral horns, exuded a solitary beauty. The space-time inhabited by the aloof beasts was not Insa-dong at six o'clock in the evening. The atmosphere of a distant place and time hit him viscerally. Where could this be? As he ambled along, Su-hye's voice snuck up on him.

"Hey, here you are."

She sounded casual, as if greeting a person she had had dinner with just a few days before. He had seen her photos in papers and magazines from time to time, but it had been a year since he had laid eyes on her. At the time, the first typhoon of the year, having flown across tropical seas, was sweeping through the city. Myeong-jo couldn't bring himself to enter the funeral parlor to pay his condolences at Ha-yun's funeral and turned back at the doorway. Still vivid in his memory were his glimpses of Su-hye, who was so emaciated that he feared she might topple over at any moment, and Ha-yun's face in the funeral portrait, beaming, white teeth exposed.

"Your work has changed completely. If I'd dropped by here randomly, I wouldn't have known you were the artist."

"Yeah. Once I stopped obsessing about selling my art, my style changed without my realizing it."

She sounded indifferent, as if she were talking about someone else. She was right though. If her works were not purchased by national or private museums, they might not sell at all. They weren't suitable for a personal collection. They were too big for an apartment or a residential building, and the impression they gave was too intense for small spaces. Su-hye had earned her reputation as a sculptor, and her sculptures of human forms had made the list of coveted collectibles for art buffs. Her sculptures, with their sharp facial lines and smooth features, were lovely, tempting viewers to run their palms over them. When Myeong-jo told her they were pretty, she responded, "They should be." It was a simple response, but the look on her face hid something deeper. Her pieces usually sold out during the opening. On such days, she'd offer her back to Myeong-jo and mumble in a gloomy voice, "How much longer am I supposed to be doing this? My shoulders hurt so much, they seem to be breaking." When he gripped the nape of her neck until it almost hurt, she'd let out a long sigh, *whewwwwww*, as if releasing something from the depths.

With Ha-yun's death, her compulsion to sell as much as she could disappeared. And with it, the tie between her and Myeong-jo was severed. Su-hye refused to explain this puzzling, seemingly causal sequence of events. It was a unilateral decision, too resolute for him to overturn. Even if the motivation to sell a lot of works was gone, she still had to sell something, Myeong-jo thought. Enough for Su-hye and her daughter to make a living, and enough for her to move on to her next project, if nothing else. At any rate, the bison exuded excessive forlornness, uncharacteristic of an animal.

"They look cold somehow."

At Myeong-jo's comment, she looked around the room as if seeing it for the first time.

"You think so? These guys are from the Ice Age. Lived about 30,000 years ago. They went extinct a long time ago. I wanted to fill the floor here with thick ice. I thought of giving it a try, if just for today, but gave up. I thought people might think they were standing on an ice rink, rather than in the Ice Age. What do you think?" she asked tentatively, It wasn't clear whether she was asking about her idea or his impression of the installation in general.

"They're captivating. Put together some specifics for me. I might be able to create a video game character with an image like this. If I end up using it, I'll pay you royalties, of course."

"Ha!" Su-hye let out her abrupt, distinctive laugh.

Her laugh was like an enormous, swollen soap bubble bursting. He could identify that laugh of hers with his eyes closed.

Once, while sitting on the sofa channel surfing, he had come across an image of Ha-yun on the screen. He was in a North Korean city, in a place that looked utterly dreary and depressing, not because it was winter but because of the bleak landscape behind him. Ha-yun was speaking with a medical official. Myeong-jo stared at Ha-yun. His face bore no trace of selfishness, almost like an imbecile's, and his personality, which so frustrated Su-hye, was clearly imprinted on his face.

"He sounds so nice and kind, doesn't he?" Su-hye would say, shaking her head, "But he always gets his way at the end of the day."

After exchanging a few words on TV, Ha-yun and his interlocutor burst out laughing, and the laughter of a woman, somewhere outside the camera frame, joined in. That laugh belonged to Su-hye. She didn't appear onscreen until the end of the program. Myeong-jo didn't tell Su-hye that he'd seen the documentary. She'd constantly expressed her frustration over what Ha-yun was doing—so why had she gone, and laughed along, for that matter? He was displeased. Oddly, Myeong-jo remembered for the longest time that abrupt, cheerful laugh, which matched the bleak scenery even less than the laughter that he'd heard when they were face to face.

"Why are you laughing? I'm serious," Myeong-jo insisted.

"Did kids tell you they'd rather watch bison roaming around, because they're sick of that female character in video games who runs around, flashing her white panties under a short skirt?"

Myeong-jo laughed along, but he hadn't been completely joking. When he first saw the bison, a fleeting thought had occurred to him: How about creating a computer game set in the Ice Age? But feeling timid in the face of Su-hye's laughter, he faltered. "What I'm saying is that they're unique and attractive."

A continuous stream of people passed by, smiling at Su-hye. The official opening hour must have been drawing near. The curator called Su-hye over. The plastic wrap covering the food was taken off and wine was passed around. A man in horn-rimmed glasses stepped forward and delivered brief congratulatory remarks, which was followed by Su-hye giving a speech. Myeong-jo stood far in the back and took in the scene, as if watching a silent movie, a glass of lukewarm cola in his hand. The voices sometimes reached him and sometimes didn't.

Was one year long enough to get over a person's death? Su-hye's shoes, which he hadn't seen before, were so shiny that they seemed as though they'd give off a strong rawhide smell. He hadn't seen her white sleeveless dress before either. When he'd listened to Su-hye's choked grief-stricken sobs on the phone, he'd felt suffocated, as if clumps of sand were falling over his head. There were tears he couldn't wipe away from her face. Su-hye—who had constantly hurt Ha-yun and been nasty to him whenever she felt like it, but said that ultimately she was the one who'd gotten hurt—was crying inconsolably. A year had passed since then, and Su-hye had staged an exhibition with new sculptures, in a new pair of heels and a new dress, smiling brightly before all these people—just like that.

Did he want her to remain the same? What did remaining the same mean? After all, people were a mix of what could be changed and what could not be changed. Just as the sound of her laugh hadn't changed, her feet, while clad in new shoes, would not have changed either. She had the most exquisite feet. Shapely with just the right amount of flesh. They didn't have any corns; they were like a child's feet, each toe with a distinct expression of its own, like children from different families. Her big toe in particular, its tip tilted up slightly like a traditional Korean sock, was the prettiest. He loved playing with her toes when he was with her. When he tickled them with his fingers, she would let out her abrupt laugh and give him a reproachful look.

"Why my feet, of all things?" She'd ask.

"Your feet aren't too bad. Your hands are misshapen."

Her hands were rougher and thicker than her feet. The backs of her hands habitually sported new scars that covered the old ones, and the undersides of her nails were always crammed with sawdust or dirt. Stretching her arms and turning her hands in the dark, Su-hye remarked, "These are laborer's hands."

When he lay down with his cheek touching her feet and closed his eyes, the dark room floated up like a small roofed boat, and floated away, out of sight. Those were really warm, sweet hours.

Once he told her a story. A long time ago, there was a beautiful geisha in Japan. An old man who loved her asked her for a favor on his deathbed, saying, When I'm breathing my last breath, tread my face with those feet of yours . . .

If he had loved Su-hye's unshapely, rough hands, would his relationship with her have unfolded differently? When he told her the story about the geisha, Su-hye brought up Ha-yun out of the blue. "He . . . he likes my hands."

Now it was all over. No longer would he cuddle her feet in the dark as the outside world faded away. Love was different from the waves of the sea, so never would there come a time for these tides to swell again after their ebbing. Picking his way behind the backs of the crowd, he left the gallery quietly. On the hanging screen draped at the entrance, a beast with a sullen expression was printed, as if finding it hard to adapt to this sweltering, damp city. As the screen fluttered in the breeze, the animal appeared to be ambling toward some destination. Whiffs of broiling pork and mackerel flooded in from a narrow alley nearby.

Even with her back turned, she knew.

He was pushing the door open, taking a step outside. He was the kind of man who found excess more uncomfortable than scarcity. Whenever she had an exhibition, he would first send a plain, simple pot of flowers before coming to look at her works in silence, then he would slip out while the opening ceremony was under way. When the after party was over, he would make sure to come and see her briefly, however late it was. This time she half thought he would come to the exhibition and half thought he wouldn't.

When Ha-yun was alive, she'd talk with Myeong-jo for almost an hour on the days when they didn't have a rendezvous. Why had she cut him out of her life so aggressively after Ha-yun was gone? She was the one who announced that she would stop seeing him, but she had no idea why she felt the way she did. Maybe she needed a sacrificial lamb to alleviate her vague sense of guilt. She'd been friends with Myeong-jo since college, before she'd met Ha-yun. There had been times when her feelings for Myeong-jo had skirted the line between friendship and love, but she'd never developed a passionate love toward him. She only realized belatedly, after her marriage to Ha-yun, that it was because she and Myeong-jo were too alike. Their school friends used to tease that nothing would ever happen between them, even if they were the only ones washed up on a desert island.

Su-hye got involved with Myeong-jo when her marriage to Ha-yun began to slowly exhaust her. To vent her inner turmoil, she found it more comfortable to talk to a male friend rather than a female one. Myeong-jo always drew neat lines, both in his relationships with people and in business matters, and never crossed them. He was a good listener and counselor, who wouldn't reveal any information he'd been entrusted with. One day, it occurred to her that she couldn't refuse him if he wanted to make love to her. After sleeping with him for the first time, she wondered whether she yearned for the relationship more than he did. Having sex with him immediately created a fatal intimacy. Myeong-jo was no longer an old friend but a budding lover. From time to time, she'd ask herself what kind of relationship they had. The relationship felt too anchored to be labeled adultery. Ha-yun liked Su-hye's hands, and Myeong-jo liked her feet. The two men didn't conflict inside her. She wasn't sure when this happened, but Myeong-jo knew more about Su-hye's mundane worries and family problems than Ha-yun did. Looking at herself, who didn't suffer from a guilty conscience even on days when she'd lain next to Myeong-jo with his arm around her, she thought that human beings had a lot of misconceptions about themselves. When she announced that she didn't want to see him anymore, Myeong-jo gazed quietly into her eyes. He couldn't have read anything there, for Su-hye herself didn't know the reason for her decision.

So she's not coming after all?

Su-hye craned her neck to look at the other side of the door. The day the brochures had been delivered from the printer's, she'd put a copy on her daughter's desk. Su-hye checked the next day but it remained right there, untouched. Hyeon hadn't opened it or thrown it in the trash, simply left it there as if it didn't exist.

The previous night, mother and daughter had had a shouting match. If the daughter hadn't set her mind on tormenting her mother, she wouldn't have done it on that day, of all days. Su-hye was in the gallery arranging installations late into the evening, with no break for supper, moving the bison and sweating profusely, when her daughter's homeroom teacher called. Hyeon had taken a classmate's MP3 player. All thoughts and feelings were wiped from Su-hye's brain, and the back of her head stung as if she'd been electrocuted. Hyeon had stolen it? Was that possible? She was speechless.

The teacher explained, "I know she's not the type of kid who'd do such things, so I don't understand it, either. I called up the girl who had lost her MP3 player to return it and told her that Hyeon must be going through a hard time emotionally. The classmate said she understood. She is not a close friend of Hyeon's, but she is a thoughtful kid, so everything has been settled. But I thought you, as her mother, should know about it. I've been aware since the new school year started that Hyeon has been having a hard time."

The homeroom teacher must have heard from Hyeon's previous teacher that she'd lost her father. Su-hye thanked the teacher and apologized several times before hanging up. An MP3 player? Hyeon already had one, so why would she take someone else's? Su-hye felt her brain might explode at any minute, but she couldn't just head home, leaving behind all the gallery staff who were helping her out. Instead she treated them to dinner and arrived home late. All that time, she' thought she was going crazy. Hyeon was watching a comedy that she had downloaded onto her computer. She was giggling, with her feet resting on the desk; her face bore no trace of guilt. Hyeon didn't turn her head, though she was aware that her mother had entered the room.

"Let's talk."

"I've got to watch this."

Only when Su-hye angrily turned off the computer did Hyeon bolt up from her chair and yell, "Why are you making a big deal out of it, pretending you care about me? You don't care about anything, except for your art, Mom. You were never here when I needed you. You lived in your studio and Dad and I lived here.

Why do you care how I live, all of a sudden?"

"You . . . why did you do it?"

"I don't know." Her tone was almost cheerful, as if she were talking about someone else.

Trying hard not to sink to her daughter's level, Su-hye lowered her voice further. "If you don't know, who does?"

"You can say that again."

"What do you want me to do? Tell me."

Now Hyeon pretended to be deaf, her mouth clamped shut.

"Tell me. Why did you do it?"

"You told me, Mom, that you don't like goody-goodies."

Speechless, Su-hye just stood there. Meeting her daughter's glaring eyes, she wondered whether Ha-yun, at one point, had perceived such venom in her own eyes. When she placed her hand on Hyeon's shoulder, her daughter shook it off violently. Her parents had never fought in her presence, but Hyeon was so perceptive that she could read the mood in the house from the moment she opened the front door, and would do her best to lighten the mood in her own way. After Ha-yun's death, Su-hye had often acquiesced to her daughter's tantrums, thinking, If you can tolerate the sorrow of losing your dad this way, go ahead and do what you want to me. This time, however, she couldn't just turn a blind eye. Life tossed unbearable things her way now and then, as if to taunt her: What about this? Can you still handle it? There was no magic solution. All one could do was keep walking. One couldn't stop on a path lined with flowers, nor jump over an icy patch on the road.

Now, standing in the gallery, Su-hye realized how swollen her feet were. They hurt each time she took a step, her shoes pinching her toes.

As soon as he returned to his office, Myeong-jo placed the exhibition catalogue on the table and washed his hands. He had endured it all, behaving nonchalantly as if nothing bothered him, but something remained unresolved between the two of them. He pulled out a bottled coffee drink from the fridge, took a sip, and picked up the catalogue. *There has to be a sentence that's meant for just me, like a secret code.* That was what he was hoping. Flipping over the cover that featured a bison against a bluish background, he came upon the artist's statement.

. . . A year has passed.

Only after he was gone did I realize that all of us are carrying a chill in our hearts as heavy as the weight of the universe. Just like the bison who lived during the Ice Age, we've been thrown here, though we don't know from whence we came or why, and we must walk on ice, fighting off the cold with our entire bodies. After he was gone, what seized me was not sorrow but an intense chill. Just like Texas Sage, which is a flowering plant that is unusually susceptible to pollution, he was an individual who felt others' chill as if it were his own. The bison never knew to the end, why they were thrown to the thick ice and endless snowy fields. I wanted to cross the eons and amble among them.

. . . He gave me the clay and I crafted the bison with it.

The moment he read the final phrase, a fierce jealousy flared up, almost to the point of exploding. He shut his eyes tight. He had never been jealous of Ha-yun when he was alive. But that was clearly the result of arrogance. He wasn't jealous of Ha-yun because he believed that nothing but a formal link remained between Ha-yun and Su-hye.

"I married him knowing that he was exactly like that. But I go through every day, every minute, with the realization that knowledge and experience are two different things." That was how Su-hye always concluded her complaint about how hard Ha-yun made her life. Those words were not intended for anyone else;

it was a closed-circuit reminder to herself, circulating from her lips, to her eardrums, to her brain, to her nerve endings. It was a way of clarifying that the issue had nothing to do with Myeong-jo. Ha-yun was a person who existed in that closed circuit. That closed circle was inseparable from Su-hye, and in order to have Su-hye, Myeong-jo had to embrace it too. But early the previous year, Su-hye suddenly announced that she'd made up her mind to walk out on Ha-yun.

"I told him we should go our separate ways." Su-hye's voice was composed. Myeong-jo was stricken. How could he put it? He'd accepted Su-hye's family as part of her. It sounded odd, but he'd genuinely hoped that her family would get along, that its members would be healthy, that Hyeon would do better in school, and that Su-hye's exhibitions would be successful so that they could move to a bigger apartment. The secret rendezvous between him and Su-hye were peaceful, rather than intense. After making love, Su-hye would lie with her pubic bones digging into Myeong-jo's waist, speaking about the details that troubled her and asking for his opinions. She'd take a short nap while he was rubbing her feet. He thought neither of them wanted anything more.

"I told him I don't want anything. Not Hyeon, not the apartment. I told him to take it all if he wished. But my voice sounded cunning even to my own ears. If we do separate, I know he'll leave empty-handed. Otherwise, would I have said that?"

Listening to her, Myeong-jo remembered Ha-yun's eyes. He'd seen his images in newspaper photos and on TV, but he'd met him only once. At one of Su-hye's exhibitions. "This is my husband. This here is my college friend. I've mentioned him once or twice, haven't I? Lee Myeong-jo." Su-hye's introduction was short. Ha-yun's gaze was sharp, with an intensity that pierced through people, objects, and even relationships. Myeong-jo knew too much about him. Not only what he did, but everything rang-ing from his daily habits to dietary preferences to temperament. Out of habit, Myeong-jo pulled out a business card and accepted Ha-yun's in return. Ha-yun's card offered little information compared with what Myeong-jo already knew. Glancing at it, he said, "You're doing really meaningful work." Ha-yun didn't answer affirmatively or negatively; he simply draped his arm around his wife's shoulders and said, "My wife has been doing a lot for me." Yet, Myeong-jo didn't feel a speck of jealousy.

When Su-hye confided in him about wanting to get a divorce, Myeong-jo asked, "How did he respond?"

"Looks like it was a great shock. He doesn't eat much these days. It makes me nervous. It would be better if he'd exploded with fury. He's soft-hearted. He's like a child. Because he's like a child, he's been doing what he does all his life."

Afterward, Myeong-jo couldn't see Su-hye for a month. On the phone, she said, "He's in bad shape." Her voice had changed so much that she sounded like a stranger. She added, "It's been about ten days since he was hospitalized." Her voice was low and husky. "They say it's cancer. It began in his stomach, but has spread to other organs . . . How is it possible? This fast?" Su-hye spoke incoherently, but Myeong-jo grasped the situation right away. Ha-yun's illness was terminal. Myeong-jo remembered Ha-yun's face when he'd said, "My wife has been doing a lot for me." A chill passed through him. Myeong-jo only managed to say, "He was in good health, wasn't he?"

She replied, "They say it's spread faster because he's young and healthy. We shouldn't have come to the hospital. Since he was hospitalized, he's been getting worse by the day."

During this period, Myeong-jo saw Su-hye only once, at a café near the hospital. She looked so drained that he ordered a tomato juice for her. She said she was having trouble keeping even water down, and swallowed some juice with difficulty, as if taking medicine. She was so gaunt that his heart went out to her.

It was a warm day and she was wearing a long-sleeved T-shirt, but she kept hugging herself.

"I should have put up with it for a few more days," Su-hye mumbled in a hoarse voice, looking out to the street.

It was the season when girls walked around with their backs exposed in the shade of lush green trees. The world was so vibrant that even the stones seemed to be breathing. She said that Ha-yun had been admitted to the hospital exactly fifteen days after she'd demanded a divorce.

Myeong-jo said, "If he's terminal, then the disease began years ago. It all comes down to statistics and fate. It's nobody's fault."

Su-hye shook her head. "That's not what I'm saying."

He knew exactly what she meant. If she hadn't brought up the divorce when she did, Ha-yun could have settled his worldly affairs and closed his eyes peacefully. How shallow emotions were in the face of absolute fate! After Ha-yun's death, Myeong-jo's relationship with her came to an end. It would be a lie to say he hadn't entertained the thought of what would happen in the future, while Ha-yun was fighting his cancer. Myeong-jo vaguely assumed that nothing much would change. At the time, he'd thought that his time with Su-hye didn't stretch toward an unknown future, but lay in the eternity that circled between them. Their relationship had been that stable.

After the funeral, Su-hye told him, "You're so much like me. You know that? I don't like myself."

Su-hye's face was puffy. Every love is fated, but only while it is burning.

"You look so tired. I'll help you here before we go," the curator offered.

"I'm waiting for someone. I'll join you soon, in about twenty minutes." Su-hye sent her off, asking her to entertain her guests who were already at the restaurant.

Finally, the hall was deserted. She wasn't expecting anyone. She just wanted to be by herself in the empty hall, if only briefly. Heaving a long sigh, she turned off a light switch. The bulbs over the reception area went dark. She switched off another. Half the lighting in the gallery was turned off. A woman passing by turned her head to peek inside. Su-hye took off her shoes, placed them neatly on the floor next to the reception desk, and meandered through the bison in the dim light. A subtle tension emanated from the disharmony between their docile looks, their blurred facial features, and their horns spiraling up toward the ceiling. The animals looked different from when they had stood in her studio. A careful look at each face gave her the illusion that they were saying something. Creating them had been a staggering amount of work for just one year.

At first, she had considered using a mold. Given the size of the animals, however, that wasn't a facile solution. After much deliberation, she opted to build a basic form for each bison, crafting a frame with an upright core, on which she pasted wooden chips. This decision made her heart flutter with anxiety. She wondered to whom this unyielding spirit of hers was directed. To begin with, would the forms be created at all? Each attempt would produce a different proportion and balance, so would she be able to create a sense of unity between the different sculptures? She felt lost and mused that it was a form of self-flagellation. She had to work with bonding glue all day long. Though she kept the windows open, the stench of the glue seeped into her nose, eyes, and skin. The glue burned off her fingerprints. Her palms bristled against sandpaper, turned into coarse brushes. She could stick to this process because she didn't know what the end result would be. She was holed up in her studio, as if trapped between the strata of the Ice Age. She wasn't sure whether there would be an end to it all, but here they were, the bison, each sporting imperious horns.

With his death, Ha-yun whisked away the nets that had bound her, layer upon layer. When she had yelled that the knots around her neck were choking and stifling her, and that she could no longer put up with it, she hadn't imagined that they would be untied in a flash. Since she believed they'd never come off, she ranted and raved at Ha-yun.

In the winter before his death, she'd spent most of her time in her studio with the excuse that she was preparing for an exhibition. It was unimaginably hard to be with Ha-yun. He wasn't a bad person who deserved her contempt, but she couldn't tolerate him. This made her more depressed and exhausted than she would have been if she were quarreling with a person who'd actually done something wrong. When she caught herself sounding cunning and selfish when she told him off, she was dumbfounded, thinking it was all so unfair. Whenever she could, she stormed off to her studio.

In her studio, she couldn't focus on her work. She'd idly riffle through magazines or take long naps, heavily laden with dreams, on the sofa bed in the corner. Or she'd hug a bag of popcorn, tossing handfuls into her mouth until the bottom appeared, as she looked vacantly out the window. She'd sit in a stupor and surf though channels on the TV. An hour flew by easily if she lingered one minute on each channel. When she came across a comedy, she would watch a skit all the way through before moving on. Sometimes she laughed aloud. Ha ha. The sound rang unfamiliar, as if coming from a stranger.

She now understood: She shouldn't have accompanied Ha-yun the second time. When she went to North Korea with him for the first time, it had been an unofficial visit. They were newly married then. The unfamiliar has the power to fascinate you and make you feel more generous. That was how she felt about Ha-yun and his work. They didn't have an official itinerary in Pyong-yang, so they headed directly for N City, where a research center was located. The people there were frank about the scarcity and strain they were working under and asked in dignified demeanor for their help. She admired Ha-yun then for the way he worked with no personal gain in mind. Come to think of it, that wasn't actually the problem. During her second visit, too, the North Koreans asked for his help with dignity. Everything hinged on how Su-hye felt, in fact. A quick look revealed that in early spring N City and the surrounding villages were extremely bleak. No improvement was detectable. Instead, out there, where a cold wind blew ceaselessly, everything—people, animals, scenery, and buildings—was as dilapidated as could be. Something made it impossible to turn a blind eye. The link with N City was an official affair, but supplies were handed over through unofficial channels to places that North Koreans wanted to keep under wraps. Their requests, which began with drugs such as ethambutol and rifampicine, had extended to include more and more varieties. After X-ray machines were sent upon request, they complained that the machines remained idle because there was no film, and after the film was delivered, they demanded generators, saying that a shortage of electricity rendered the machines useless. When the machines broke down, the North Koreans insisted that they be repaired. Everything was in this vein. Tubercolosis is a consumptive disease. Drugs alone can't cure it. They had to have food. Appeal after appeal kept coming.

If insufficiency was apparent at the official level, things had to stop there, but Ha-yun just couldn't do it. The problems could not be solved by one individual. Constant giveaways didn't result in any sign of improvement; rather, the holes grew larger. Su-hye was angry, but she remembered the sallow, gaunt face of the doctor at the research center, who didn't seem to have an ounce of fat on his body. If she hadn't seen it all, she would have thrown up her hands, saying, I can't do this anymore. When her irritation had passed, the sad gleam in the eyes of the weak would come to mind, leaving her feeling sad and resigned.

After her second visit to the North, she felt like a deflated ball that would never bounce again. She couldn't look Ha-yun in the face. The feeling was too complicated to put into words. How could she explain it? When she looked him in the face, she thought, *Yes, you're the good guy*, which was soon replaced by resentment. *Then am I the bad guy?* She felt as though she'd taken the first, and then the second, step into a bog; the more you kicked and screamed, the deeper you sank. When she was at home, she ticked like a bomb of gloom.

"I don't like freshwater fish," Su-hye snapped at Ha-yun on the eve of their return to Seoul, as soon as the door to their hotel room clicked shut. He remained silent. Putting down her handbag on the table with a thud, she shook her head. She said, "I don't like 'passionate welcomes' either."

The man named Song, who'd come all the way to the airport to meet them, had grabbed Su-hye's hands, saying, "We welcome you passionately." Song had met Ha-yun before. It was not that he gave off bad vibes. It would have been the same if they'd been met by someone else. Su-hye followed Song around downtown Pyongyang as he guided them, and regretted constantly that she'd come along. What had changed since her first visit to the North, to N City?

The lunch menu featured spicy freshwater fish soup. Song repeatedly urged her to have more, saying that the fish was a rare delicacy caught in the Taedong River, but she only went through the motions of sipping the broth a few times, then stuffed herself with rice, kimchi, and other vegetables. She didn't care for freshwater fish at all. At his urging, she had reluctantly drunk a little bit of broth and found it pretty tasty and not fishy at all. Still, she made sure not to spoon up any of the fish, as if in protest to Ha-yun, who was well aware of her dietary preferences, but refused to put in a word for her sake.

Afterward, they passed clean, orderly streets on their way to visit a kindergarten, and the children there extended another "passionate welcome." Su-hye didn't feel that it was the first time she was visiting the kindergarten. Nothing was new. The scenes unfolding there were what she'd seen on public television again and again, until she got sick and tired of it. The children wearing large red flowers in their hair sang children's songs in a high falsetto, just like the popular "trot" singers in the South. The hand motions of the children, wearing the same smile as if created from the same mold, were too artificial to be called cute. *Just look how unnaturally they move their shoulders!* She shuddered. It bothered her that their synchronized dance didn't deviate in the slightest from one child to the next. How relentlessly they must have been pushed to practice!

Earlier, Song had explained, "We've distributed the antiparasite tablets you sent us last time. Almost all the children in Pyongyang kindergartens and daycare centers received them, but woefully the number of tablets fell short, given the demand in the entire republic. To distribute just one tablet each for growing children, we'll need two million in total."

Ha-yun nodded again. *Two million tablets?* Su-hye thought, *Do you know how much a tablet costs?* Simple arithmetic yielded an astronomical sum. *So what now? What do you want me to do? Why you and I, of all people?* Su-hye gritted her teeth. The children with their red flowers kept singing and dancing similar numbers. Looking at them, Su-hye became more angry, for it looked like they were bullying her into promising what she couldn't deliver, as if pulling her reluctant finger into a pinky promise.

The children in front of her looked in excellent health. Su-hye shook her head. She saw in her mind's eye the pasty faces of the children who were wandering around some nameless border, neither N City nor Pyongyang, with anxiety in their eyes, jumpier than the old-fashioned videotape itself, which had been surreptitiously taken by an anonymous artist. Starvation and cold pushed those children to become almost feral. Even if two million anti-parasite tablets and hundreds of thousands of TB drugs were sent, they would never reach those nomads. Even if a whole set of baking appliances was transferred to build a mammoth bakery, not a single bite of bread would ever enter the mouths of those children. The kids, scrawny as undernourished animals, roaming about the border areas and picking through the trash for dirt-covered greens and discarded food, were children of another country, who belonged neither to this side nor that. Su-hye was disturbed by Song's strong, confident gaze; he kept saying the words *two million tablets* as if they were nothing, as if he were asking them to return something they had merely been safeguarding for him. This was after he had showed off the city to his heart's content, as if he were living in a self-sufficient paradise on earth.

It rained on the way back to the hotel. The apartments in Pyongyang were being dyed dark gray, and people hastened their footsteps for home. Some were shopping at a vegetable seller's. Though the details differed, in the grand scheme of things, the scene was no different from anywhere else; it was the very picture of people going about their daily business.

N City had melted her heart but now Pyongyang triggered a negative reaction. Gazing out at the fading city amid the rain, Su-hye felt her heart tangling up. Many things had changed— the most obvious of all was her relationship with Ha-yun. It was not clear which came first: Did the aspects of him that had once fascinated her so much make him insufferable now? Or was it the other way around? For all she knew, Ha-yun would stick to this work until the day he died, and she couldn't extricate herself from it all either, as if she were caught in a net with him. At this thought, she ended up exploding at the hotel.

She didn't exactly mean that she disliked the freshwater fish and the passionate welcome, but the work she was doing with him she now found tiring. Ha-yun couldn't have been oblivious. It hadn't been just once or twice that they'd squabbled over the issue. More precisely, Ha-yun had always listened quietly to Su-hye's stream of snappish accusations. She found it harder to stand him when he reacted the way he did. Ha-yun's eyes, calmly looking at her, reflected Su-hye like a mirror. In the hotel room in Pyongyang, Ha-yun gathered up the clothes Su-hye had thrown to the floor and put them on hangers.

He said, "You're not a child. Did you have to protest the way you did, making your feelings known? You've worked so hard, behind the scenes and on the scenes as well . . ."

She shot back, "Everyone wants to live for a beautiful cause. They want to be good guys. All of us are like that. So am I. But this isn't right. Where's the end of this work? Why do you have to pour the money I've worked so hard for where it doesn't leave any trace? I want to spend what I've earned on myself and Hyeon. I want to save for retirement, too. I'm no Mother Teresa. What now? Anti-parasite drugs? Antibiotics? What else do they say they need? What disease do you have to carry on your back next time? Even God can't do anything about poverty in this world. I thought I was going crazy all day because of all this gloom. What fool would try to plug these holes with money from his own pocket? What's left for us? All we get is criticism that we're just throwing money around."

He said, "It doesn't matter what people think."

"I don't want to live with an angel. I want to live with a timid guy who's selfish, cowardly, and only looks out for his family."

"You're not a cynic."

"I shouldn't have come. The kids at the kindergarten looked healthy and happy. More than me. Where are the children we wept for while watching the video? Convince me."

Ha-yun frowned. "It's not simple. I know that."

He was going to add something but stopped, looking Su-hye in the eyes. Those eyes of his were deeply sunken, as if tears were flowing behind his eyeballs. He was always busy, requesting donations from corporations and individuals, traveling to give lectures, and assigning donated goods to needy places, but to her, his work seemed no better than pouring water into a broken jar. In her eyes, he was a person who'd started an impossible deed and was waiting for a miracle. Other than the aid that could be documented, all expenses were replenished from his own pocket. Whenever Su-hye had an exhibition, Ha-yun already knew where he would spend her tidy earnings. That night, when she looked into his eyes in the hotel, Su-hye felt driven to despair. She realized she could no longer put up with Ha-yun and his work. She drove the final nail in the coffin, "This, this is the wrong goal."

After her return, Su-hye practically lived at her studio. On that fateful day, she was taking care of unnecessary chores there. She hadn't been able to do a thing about her work. During lunch, she talked with Myeong-jo for over an hour. He asked her to have lunch with him, but she wasn't in the mood. Before hanging up, she said, "How could I have endured it all these years? If I hadn't had you to listen to me, I would have gone crazy." In the afternoon, she watched a documentary about the ecosystem of the Kuril Islands until the closing credits rolled, wondering whether people favored animal documentaries because they didn't have to look at human beings on screen. The cold at the start of winter was more formidable than that at the end of winter. When she wasn't working, the room felt chillier. Irritated, she said, "Why won't this cold go away?" She haphazardly put away the things that she'd spread out on her worktable but never got around to doing anything with, and then left her studio. She was thinking of going home and soaking in a hot bathtub.

Remembering the empty refrigerator at home, she stopped by the supermarket and bought whatever caught her eye. When she'd turned into an alley, it was a struggle to walk on the three-day-old snow frozen in dirty clumps. The plastic shopping bag full of potatoes and onions seemed to be growing heavier, so three times she had to put it down on the snow and rub her fingers to ease the pain.

It looked like no one was home. The living room was dark and a sour kimchi odor hung in the air. She couldn't put down the plastic bag with its soiled bottom, so she struggled out of her shoes and headed straight to the kitchen. Ha-yun, who was eating ramen at the table, stood up awkwardly and held out his hand, probably intending to take the bag, but she brushed by, went over to the sink, and put the bag down on the counter. Her cramped fingers tingled. If he hadn't been eating ramen at four o'clock in the afternoon, if he had been eating it with the light on at least, Su-hye would not have blurted out what had been festering inside her.

"Let's get a divorce."

About half of the ramen remained in the pot. She should have waited until he was done. She was instantly pleased, thinking that she had done what she shouldn't have. Ha-yun looked down briefly at his ramen, brought the pot to the sink, tipped it over, and turned the tap on. All without a word.

She said, "Why is our life so disappointing? Your mind is fixed so far ahead, and it's difficult and lonely for me. All that's left of me is a shell. Let me go."

When he turned the water off, she could hear the loud ticking of the clock's second hand. She'd always thought Ha-yun was stronger than she was, but he was not, not at four o'clock that afternoon.

Standing among the bison, she felt as if she had been buried between the transparent strata of ice. Where could Ha-yun be now? In her memory, he was always frozen in a single still image. He was dumping the ramen in the sink. When she tried to assemble a moving image, with him sleeping, smiling, weeping, and talking, all these scattered memories receded, leaving only his profile as he poured out the ramen.

The blizzard's knife-sharp wind raps against their leathery skin. The bison silently cross the blue, frozen Lake Baikal and walk on and on, passing plains and hills. They walk through winter, spring, and summer. They pass the Korean Peninsula, cross the frozen Bering Strait, and enter Alaska. The conditions of life don't change. Where they arrive is exactly the same as where they've left. In order not to freeze to death, they must walk without stopping and lick moss to fill their empty stomachs. Everything—eating, loving, and walking—is arduous. As they breathe the last breaths of their harsh life, the bison freeze in place like rocks.

Beings that withstood the conditions of the Ice Age with nothing but their own body heat, herbivorous mammals that did not fight, lives before the advent of desire . . . the lives beneath the strata.

Su-hye knew that her cunning had made her choose animals that lay buried underground as a monument for Ha-yun. Just as she had said she'd give everything to him when they divorced. Just as she had said she disliked freshwater fish. Just as she had said those things instead of saying that she wanted nothing to do with his work.

The whirlwind in her heart, whether consisting of pain or guilt, would be buried in the frozen strata. After the exhibition was over.

Her back hurt. If only she had said that the spicy freshwater fish had tasted good—though she still would have fought him when necessary.

"You stopped smoking? That's good," Su-hye muttered, as if to herself, and then lit up. "As if you'd live forever. Ha!" She contradicted herself this way in the same breath and then grimaced.

"Come right away wherever you are." When Su-hye called, Myeong-jo had been in his office. There was always so much to do. Well, not really. He had been waiting for her call. Su-hye was waiting for him in front of the unlit gallery, thinking, *If he's done with seeing me at the end of every after-party, then so be it.* When she greeted him with the words, "That was fast," the faint whiff of liquor and stew drifted toward him.

The air was sticky and the street was dirty. The plastic trash bags, put out by the stores, were piled up next to the stone caskets, and the air of stale alcohol reeked in place of the excitement and heat that had filled the street earlier in the evening. As if she had called him reluctantly, Su-hye had said that she wanted to drink coffee, but she didn't want to drink it alone. No other customers were in the café because it was almost closing time. He had thought they still had things to sort out, but face to face he wondered if there was anything left that they needed to talk about, really. He drank his coffee without speaking, feeling it would be silly to ask how she had been all these months.

"Myeong-jo, I wanted to part with him, but not that way. You know, though it was a short period of time, I did everything in my power. I boiled elm bark and made him drink the coagulated liquid, which was thick as mucus, and I bought maggots, though they looked absolutely repulsive. I knew that it made no sense, but I clung to alternative medicine and made him more miserable. I learned pain was a cruel thing. I knew what great pain he was in, but I couldn't feel the tiniest bit of what he was feeling. I saw that he was sick, very sick, and that he was hurting tremendously, but I could never actually feel his pain. When his doctors said they would stop giving him drugs, only painkillers, I put him in the car and took him to a retreat for prayers. I'd only attended Sunday school when I was seven. I pleaded not with God, but with him. Cling to Him, please. Ask Him to let you live. They say cripples walk and cancerous tumors break down and are flushed out of people's bodies. He shook his head. He said that he'd like to, but he didn't have any energy left to pray."

Su-hye's voice was calm. Only the skeleton of her story was left, because she had chewed on it over and over in her mind.

"Everything I did, from the time he was diagnosed to the time he closed his eyes, I did from the bottom of my heart."

"I'm sure you did."

Su-hye shook her head. "No, that's not true. Around the time he got sick, I showed him the worst side of me, when I brought up the divorce. How torn his heart must have been, looking at me running around in a frenzy as if I had been the most devoted wife in the world! When everything was over, I wondered if I'd wanted him to survive, to recover his health, so that we could resume our fight and see who would win, and then he'd be free to do whatever he wanted."

A sympathetic ear was probably what Su-hye needed, not coffee.

"It's nothing like the love that I realized belatedly after he was gone. You know, petty things—my irritation, hatred, anger—are part of me. I thought I could fly away if I could shake them off. I thought a big hole had been drilled into me. As I shaped the bison's horns into spirals, pasting nail-sized wood chips one after another, and filled the heavy, gigantic bodies one inch at a time, I asked myself, How did you guys endure those days, standing on the ice? What warmth did you have to embrace in order to endure the absolute emptiness, because you turned into ice blocks as soon as you breathed your last?"

"What did the bison tell you?"

Snorting, Su-hye examined her palms as if she'd never seen them before. The unhealed scars were still vivid.

"They told me to keep walking. To just keep walking past ice, meadows, flowers, deserts, and heaps of stone."

The café owner pointed to the clock. They left and walked

toward Anguk-dong. A drunkard staggered in and out between the bags of trash lining the street. Passing the gallery, Myeong-jo unconsciously turned his head toward it, and Su-hye stopped in her tracks.

"Earlier today, I happened to look out and noticed that you were standing right here. You were standing awkwardly, caught in the middle of the flash mob. You didn't collapse like the kids did, and you didn't march off, either. I found it funny, but if I'd been here, I'd have done the same thing. We're so alike."

He'd never thought the word "alike" could carry such a daunting ring to it. A speeding taxi came to a crawl near them. Su-hye raised her hand to flag it down. She looked at Myeong-jo, standing on the other side of a black stone casket littered with disposable food containers. Her eyes told him that they would never see each other again. When the taxi disappeared around the corner at the end of the street, Myeong-jo looked around him as if he'd never been to the neighborhood before.

The streetscape was completely different from what it had been at six o'clock in the evening.

In the Wind

How can I describe it?

It looked like a flower with a single layer of four petals. The bottom of the Petri dish was almost visible under the translucent flower whose oval boundaries shimmered in rainbow colors: yellow, light green, green, sky blue, and purple. I couldn't take my eye off it.

"The colors are so gorgeous."

"It doesn't actually have colors. You can't see it with the naked eye so we've lit it for clarity."

As I stared at it through the lens, it seemed to be quivering ever so faintly like heat haze.

"Uh, is it moving now?"

Dong-jae didn't answer. I took my eye off the lens and glanced at him. His expression was unexpectedly complicated. Actually, he could just have been wearing the guarded smile of any veteran fertility doctor who didn't want to give his patients too much hope. It had to be my intuition that read complexity on his face. How could cells move? Even without his answer, I knew that cells did not move. Still, I could do nothing about my racing heart.

"Dr. Cha, why does it look like it's trembling, like a bud that's blossoming?"

Dong-jae plunged his hands deep into the pockets of his white coat. "Moving? That's possible. All beings . . . are probably moving."

What was the difference between moving and trembling? He was too restrained. I was a little offended that he was not swept up by my excitement, which was practically causing me to hiccup. Yes, I knew. What was trembling wasn't what lay on the dish, but me. I pressed my eye to the lens again. If Dong-jae had not been standing there, I could have looked at it forever. Click! Dong-jae turned the switch off. The light disappeared. The petals lost their colors. Only the colors were gone, but the embryo instantly retreated far away, growing faint as though it had moved into a different dimension. The petals now looked like a few droplets of foam that might burst at any moment.

"This . . . is this life?" I asked, my eye still glued to the microscope.

He and I knew each other too well. He clearly understood that this wasn't the question that I'd wanted to ask. He knew what it was that I wanted to confirm. It had been a while since I'd stopped discussing this particular issue with anyone else but him, revealing what I really thought, just as a person who had undergone psychotherapy felt at certain moments that her psychiatrist was God, a lover, or her only soul mate in the universe. Now, however, I couldn't bring myself to pose the question I really wanted to ask, even to him.

What I wanted to learn was the statistical probability, not whether the cells were trembling or moving, or from which point of cell division the embryo could be classified as life. The odds of probability: for a brief moment before throwing out the question, I had been tempted to say "the baby" instead of "this."

He replied in a soothing tone, fully aware of my thoughts. "It's just the beginning."

This had to be the only thing he would say, having observed every single phase of my yearning, anxiety, failure, despair, and then uncertain hope that flared up again at the end of this cycle. I, too, was aware that I should keep my calm, instead of harboring even the tiniest mustard seed of hope, until the moment I held a baby in my arms, who was taking its first breaths with its own nostrils. The scar of each failure smarted as much as the first one. I willed myself to remain cool, telling myself, This is still an abstract concept. Yet, my heart kept fluttering like the petals on the Petri dish. Each of those petals had to contain tiny arms and legs, dark eyes, soft lips, and red chubby cheeks.

"Will it be transferred tomorrow?"

"We'll do it in three days."

"Why is that?"

"We'll do it after it's more developed. When it reaches the blastocyst stage, the cells double, and the success rate increases. This is the best one so far. I would give it a B grade."

We had done the procedure several times, but he'd never taken me to the lab to show me an embryo. Was he implying that he was that confident this time around?

As he opened the door to lead me out, he said, as if he had just remembered, "Oh, Yeong-jo came to see it yesterday."

My husband? Why had he suddenly stopped by? Even when he had to come, he'd given me the impression that he was dragging his feet, making me nervous.

"Did he say he wanted to see it?"

"I asked him to come. Thought he'd be curious."

I answered vaguely, Oh I see, but my thoughts were all jumbled. Saying that he would get in touch with me again as things progressed, Dong-jae raised his hand in farewell and briskly strode through the back door that was connected to his office.

I slowly walked by the patients sitting and waiting in the hallway. A woman with a youthful face was leaning against the wall, with her round belly thrust out. Her upper body heaved every time she breathed. The hallway was crowded, all the way down to the end. It seemed like I had held up the doctor too long.

Before I became Dr. Cha's patient, I had called him Dong-jae.

I had stopped going to church by then as well, but at one point I joked to him that he should come to Mass, having learned that he, the confirmed faithful, did not attend Mass. "There are a lot of women in the church, so your patients will double." Dong-jae answered, "Do you want me to close shop? Fellow believers can become potential patients for other doctors, but that's not the case when it comes to obstetricians." I thought that made sense, and also thought that as the wife of his friend, not just a fellow churchgoer, I would feel even more uncomfortable. But that was only my way of thinking. Yeong-jo believed that there was no reason for me to settle for second best when Dong-jae was the best in his field. I'd known that as a renowned fertility doctor Dong-jae had a waiting list of six months, so I thought it was out of the question that I'd become his patient.

"How can I go see him?" I said, and went to another doctor. On the day the second procedure turned out to be a failure, I silently shed fat teardrops. Yeong-jo, sitting next to me, called Dong-jae and made an appointment. Informing me of the date and the time set for the following week, not six months later, he glanced at me, his eyes saying, See?

If I didn't take my feelings into consideration, Yeong-jo's choice seemed to be right. Dong-jae was an outstanding fertility expert and at the same time played the role of a thoughtful psychiatrist. From the first day of consultation, I started calling him Dr. Cha. That was the only thing I could do. That was my feeble acknowledgment that I couldn't bring myself to spread my legs before him and show him my reproductive organs while calling him Dong-jae.

One could reach the lobby only after passing through the pediatric department around the bend at the end of the hallway. Could this be a marketing gimmick? Babies are always adorable, even when they cry in pain. Once I had stopped and lingered over a baby who was crying his heart out, showing his uvula, before

I managed to tear myself away. When I passed mothers holding babies, I inevitably imagined myself sitting in one of those green chairs with a baby in my arms. There couldn't be a better stimulus than this for firming up my easily frayed resolve to soldier on for further fertility procedures.

I walked across the lobby and pushed the heavy door to step out of the building. The July sun, as intense as heated metal, burned my skin. Why was I always so drained after doctor's appointments, even when nothing had been done to me? Today I hadn't even gotten a shot. If I got pregnant in July, the due date would be spring. The shimmering, colorful embryo, just like flower petals in early spring, kept floating up before my eyes.

As I ambled down a sloped cement pedestrian path, hope began to ferment in my heart, sending up bubbles of excitement. All through the previous procedures, I had shifted back and forth between hope and despair. If I had experienced abject despair whenever Dong-jae had said, "Looks like we've got to hope for better luck next time," I would be overcome with a real sense of loss if the procedure failed this time. I might not be able to eat for several days, seized by the vision of the petals that had been washed away, and for all I knew, I might go slightly crazy as if I'd lost a real baby. Was it possible that Dong-jae wasn't aware of my fragility? Why had he shown it to me, and even to Yeong-jo?

While I waited for a taxi, the heat of the sizzling sun, every ray of it, poured down on my face. But I didn't even feel the heat.

After I got into the taxi, I gave the taxi driver the name of the wedding hall at Sinsa-dong, where my cousin's wedding was to be held, and closed my eyes. I was not sure if I could make it on time. I was reluctant to ask a fellow teacher to take over my class too often, and so I tried to schedule doctor's appointments on days when I didn't have to teach immediately before the lunch break. Then I could combine the free period with the lunch hour. Today, however, I had to attend the wedding, so I had no choice but to ask Ms. Roh to cover my fifth period.

The traffic wasn't too bad, fortunately. At the entrance, I checked my cousin's name on the list of the day's wedding couples before walking up to the second floor. I caught myself being careful with my footsteps. Mom, who had arrived earlier, cast a critical eye over my outfit. She seemed to disapprove that I hadn't dressed up. Mom lived and died for appearances. No one would have cared if she occupied herself with these concerns, but the problem was she imposed her ways on the people around her. Her face paled at the sight of me clad in unmatched separates and wilting from the intense heat, my eyes sunken in their sockets, as I entered the hall where all our relatives were gathered for the first time in a long while. She chided me in a voice that reached only my ears, "You don't have a formal summer dress? I know you play with snot-smeared kids, but still . . ." I was tempted to say, "I've been at the doctor's," but decided to say, "No, I don't."

"You don't even have a child to take care of, and look how you're dressed!" She never failed to make a disparaging remark whenever there was an opportunity.

I'd never been grateful for Mom's frankness. Why did she feel such intense rivalry with her own sister? Mom felt her husband ought to make more money than her younger sister's, and everyone in the world should know about it. The groom being married to her niece today should not have a better job than her own son-in-law, and, if he did, at least he should be shorter than her son-in-law. Living this way, it was no wonder that she was always tired, angry, and depressed. If my cousin was to get pregnant with a honeymoon baby, Mom would certainly sink into another bout of depression. Not because of her sympathy for her own daughter, but because of her injured pride.

My cousin was the same age as I was, so she was getting married rather late in life. Surrounded by her friends in the bride's waiting room, she was trying hard not to smile too broadly, pressing down the outer corners of her eyes with her palms, but even when she remained expressionless, tiny wrinkles were evident around her eyes. Standing behind her friends, I observed her thrilled expression. When she spotted me over the photographer's shoulder, she waved at me. Though her shoulders were bare, the layers of her spread-out skirt made her look uncomfortably warm. Her forehead was already glistening.

I squeezed her hand veiled in fancy lace gloves, and said, "You look stunning. I wish you all the happiness in the world."

She smiled, her eyes almost weepy. When we had been in college, we often spent time together, watching movies, talking about our boyfriends, and going to the beach together. Had I looked like this on my wedding day? I didn't know what expressions I had worn that day, but I had been thinking obsessively about Yun the entire time I was in the bride's waiting room. I asked myself, Is this the right decision? Am I starting something that I'll regret?

Yun, the guy who had said he would never have children.

He'd said, "I can't be optimistic about the world my children will grow up in. It's irresponsible and absurd to bring children into this world, especially if I can't be optimistic about it, and without asking them first if they'd like to live in it even though it will be tough. I'm sure the children will be adorable when they smile. I'm sure my heart will go out to them when I see them toddling around. I'm sure I'll momentarily forget that life is a roiling sea when I hear them call me Dad for the first time. But casting a life into the world for such momentary, selfish satisfactions, well, that's the definition of irresponsibility."

When Yun happened to mention that he wouldn't pass on his genes, while discussing some other innocuous thing, I interpreted that as, I don't love you enough. My idea of love at that age was that he could change his tragic worldview in a flash if he truly loved me, however rock solid his beliefs.

I vividly remembered how Yun had occupied all my thoughts as I'd sat like my cousin was sitting now, waiting for someone to escort me out. It wasn't that Yun and I had gone our separate ways over the issue of unborn children at such a young age, but if I went backward from the point of our irreconcilable alienation, it all began when the clash between genes and love occurred.

Then, was my persistence to have a child by any means, and Yeong-jo's obsession with it, a pledge of our fierce love for each other? I could answer that all too easily: no. I didn't know what it had been like earlier in our marriage. Emotions are hard to remember.

If I had married Yun but not been able to conceive, would we have been happy? It was impossible to know. Life is unpredictable. Only after things became irreconcilable did I think that what Yun had talked about perhaps had nothing to do with our love or marriage, but a dark, vague forecast about the future of humankind. Then why had Dong-jae shown those flower petals to my husband, and then to me?

I wasn't ready to be interrogated by my relatives, who made it their business to poke their noses into other people's affairs, so I slipped into the wedding hall through a side door and stood in a corner, with my back to the wall. My cousin, gliding in hand-in-hand with her father, looked as though she belonged in a romance comic. A long time ago I'd realized that the surreal accoutrements of a wedding are meant to shield the couple from the stark reality of marriage. Slow steps and a happy smile. The room turned blurry. Why was I like this? I didn't know when this started to happen, but whenever I watched a bride's back as she walked down the aisle to the tune of the piano, my eyes welled up with tears. My life wasn't particularly unhappy and I didn't nurse bitter regret over my marriage to Yeong-jo, but tears surged at unexpected moments. I opened my eyes wide to prevent the tears from falling. I was being too sensitive.

After the ceremony, while the newlyweds posed for photos with their relatives, I stood in the back row. Then I said, "Mom, I have to dash off," and she poked me in the side, startling me. Glaring, she whined, "You can't just put in a brief appearance like this and disappear. Stay and eat with us at least." For some reason, lies tumbled out effortlessly when I was with her. "I'm sorry, I need to stop by the clinic and then head to the school as soon as I can." "Why didn't your husband come?" she demanded. "It's the last family wedding in your generation." I said, "How can you expect him to attend a wedding on a weekday? He was trying to make it but I told him I'd come on behalf of both of us." She asked, "Do you really have to go to the clinic today? I have something to tell you." I replied, "I've got to go. Will call you in the evening." She glanced at my belly and commented, "It's not absolutely necessary to have children, you know." She didn't say this to make me feel better, nor was it a nod to the old saying "No children are bliss." It was a childish complaint on her part: *Well, what's the use of having children like you?*

Did she have to go around broadcasting her unhappiness? Mom was so attuned to her sister's laughable desolation at marrying off her daughter, who would set up her household a mere stone's throw away. And she felt most keenly her own anguish as a mother whose daughter was less pliant than other people's children. But why did she fail to read her own daughter's twisted heart? I had compressed my troubles into a tiny ball and kept it out of view. It wasn't because I was strong. People who haven't experienced it will never realize how intolerable it is to attract looks of pity for several years running, not just for a day or two.

I bought a cheesecake near the wedding hall before returning to the school. I had to teach the remaining period. I was so exhausted that my legs had grown numb. After the end of classes, some of us teachers gathered at Pak's homeroom—she was the head teacher for the sixth grade—and shared the cake. These days I found myself gorging on food, even when I wasn't hungry. Ravenous ghosts seemed to lurk inside me and wake up as soon as something slid down my throat. The four of us women polished off the cake, which was far from small. I was thankful to my colleagues, who took turns covering for me when I had to go to the clinic, but putting up with their chatter afterward was a chore.

"I fight with the kids all day long, and then go home," Pak began. "The venue changes, but the war still goes on. Sometimes I can't believe what a mess two kids can make. The whole apartment is one huge trashcan. Cookie wrappers, milk glasses, and Lego pieces . . . Teacher O, aren't you lucky to find your place exactly as you left it in the morning? Since I'm harassed by kids day and night, I wish I could live in a world where there were no children. That's exactly how I feel. By the way, next time, get shaved ice with red bean on top. They pack it to go in the bakery around the corner. Since I talk all day, by the afternoon I can smell something metallic drifting out of my throat."

Since she was saying this to make me feel better, I was obliged to listen with a polite smile. Pak was like that. She would say, "A fertile period? If I just lie down next to my husband. . ." Then she would raise her fingers to indicate the number of abortions she had gone through.

I cleaned up and gave my profuse thanks again before returning to my empty classroom and plopping down in my chair. I was supposed to have a conference with Ji-eun's mother, but I hadn't heard from her yet. The day before when I'd told Ji-eun that I needed to see her mother, it had been before I'd gotten the call from Dong-jae. With the summer vacation approaching, the older kids were behaving badly. Compared to my previous school, this one had unusually precocious and cheeky children, most of whose parents worked late into the night running small neighborhood businesses. Ms. Roh, new to the profession, opined that it just meant the world was changing fast, and that this area wasn't an exception. Not all the kids in this school were growing up too fast, though. I'd say two or three children in each classroom didn't strike me as elementary school students. It wasn't simply because they had overly developed bodies. Dyed hair and pierced ears were no longer a novelty either. After doing whatever it was they did at night, roaming about somewhere, some kids put their heads and arms on their desks and slept through all their lessons. When I reprimanded them, they stared at me instead of looking down, and those eyes drained my energy. Yesterday I thought they needed some discipline and decided to check what they had in their schoolbags.

I made an announcement as soon as we entered the classroom after the morning assembly. "Everyone stand up." The kids didn't budge, eyeing each other and talking in low tones. I rapped the lectern with a plastic ruler several times. "Now go to the back of the classroom, all of you, and stand there," I ordered. There was no need to check all their bags, but I couldn't just search a few, so I started opening bags from the front, one by one. I arrived at Ji-eun's desk, in the second row from the back. In her bag, which contained no textbooks, I caught a glimpse of balled-up clothes and hair wax. As I took the clothes out, I spotted a cigarette packet with the plastic wrapping still intact. I opened a zipper inside the bag. Hairpins, a comb, lip gloss, cosmetics, and a packet of condoms. She was only twelve. I was dumbfounded. I couldn't bring myself to take it out in front of the kids, so I took her bag to the lectern and only then did I move the condoms to my desk drawer. "Kim Ji-eun, come up here!" She marched up in confident strides. I rapped her forehead twice with the attendance book, but she remained immobile. I was afraid, most of all, that I'd fly off the handle. "Take your bag and return to your seat. Tell your mother to come see me tomorrow." Instead of being embarrassed, she held her head high and kept her gaze down, as if she were proud of what she'd done. Her expression said, It's just my luck that I'm in this shit.

In the morning I asked, "Did you ask your mother to come?" And she answered as if she were talking about something that didn't concern her, "Says she can't come early, though." What could she have learned from a mother who didn't bother calling the homeroom teacher when she was going to be late for a meeting? I was peeved. In any event, because I was the one who had summoned her, I would have to stick around. I regretted, belatedly, that I hadn't gotten her phone number. Even if she showed up, what could I tell her? I felt despondent. Here I was, teaching children's songs to kids who changed into tank tops after school and spent their time singing karaoke. When I had mentioned the condoms over cake earlier, Kang, who was thirty-two and single, slammed her fork down, and exclaimed, "God, I've never done it myself, and here they are, these baby students of ours . . ." Pak, who was frank to a fault, ruffled her feathers by quipping, "About that, Kang, your problem is more serious."

It was odd. Why did I feel so disturbed? I was at the point in my cycle when hope and yearning should be bubbling up. Dong-jae had said, "The chances are much better now; the best grade we've had so far." But what was this depressing obsession that had plagued me all day? Why had Dong-jae taken the trouble to invite me to the lab and show it to me when I hadn't requested it? Why hadn't my husband told me that he'd seen it the day before?

This very morning, Yeong-jo had discovered a hole in the toe of his sock while putting it on. He crumpled it and shoved it back into the dresser drawer. His expression was a mixture of odd fury and irritation, which he would never have shown anyone else but me. He seemed to be saying that he couldn't imagine throwing it away with his own hand into the trashcan that stood right next to the dresser. That was exactly the point where Yeong-jo and I stood these days.

Earlier today, had I wished, with my eye glued to the microscope, that he wouldn't be the father of "the baby"?

Possibly.

Dong-jae might know more about the person I lived with than I did. Just as Dong-jae knew much more about me than Yeong-jo did. A fetid smell drifted out of the flower vase on my desk. The flowers looked perfect. I jumped up, took the vase outside, threw the flowers into the trash, and turned on the faucet to rinse the vase. As I poked my fingers into the narrow opening of the vase, my fingertips touched something slimy. I felt like throwing up. This was not an unfamiliar sensation. While waiting for the implantation, I always imagined myself to be in a state of queasiness and then felt nauseated at times. When the embryo failed to take hold and leaked out of me, the imaginary nausea disappeared without a trace. I meticulously washed my hands with soap and smelled them. Something unpleasant seemed to come from inside my nose, not from my hands. As I walked along the corridor, with the empty vase in hand, I became convinced that it wasn't for a higher likelihood of implantation that Dr. Cha wanted to wait a few more days.

The doctor's office hours should be over. Pressing the key on my phone to speed dial his number, I shut my eyes tight. You're so slow, I scolded myself. I came to understand that Dong-jae had given me a quiz, but I had no idea what it was about.

"Dr. Cha? It's me. Is it an okay time to talk?"

"No one is here. Go on, please."

"I'll go straight to the point. Did my husband say he didn't want the baby?" I asked flatly.

"That's not something I can answer." Dong-jae evaded my question in a calm, indifferent voice.

"Then what can you tell me?"

"You asked me when you were here. At what exact moment can we call it a life?"

How far would he detour before telling me what I wanted to hear?

"As a doctor, there's an answer I could give, but what meaning would it have? I thought it would be meaningless to give a biological reply and that was why I didn't answer."

The summer evening felt languid. In the dim light, the geraniums on the windowsill were sensuously red. I had never thought that those strong, fecund flowers were beautiful.

Dong-jae continued, "You commented that it looked like flower petals, didn't you? Even though it looks like that, it does not have vegetable properties."

"I am not in the mood for playing twenty questions," I muttered to him, but I understood what he was saying. That we should look at the thing itself, not the obsession my husband and I had poured into those flower petals, that we should discard the illusion, like a pair of overgrown kids, that the universe revolved around ourselves, that the thing we had peeked at through the microscope was not the flower for the beholder, but a life that had begun to exist in its own right.

Was it really a child that Yeong-jo had wanted so persistently for the past eight years? For him, having a child could have been one of the tasks that he had assigned himself. Something like a goal for which one is supposed to do one's best until it is achieved through adequate planning, effort, and investment. If I told him that at some point having a child turned into a sort of defiance over an elusive thing, would he deny it?

Ironically, infertility might have helped us maintain our marriage, as it were, obscuring other problems between us. Yes, we were already at a point of no return. Yeong-jo must have heard about the higher likelihood while talking on the phone with

Dong-jae, and only then could he have realized, as if scorched by fire, that the object of his desire and obsession had its own stark existence; also the significance of the relationship involving three people, not just two.

I asked indifferently as if discussing other people's affairs, wondering why I was asking Dong-jae this, "Is he seeing someone?"

It had been a long time since Yeong-jo and I stopped having sex. Come to think of it, from the perspective of the monkey in Jared Diamond's book, *The Third Chimpanzee*, it had been a long time since I'd stopped being human. Monkeys are curious. Why do they do it secretly? Why do they do it year round? Human beings are strange. Well, my husband and I didn't do it secretly, and moreover we didn't do it year round.

What remained between us was a mechanical union: checking my temperature, confirming ovulation, and pouring a fresh sperm sample onto an ovum within the prescribed period, according to the schedule set by Dong-jae. As the producers of sperm and ova, we had experienced more pain than pleasure. My husband would vent his frustration and then it would all be over for him, but whenever eggs were harvested, I was subjected to fresh suffering.

The physical pain was the easy part, however. When hormones were injected and blood was extracted, I felt dizzy and nauseated. "Is it supposed to be like this?" I asked once. The nurse asked back, "What's the problem?" "Whenever I get my blood drawn, I feel dizzy and queasy." She glanced at the syringe filled with blood, and shook her head. "No," she said, "it has nothing to do with it. I wonder if it's psychological?" As a matter of fact, every time I was poked by a needle, I felt as if a corner of my soul was being pierced, leaving behind enormous pain, and then I felt invaded. The most painful moment of all was not receiving the injections or having the eggs extracted, but when I was leaving the clinic after confirming that leakage had occurred and that the implantation had failed for no discernible reason. Dong-jae would notify my husband of the results. Whenever I returned home and saw Yeong-jo's annoyed face as he maintained his silence, I'd be gripped with intense hatred.

Some time ago, I woke up in the middle of the night and, feeling thirsty, headed for the kitchen when I heard a sharp but muffled moan. If I had known what I'd witness, I would have quietly returned to bed, still thirsty, and lain down, though I wouldn't have fallen easily back to sleep. I'd thought Yeong-jo, who was sitting in front of the computer, had had a heart attack or something. In the dark, the screen was vivid. Yeong-jo was gripping his penis before a naked woman, whose legs were spread out as if she were doing calisthenics. Holding my breath, I was compelled to return to the bedroom. I felt disdainful toward myself for some odd reason, even though I knew that what Yeong-jo felt toward the woman on the screen was lust, which would be followed by a sense of disgust, and that nothing existed between them.

I wouldn't blame Yeong-jo even if he were in some passionate relationship with a woman, whom he wouldn't have to supply his sperm to under stressful conditions. I asked Dong-jae whether Yeong-jo was seeing someone because I wanted to clearly understand the question Dong-jae had thrown me earlier in the day and I wanted to sort things out.

"I can't answer that either," Dong-jae answered flatly, as if he wouldn't allow any room for my active imagination.

"Dr. Cha, what should I do now?"

"What could I possibly tell you?"

"Doctor, can't you even tell me that much?"

My voice sounded precarious. He tactfully dodged my question, asked in a tone that wasn't indulgent, rebuking, or lamenting. He simply blamed himself. "Doctors are fools when it comes to everything else but their own specialty."

After hanging up, I stood by the windows and looked down at the playing field. What was I supposed to do now?

Yeong-jo was the kind of man who was cut out to be a husband rather than a lover. He was serious about trivial matters, wanted to possess a bigger house, and desired to fill it with his belongings. Just like all the ordinary men in the world.

If I'd started seeing someone after my feelings toward Yun had been completely resolved, I might have wandered around to find a soul similar to Yun's. As a woman in my twenties I believed that if I couldn't overthrow my boyfriend's view of life, it couldn't be love. It sounded to me as though I wasn't the one he loved most in the world, as if he'd said I was nothing to him. My blood turned cold. It wasn't as if Yun had been more mature than me, so he couldn't nurse my wounded pride. We had been so young then.

Soon after I parted with Yun, I met Yeong-jo and married him as if to prove a point. I chose a man who wanted to have a child sharing both of our blood, a man who'd be the first to load his family and valuables into his car at the sign of a hurricane and take refuge in a safe place, a man who'd protect his wife and children with his wits and muscles if a burglar broke into his home, a man who'd risk his life for his family in a seven-year drought by crossing the desert and returning with food on his back. Yet, for better or worse, no such calamity happened and eight years of our marriage went by.

Now the sun had gone down but it was still light outside. Several boys were playing soccer in front of the cafeteria. With nothing better to do, my eyes followed their ball when the front door burst open without a knock. An old woman, whose short permed hair was entirely gray, poked her head in and said, "I wonder if this is my Ji-eun's class? She said the Sixth Section . . . Oh, why are you sitting in the dark?"

I sat her down and pulled up a chair for her. She kept bowing her head, calling me, "Teacher" at the end of every sentence even though I was many years her junior, saying that she couldn't come earlier because she had to work during the day. I was at a loss as to how much I should tell her, but she brought up what I was supposed to. "Teacher, I know how much of a headache you have because of that girl. She's just like her mom, so she's footloose and wanders about at night just like it's daytime. The kid is taller than me and stronger, too. Can't give her a beating. Even animals know how precious their cubs are. But not her mom. Why did she have the kid when she wasn't going to look after her properly?"

I had no choice but to listen to the endless story the granny poured out. Her son had left home first, followed by his wife, and the bastard and the bitch had never phoned to check on their daughter, not even once. She complained she didn't know how to feed her granddaughter. *Why were people's stories of suffering always the same, just like a continuous wallpaper pattern? Why did Ji-eun's mom have her if she wasn't capable of raising her?* As I listened to the granny's long-winded lament, the flower petals on the other side of the microscope floated up in my mind and lingered there. The granny didn't even ask why her granddaughter's teacher had summoned her. What could I tell her, an old woman who might not know what a condom was? A teacher-parent conference was an impossibility from the start.

She continued, "When she crawls back home, miserable hole that it is, and sleeps on her stomach like a baby, my heart breaks. Teacher, please teach her what's proper and make her an upright person." The granny stood up after spilling out everything, saying, "I had nothing to bring you, so . . ." She insisted on giving me the plastic bag she had brought, and then walked down the dim corridor. A whiff of fishy stench had been drifting out of the bag all along. I couldn't bring myself to show her what I'd kept in the drawer. What was I supposed to do? I couldn't just ignore the situation. Was I supposed to scold the child and tell her that she shouldn't be sexually active yet, young as she was, or should I teach her to use condoms?

After sending the granny off, I returned, pressed the button on the electric kettle, and took out a mug from the shelf under the lectern. The inside of the mug was discolored a dark brown. As I opened the lid of the tea tin and pinched some tea leaves, the phone rang. Mom. Should I ignore it? As I poured the boiling water, the leaves floated up and circled around in the mug. I knew that tea became bitter if piping hot water was poured, but I ended up doing it every time. I had stopped caring about the small things in life for a long time. Such indifference turned a person into a wasteland. The phone started ringing again.

"Yes, Mom."

"Would it kill you to pick up the phone and call me first? Why do I hear an echo?"

"I'm in an empty classroom. I'm still at the school."

Ignoring my words, she pressed on right away. "I'm not going to live with your father anymore."

She must have read a newspaper article that so-called twilight divorces were in vogue.

"Now what's the problem this time?"

"Your father's made me suffer all my life. I'd be happy to see him suffer living by himself, if nothing else."

It was nonsense that he had made her suffer all her life. It wasn't as if only he had led a comfortable life. It had been years since she had gone through menopause, but Mom was still in the grips of depression that had started back then. My father had been a victim of her weeping, which broke out at the drop of a hat. Once formed, a relationship meant bondage to another person for a lifetime, so why did people want to weave new webs of relationships? I had heard about Yun from a college friend. He was married and had a son. When I heard that, I didn't feel a thing. Did he even remember what he had said a long time ago?

Floating in my head were the flower petals that would divide themselves quickly in the dark lab. Just the thought of them made my heart race.

"Mom, it's too late for you to get a twilight divorce. The glow has already disappeared and it's midnight for you. Fight and live together, just like you're doing now. What fun will there be if you don't have Father to nag?"

"Anyway," Mom said, "This afternoon I went to your place with some goat bones and put them on the stove. I've already drained the blood, so all you have to do is cool it down and skim off the fat at the top. I put it on low heat, so it should be okay until you get home."

I burst out, "You brought me bones? How can you expect me to boil them on such a hot day? If I were pregnant, the heat alone would cause a miscarriage."

"Watch your temper. I'm worried about you, that's all."

"I'll take care of everything myself. You said it's okay not to have children."

"Ha! You'll take care of everything yourself? How old are you? If a woman's body is cold, her husband won't go near her. Think it over carefully."

She would jump up and down in anger if she knew that half of the packets of Chinese medicinal brew she had sent in the spring were still untouched in my refrigerator drawer. I lowered my voice, "Okay, thank you, I'll eat it with gratitude." Then I hung up. Sitting absently with my chin cradled in my hand, I opened the directory in my cell phone and scrolled down, checking every number. More than a hundred numbers had been saved. I lingered over each name at the top of the list, but there was nobody I could call at the moment. No one I could ask whether I should let those flower petals be inserted into my body, with the belief that they would magically heal our messed-up relationship, whether I should let them splash down the lab's drain, or whether I should think of the baby and Yeong-jo as two separate issues. Yeong-jo's number came up on the screen. *You cowardly bastard, you're pushing all the decision-making on me.* I drank the cooled tea, rinsed the mug, and placed it upside down. Scanning the darkened classroom, I left with the plastic bag emitting whiffs of fishy odor.

The playing field was damp; a brief shower must have passed just minutes ago. Only a few cars remained here and there in the parking lot. Next to my car was a tiny golden Daewoo Matiz. There were splotches of brown dirt, probably from a dusty gust of wind. I got into my car and placed my purse and the plastic bag on the passenger seat, but soon moved the bag to the floor. The fishy smell flooded my nose whenever I inhaled. After turning on the air conditioning, I rested my head on the steering wheel, my arms draped around it. Did I really want a baby? Or did I not want to appear inferior? Could I love the child while hating its father? If the embryo were from a stranger's sperm, I would make a decision by myself, and raise it as just my child . . . but now the embryo . . .

I suddenly remembered that my mother had turned on the stove in my kitchen. Who could I blame? It was all my fault; I'd failed to explain to her that the problem wasn't something that could be fixed with a bowl of soup.

As I was about to reverse my car, I noticed that the Matiz was already backing up. The driver seemed to be in a big hurry. The car didn't look familiar. Visitors to nearby shops sometimes surreptitiously parked there while tending to their business. The back of the Matiz almost collided with my bumper before the car raced off. It disappeared out of sight, but I soon found it again at the traffic light at the main road. It was dusk, but neither the Matiz nor my car, idling behind it, had lights on. As soon as the left-turn arrow appeared, the Matiz darted out. I noticed a taxi speeding from the left. I gasped. The sound of the cars colliding rang out. Momentarily, the street grew silent, as if submerged in water.

People rushed over. The taxi had crashed into the front door of the Matiz. The taxi driver backed up and people tried to open the Matiz's door on the driver's side, but the smashed door wouldn't budge. The taxi driver, who had obviously run the red light, shook the door, almost in tears. The head of the Matiz's driver, sagging heavily toward the left, wasn't moving. When the left-turn arrow lit up again, I backed up a little and made my way through the crowd. If the man hadn't been in such a hurry, I would have been in his place. Had I dodged my own fate or was I meant to be a witness to another person's fate?

When I stopped at another light at an intersection, I turned the sun visor down and checked my face in the mirror. My lipstick had been wiped off, leaving only the outline. The skin under my eyes, smudged with mascara, sported faint wrinkles, resembling a tiny bird's footprints. For most people, their final moments came unexpectedly, like the guy in the Matiz. As I was rubbing off the dark smudges under my eyes, honks came from behind. The car in front of me had already zoomed off. The fishy smell grew overpowering. The moment a life comes to an end, it starts to rot. The flower petals would bloom into eight parts tomorrow, and double again the day after tomorrow. And then what next?

If I had arrived at the light before the Matiz, I would have died, and I felt angry and fearful. The moment I saw the fallen driver's tilted head, I realized that I was angry at two things, myself and Yeong-jo. I also harbored two kinds of fear, a fear of myself, who always failed to conceive, and another fear of the loss that Yeong-jo would feel. He always laid his problems on top of mine.

Steam spewed from the stainless steel pot, its lid rising up and down. Entering the apartment, I found it steamy like a sauna. My anger at my mom flared up again; she just had to come and put a soup on in this sweltering weather. My explosive fury about everything was certainly the symptom of an illness.

Yeong-jo wasn't coming home. He had long ago stopped calling to tell me that he'd be late, that he had plans for the evening. I had no appetite. I opened the plastic bag that had begun to give off a revolting stench and found a fat scabbard fish, cut up into several pieces. I was about to throw it out, but changed my mind. I rinsed it and stored it in the freezer. If it lost its moisture and began to stiffen on the edges, I would be able to throw it out without a sense of guilt. Now that the fish had been taken care of, what was I supposed to do with the full pot of soup? As I stood there, sweating profusely, the phone rang. It was Dong-jae's number.

"This is Dong-jae," he said, without saying anything further. "Yes," I replied, and waited for him to continue.

"Where are you?" He asked.

"I'm at home."

"Ah, yes."

I could picture him hesitating. I quietly waited for him to speak.

"The thing . . . I mean, it's stopped moving."

By "the thing," he meant the flower petals on the Petri dish I had seen in the morning.

"What do you mean, stopped? You said it doesn't move, didn't you?"

"Well, that is, it's stopped dividing itself."

I didn't ask what that meant. No such thing had ever happened before. The embryos had never failed on their own; they had just been flushed out of my body, having failed to implant themselves. Hadn't he said that the embryo was in unusually good condition that very morning? Dong-jae didn't mention a "next time." His silence, coming from far away, overwhelmed me. "I understand," I managed to say, and hung up.

The kitchen was filled with an unpleasant greasy odor. As I opened the lid of the pot, hot steam assaulted my face. After all the steam had left the pot, I could make out a brain floating among the haphazardly stacked bones. The hollow eye sockets, the clamped teeth. Hot bubbles were surging out of the eye sockets. I looked at them blankly for a while and started to skim off the ugly tangles of fat and specks of dirt with a ladle.

Something had been on the verge of blooming, but had disappeared in the wind. It was invisible to the naked eye. The invisible did not exist. Nothing had changed. Ladle in hand, sweating profusely, I kept skimming off the yellow fat as it boiled up and congealed. The goat brain emerged pale in the now clear broth.

I took out the leftover dish of bellflower root and radish salad from the refrigerator, dumped everything in a bowl, and added exactly one scoop of rice from the cooker. I added a dollop of red pepper paste and a few drops of sesame oil. Sitting with my back against the sink with knees raised, I put the bowl on my knees and mixed the rice with the leftover vegetables. The bellflower roots gave off a slightly sour smell; it was starting to go bad. The rice was bland in some parts and then too salty in others because I hadn't mixed the red pepper paste well. I polished off the bowl of rice, and still sitting, raised my hand over my head to drop the bowl into the sink. As if a long stake had sprouted from the floor and impaled me through my backbone, my neck, and emerged through the top of my head, I sat immobile in the same spot, listening to the broth sizzling in the pot.

Other than the *pah pah* sound of the bubbles, everything had returned to the way it was yesterday. I shuddered violently at the thought that nothing had changed.

My Son's Girlfriend

Why do I feel the apartment is so deserted when I'm left alone?

If I were to be photographed, standing in the foyer after send-ing off the last member of my family, the image of a woman would be captured, looking as though she might disappear into the cracks of the shoe cabinet like a puff of smoke, the image so faint that it would be hard to make out who she was.

I lock the front door, return to the living room, and turn on the stereo. Sliding open the veranda door, I step out. I'm not seeing off my husband, who has just left. The sparse remaining cherry petals are surrounded by light green leaf buds, which seem green-er than yesterday. The landscape of blossoming flowers is more striking on an overcast day like today. Symptoms of a cold have lingered in me all through the weeks of transition between winter and spring. The breeze seeping into my housecoat feels ticklish against my skin, and I feel my cold is about to depart, finally. As I get older, the tail end of winter seems more intolerably persistent. With my hands on the railing, I look down. A dark solitary figure is moving about the empty parking lot. Just like a wound-up doll, its legs move to and fro with mechanical regularity. It's my hus-band. He approaches his car, opens the back door, puts down his briefcase, takes off his jacket, and hangs it on a hanger. Even on a bitterly cold day or a rainy day, he gets into the driver's seat only after taking his jacket off and hanging it up. He opens the door to the driver's seat and gets in. He doesn't look up.

A car drives out of the apartment block's courtyard. My husband will wait until it passes. The right-turn signal of my husband's car starts blinking at the exact moment the other car passes by. Is there any other man who turns on the right-turn signal as he leaves an empty parking lot at ten o'clock in the morning? It may be easier to find a man who keeps shuffling his car back and forth in a blizzard until his car aligns accurately with the parking lines on the ground. Both describe my husband.

With his car out of sight, a long sigh escapes from my mouth. I don't do this for any particular reason. The moment I no longer see the taillight of his car, I feel as if the knot of rope binding my chest has snapped open. A Chopin melody drifts out of the living room windows. Chopin! The piano notes disperse into the air, failing to linger in my heart, and bring to mind the face of a boy I knew ages ago.

He threatened that if I didn't accept his love, he'd give up his attempt for a second year running to get into college and voluntarily join the army. He said, "Come to Cho-pin tomorrow because I have something to tell you." I had no intention of going, but I wondered where on earth "Cho-pin" was. "Where's that?" I asked. He said, "Next to Ahyeon Bookstore." I snickered and said, "You're supposed to pronounce that as 'Sho-pang.'"

At the time, I felt a sense of superiority for having made it into the university of my dreams, and I wasn't thrilled about his status as a repeat college applicant, his suppurating pimples covering his cheeks, and his complete ignorance over how to pronounce Chopin. I didn't like any of it. How stupid could one get? Naturally I didn't go out to see him. Long afterward, I read somewhere that Chopin could also be pronounced "Cho-pin," but I was too brilliantly youthful to recognize someone's sincerity, just as a searchlight erased the contours of objects in front of it.

Feeling languid, I am suddenly bothered by the plans I've made for the day. I wonder whether I should call and cancel them when I notice a white sedan whizzing in from the entrance to the apartment complex, from which my husband's car has just disappeared. The car is speeding. I have a sense that it will pass through the parking lot, but it comes to a screeching stop in front of my building and pushes its way between two parked cars. The space is just barely big enough for that kind of smooth maneuver with one turn. What's the hurry, I think, because the car goes too fast backing in, and it's no wonder that it nudges the side mirror of the silver sedan parked on the left. I seem to hear a metallic thud but it's probably my imagination. The car halts briefly before it darts to an empty spot across the way. This time the reverse maneuver is gentle and smooth. I can't read the number on the plate. A woman clad in a light green sweater gets out. Without glancing at the car she has damaged, she enters the row of apartments I live in. I'm not sure whether she's a resident or a guest. The parking lot is quiet again. I snap out of my languor. I'd better take a shower.

Later, as I lock the front door after leaving my apartment and turn around, the door of the apartment facing mine clicks open. I catch a glimpse of a light green sweater in the foyer. She's probably close to my neighbor, because my neighbor doesn't come out of her apartment to see her off. Instead, my neighbor goes right back inside after saying goodbye in the foyer. I don't look at the woman's face as I stand next to her, waiting for the elevator. The tips of her beige shoes are pretty worn out. After the elevator descends to the first floor, she bolts out before the doors open fully. No manners, I grumble to myself. The woman's light green sweater, cheerfully shimmering in the haze, as if seen through translucent glass, imparts fresh brightness, like a harbinger of spring. My car, covered with a thick layer of the yellow dust that blows across from China, has lost its color, looking a dullish brown. If the weather forecast says there will be no rain tomorrow, I'd better stop by the carwash on my way home. 1949. That's the license plate number of the car that slips out of the complex before mine. Of all numbers, it is the year my husband was born.

What's the most pleasant temperature when you're naked? I'll know the answer if I find out what the temperature is now, but I don't bother as I lie on my stomach, eyes closed. The same is true with lighting. The accurately calculated luminosity when you close and then open your eyes, and they feel comfortable, not blinded. The sound of the footsteps of the therapist who patters around is absorbed by the thick carpet. The music is flowing so softly that it is hard to make out the melody if you don't concentrate. Just as softly as the fingers touching me.

Along my spine, warm stones are placed, one by one. They feel slightly hot at first, but they have been heated so perfectly that the temperature is pleasant after you let out one long breath. I feel as though I'm lying on the beach on a summer evening, on a bed of stones that has been heated by the sun all day. The warmth gradually translates into a sense of relief, reaching deep into my skin. A moan escapes from my throat.

The therapist pushes a sheet of paper before my face and gently shakes it. "It's ylang ylang," she says, "This will soothe your mind and body, which are fatigued by the strong spring light." The sweet, languid scent of the tropical flower floods my nostrils. Waiting for me to exhale, she touches my face with another sheet. "This is eucalyptus," she says, "It's a fragrance that calms your frayed nerves. It also soothes your breathing organs exhausted by the yellow dust." I feel as if a thick green leaf has been torn off and placed under my nostrils. "Which scent would you like?" These girls know how to put their customers at ease. If she'd offered three scents and asked me to choose one, I would have hesitated, though momentarily, but it is easy to make a choice between the two. I know that whichever one I choose, it will not be a bad choice. "Give me the first one," I say. The ylang ylang scent travels through the tranquil chamber. The massage table next to me is empty. My daughter is always late, though she has nothing pressing to do.

Of course, it doesn't mean that a choice is simpler just because there is only one option.

Do-ran.

The girl's face that is on my son's computer screen floats up. I'd seen her face on his computer earlier, but I didn't ask any questions until Hyeon brought her up. My son would talk about the girls who appeared on his computer screen, even if I didn't say a thing. After a while, I'd ask, "What's going on?" And he would answer, his face without a tinge of hurt, "We've broken up," or "She wasn't anyone special to me, anyway." That would be that. What's the attraction of putting someone who's not special to you on your desktop? I would ask myself.

I studied Do-ran's face when I noticed a picture on his desktop of the two of them, cheek to cheek, beaming brightly. My first impression? Well, her face was not one that I could warm up to immediately. I don't like that girls that age have the faces of kindergarteners with overgrown bodies, but this girl in particular looked—how should I put it?—as though she was cold. Of course, there are people who cherish desolate landscapes and ignore the flower-blooming season of May, that month when everything seems to float. There are people who prefer to be holed up in their rooms rather than be part of a gathering where laughter ricochets like corn being popped. There are also men who are drawn to women who look ill, even if a bunch of vivacious, pretty young women bustle around them. You can't do much when it comes to preferences. Still, I had no idea that my son liked that type of girl. Whatever the case, Hyeon's eyes were glazed over, and he was mesmerized by her. For some time, he dropped the name Do-ran at the end of every sentence. "Mom, you know, Do-ran did . . . Mom, yesterday Do-ran . . . Do-ran said . . ." I would interrupt, "Hey, will you stop talking about Do-ran?"

"Mom, you know what? Do-ran hears me out, no matter what I say." "Do-ran? That's one old-fashioned name!" "What's wrong with the name Do-ran? Doesn't it have a nice ring to it?" "Yeah, what about her do you not like?"

I thought I'd just wait and see. A few nights ago, my son's expression was dark as he sat down next to me at the kitchen table, where I was reading the paper.

"Mom."

"What?"

"It's about Do-ran."

"Do-ran again?"

"Mom, her family is poor. Not poor by your standards, but really poor. They live in a shipping container. Surrounded by squatters in illegal shacks."

I detected an accusing tone in his voice. It stung. Was he declaring war?

I retorted, "Did I say anything? Did I say I'd go out and check on how her family is doing?"

"I don't mean to get married right away. I'm ready to break up with her tomorrow if I fall out of love. But I'll never break up with her because she's poor."

"Then go ahead and whisper your sweet nothings to each other."

"See, Mom? You're irritated."

"Why are you making such a fuss at this late hour over a girl I've never met?"

Looking at his flushed face, I thought I'd meet her one of these days. I don't think this way because he's my son, but he is affectionate and considerate of others, a good kid. His face was reddening and paling at the mere thought of his girlfriend's discomfort if she met me. But a shipping container? I was definitely bothered.

The door bursts open and Myeong enters. "Hi, Mom, I'm

here," she says, and carelessly whisks off her dress, exposing herself, and hangs it up. Then she lies on her stomach and turns her face toward me. The therapist carefully pours the oil, heated to body temperature, on my daughter's back. What is she thinking when she massages the body of a girl who is approximately her own age? My daughter lets out moans like a satiated cat when the therapist's moving hands press her massage points.

"Mom, I think I'm getting old. I miss the therapist's hands more than I do my husband's."

"Is that the kind of thing to say to your mom?"

"So I hear that your son has finally found someone he'd like to marry."

"I'm going to meet her near here this afternoon."

That fast? Her eyes are wide. I say, "I thought it would be a good idea to meet her." She says, "Whatever the case, she doesn't know her social standing." "And what's yours, may I ask?" She glares at me, the whites of her eyes strikingly prominent. Although she's my daughter, rather, because she's my daughter, I wish she'd live differently. She goes out to department stores every day and drops by the spa, complaining that her legs hurt, and she relies on a housekeeper to do all her household chores, but she still complains about every little thing, none of which are important. If she comes off like that to her own mother, who will ever find her pleasant? Right before the cooled stones on my back start to feel like foreign objects, the therapist removes them one by one. Even after they are taken off, their warmth lingers briefly. It's almost time to go out to meet Do-ran.

I search for a relatively quiet spot in the coffee shop and take a seat in a corner, but my ears hurt with the chatter of the women who fill the coffee shop. Thinking that the girl entering is Do-ran, I raise my hand. As I lower it, I spot my daughter, sitting by herself near the entrance, blatantly staring up at the girl. I didn't notice it when my daughter was right next to me, but from a distance her facial features resemble mine more and more as the years go by. Before coming here, I'd asked my daughter to join us, since she was in the neighborhood anyway, but she shook her head, saying she found it burdensome, for there was no telling what would happen between her brother and Do-ran. That was why she decided to sit near the entrance, saying that she'd just check out Do-ran. Now here she is, brandishing a finger behind the girl's back, demanding my confirmation that she is the right one. A pity that my daughter behaves the way she does . . .

Observing the foreboding, overcast sky, I congratulate myself for not stopping by the carwash. As I get out of my car, I notice that the new leaves on the cherry trees seem to be longer than they were in the morning. Squinting, I focus on those young leaves. The light green of the woman's sweater in the morning was the exact same color. The buds, peeking out from moist bases, look like exits from another world; if you poked a finger into a bud and tore it off, an entrance to another world might reveal itself.

The guard, talking to a man with short-cropped hair as they stand in the stairway, makes way for me, nodding his head politely. I brush by them and as I approach the elevator, the voice of the man reaches my ears.

"Heck, what can I do? I should pay for it if I want to keep my job. Shit. It's not small change. I have no idea how to raise that kind of money."

It's not the kind of situation that should elicit a laugh, but the ever-optimistic guard bursts into merry laughter. "Can't believe a side mirror costs as much as a small car. Ha-ha-ha."

"Exactly. I don't understand why I should be punished out of the blue like this. All I did was step away from the car just long enough to nibble on a few slices of stale beef. When I think about it, it makes me crazy."

The elevator doors close. I have no choice but to look at the profile of the woman in the mirrors wrapping around the elevator, and even at the back of her head. Right there is a face that looks impoverished, lacking any wants, a face that does not look tired but is far from lively, prompting me to avert my eyes.

Why is my own face getting more unfamiliar as I age?

I broach the subject as I set a plate of strawberries next to my husband, who is watching the nine o'clock evening news.

"What should we do about the kids?"

"Leave them alone."

"You're still so indifferent to our family's affairs, no different from when you were younger. He's our only son and inviting a new family member into our midst is a very important matter. How can you speak as if you're discussing the second marriage of our in-law's distant relative or something?"

"Indifferent? I've formed an opinion in my own way. She graduated from the same university as Hyeon. That won't be embarrassing to tell anyone, very good academic achievements, actually, and she must be smart, and she must be pretty judging by the way our nit-picky kid chases after her, and by the way she tolerates his whims, she must be much more easygoing than you. By the tone of your voice, your first impression of her didn't seem to be too bad."

Listening to my husband speak slowly, pausing here and there—he didn't even bother to turn down the volume of the television—I have to agree. I've got to give it to him: Not everyone can run a big business. I have to agree that he always views a situation from a wider perspective.

"True. I think it won't be easy to find someone as good as her these days. I can't claim I'm a good judge after meeting her just once, but she seems like a decent person, she's personable, and yes, frankly, a mother who has a marriageable child tends to have higher standards for his spouse, but ..."

"But?"

"She's from a very poor family."

I don't tell him that Do-ran lives in a shipping container.

"We're not doing so badly that we have to drool over our in-laws' money, are we? She's got to be better than the kids in this neighborhood who spend money as easily as grabbing a piece of tissue to blow their noses."

He's not completely wrong. What troubles me—how can I put it?—is not the money itself.

"I don't know how to describe it. How should I put it? She seems cold . . ."

"Cold? You mean she looks poor and miserable?"

"That's not it, exactly."

If I had met Do-ran on a different occasion, I would have thought she was neat and decent. As we left together after drinking tea, I had a feeling that she wasn't at ease. I thought she didn't feel that way toward me; it had to be the coffee shop. I couldn't pinpoint which aspects of her bothered me, but she seemed out of place there. It's possible that I reacted too sensitively; I might not have noticed if Hyeon hadn't told me about the shipping container.

"Why worry? Nobody was born with the talent to spend money. Look at Myeong. You didn't teach her, but she practically lives in department stores. What does Hyeon say? Does he want to marry her?"

"He doesn't seem to be in a hurry to set a wedding date at this point."

"Then wait and see. He isn't at an age when getting married is urgent."

I leave it at that. After cleaning up in the kitchen, I go down with a garbage bag in hand. The guard is smoking under the cherry trees. Petals strewn on the ground shine white in the dark. Dumping the garbage and turning around, I ask him, "Did something happen today?"

Words spill from the man's lips, as if he'd been waiting for this chance, bored out of his wits.

"You see, in the morning, someone shattered the side mirror of the Mercedes belonging to Unit 107. Ha-ha. The lady owner just said, 'What were you doing, not keeping an eye on the car?' But that's more frightening to the driver than the outright demand to pay for the damage, you know? Normally when the gentleman of the house doesn't go out, the driver stays in the car or waits for him outside my guard post. As it happened, the family who had a pre-wedding party last night sent down a tray of food for me. We drank just one cup of *soju* each and he was away from his car for just ten minutes or so, and that's when it happened. Now, Driver Choi isn't completely innocent, you see, because he drank on the job, but the cost of the repair is more than his salary. Just one side mirror costs two million won. That's pretty shocking."

He seems to be implying that the owners have gone too far. "Oh, I see," I answer vaguely, and turn around to leave. If I let him chatter on, I will hear an endless, predictable story, something along the lines of how Driver Choi's mother is showing symptoms of early dementia, his young daughter begs him to pay for piano lessons, and his wife is whining about how they can't raise money to meet an increase in rental deposit demanded by their landlord. More than that, I'm afraid that a longer conversation will prompt me to burst out, "Actually, this morning I happened to . . ." But two million won? Should I speak up?

My husband is still watching the news. The news seems to bring more pleasure to viewers the more shocking it is and the farther away it is from their own lives. With a bored expression, he is watching the segment about a regional city where a big fire erupted but fortunately no lives were lost. I am tempted to tell him about the side-mirror incident, but decide against it and head for the bedroom. Who was it that said after a phase of boredom in marriage comes a phase of disenchantment? Our topics of conversation are limited to what is going on in our children's lives. After Hyeon's marriage, this place will likely turn into a home for a mute couple. Until my husband made it in the world through his sheer effort, he was a real penny-pincher. It looks like he's mellowing out, judging by the way he remains calm after hearing that his son's prospective in-laws are poor.

Hyeon, who comes home late, vents his fury as soon as he sees me.

"Mom, did you meet Do-ran?"

"Yes, I did."

"Why didn't you tell me first? Why do you do things as you please?"

"Do I have to get your permission before I meet someone?"

"You're stressing everyone out."

"I didn't make her stressed."

"I mean you stress me out."

"Why are you stressed?"

"I have lots to think about."

"I don't understand. It didn't feel like I'd met her for the first time. You talk about her all the time, you know. What's there to think about?"

"I want to see her without thinking about complicated matters yet."

"At your age, shouldn't you?"

"Mom, it's not like that."

"You kept talking about Do-ran all the time, so I met her. We didn't talk about anything much."

Seeing him go to his room and slam the door behind him, my blood begins to boil. This is exactly why people say that the son is equally to blame when a conflict arises between mother-in-law and daughter-in-law. It's easier to tell your daughter what's on your mind than your husband. I call Myeong and she says, "Actually, you've gone too far, Mom. Wait and see. Kids these days, you only know for sure when they enter the wedding hall together."

"She looks okay, don't you think?"

"Do you think she's arrogant, Mom? I think she's terrible. It's more frightening when a person is busy calculating behind the mask of innocence."

I find it detestable that my daughter is crunching on an apple while speaking to her elder on the phone. I take the receiver away from my ear. The crunching noise doesn't diminish.

My daughter says, "She doesn't know a thing about her social standing. There are limits even to social mobility, you know."

"What's your own social standing, may I ask?"

Though she's my daughter, I don't care for her at a time like this. All the more so because people say that she's exactly like me.

"Mom, it's not an issue of whether she has money or not. You'll see. I think there's an issue of class between the two of them, and they won't be able to overcome it. I majored in sociology, remember? I don't think it matters that she lives in a shipping container. If it's just a matter of where she lives, you can offer her one of the apartments Dad owns, but that's not the main issue. Why didn't you marry that guy, Cho-pin or whatever-his-name-is? And why did you marry Dad instead? Mom, you read your future with that guy Cho-pin, as if you were looking into a mirror. Let's be frank, Mom, you've been a successful investor in the venture called marriage. Don't you agree?"

Now she's gone too far. She must have finished her whole apple by now. Her voice is clear as she wraps up her argument.

"We don't take after you, Mom, no matter how I look at it."

"What do you think of Hyeon?"

Swallowing the black bean noodles she was chewing, Do-ran smiles faintly.

How adorable she would look if only she smiled more brightly.

When I called her, offering to treat her to a nice meal, I promised myself that I wouldn't feel hurt even if she declined with the excuse that she was busy. Do-ran didn't ask, "Why do you want to see me again?" She simply said yes. I asked her what she would like to eat and she answered, "Black bean noodles." I had made a reservation at a Chinese restaurant, but she insisted on ordering just the noodles, saying that she didn't eat much for lunch.

"Hyeon, he's a narcissist."

A laugh slips out of my mouth.

"Do you mean that he's full of himself, despite the way he looks?"

"I don't mean that. His self-love is extraordinary, but it doesn't come off as offensive. How can I put it? It seems that he was raised that way."

She's right, quite observant for her age. He doesn't mind eating at a tacky joint, but his appetite disappears at the sight of a roll of toilet paper lying on the table in lieu of napkins. A bourgeois youth through and through—that's my son. I look at Do-ran, and the way she eats is quite endearing. She scrapes up the sauce from the bowl and eats every last drop. She sips the jasmine tea and then hands me a shopping bag politely with both hands.

"What's this?"

"I heard your birthday was a few days ago."

I open the package and find a knitted mohair scarf in Indian-pink. Bright in color and narrow and long, it would be okay to wrap it around my neck even now, well past winter. I'm moved by the unexpected present. When was the last time I received such a sincere, handmade gift?

"Did you knit it yourself?"

"The season for scarves is over, but there isn't much else I can make."

"You must be busy, though."

"Yes, but . . . it didn't take long. The loops are uneven. Some are big and some are small."

I wind it around my neck, saying, "Hand-made items are all the rage these days, aren't they?" I feel the warmth not only on my neck, but down to the depths of my stomach, as though warm bubbles were rising from there.

"That color looks great on you," Do-ran says.

As I take out a credit card at the cashier, Do-ran glances at the bill and asks the girl at the counter, "Weren't the black noodles 9,000 won?" The girl answers kindly, "VAT and service charge are added to that." Her face dark with displeasure, Do-ran exclaims, "Charging for service on a bowl of black bean noodles?" I take Do-ran to my car, sit her in the passenger seat, and drive her to a department store nearby. Is it because I've been provoked by the cashier, who was wearing an inscrutable expression as she looked at Do-ran? "It doesn't feel right to receive a gift from a young person and not give something in return," I say to Do-ran, as I get out of the elevator on the women's apparel floor, and suggest that she pick out an outfit. Wearing the same expression that she wore at the restaurant counter, she says, "I don't buy clothes in places like this." I say, "When an elder wants to give you a gift, you're supposed to say thank you and take it," and I start walking ahead of her.

People say that when shopping at a department store, you should be carefully made up and dressed up, just like when you attend a gathering of your old school friends, but the atmosphere of this particular department store is way over the top. This realization hits me again after I take Do-ran to a young casual brand boutique and see her standing there. If two women with no makeup were to stand side by side, the complexion of the woman from this neighborhood would be different from the one from a different area. If people came out wearing slippers on their bare feet, you could easily distinguish those from this neighborhood. I am aware that this isn't a function of what they're wearing. How do I put it—the difference seems to emanate from deep within, from their very bones. Do-ran is of an age where she looks pretty and radiant even when she wears something bought from a vendor at Namdaemun Market, but this is not the case here, not in this place. Do-ran stands awkwardly, suddenly giving off the impression of a girl who isn't well cared for, who fails to dress fashionably. I pick out several outfits for her.

It is incomprehensible. Standing next to the mannequin dressed in over-the-top clothing just like a big doll, Do-ran looks out of place, like an unappealing child who doesn't look good no matter what she's decked out in. When Do-ran, who neither expresses her likes nor dislikes, suddenly looks resigned, and I see the salesgirl's stuck-up expression, even though she is nothing but a salesperson in the shop, something fires up inside me. I rifle through the clothes on the hangers, select this and that, and make Do-ran try them on. She changes outfits several times, but nothing seems to suit her. I choose a yellowish jacket—nothing too eye-catching—and ask her to try it on; Do-ran takes it, looking almost exhausted. In the jeans and cotton jacket I've selected, she doesn't look half bad. We go down to the basement parking lot, get into my car, and I drive her to the nearest subway station. She is silent through the entire ride, and as she gets out, she says softly, "Thank you," and shuts the door. In the side mirror, I watch her standing there until she is no longer in my line of sight. A sigh escapes from my lips. I remember Hyeon's voice: It's not just because of the shipping container.

That's right, but . . .

As I enter the elevator, my eyes wander toward the wall, where Driver Choi put up a poster several days ago. It was a computer printout, suggesting that he had put it in the other elevators as well. The poster began, If you witnessed a collision that occurred at a certain hour on a certain day of a certain month . . . The font was so big that he ran out of space to describe how difficult it was for him to come up with the money. The poster disappeared the very next day. The guard, guffawing as usual, told me that he had received a severe reprimand, accompanied by a wagging finger: How dare he treat the residents as criminals?

At night, I confide in my husband, who is eating a slice of melon at the table, about the side mirror. Without a word, he tilts his head toward me and stares at me with a stupefied expression. From his eyes, I can understand his thoughts: You're not going to speak up after all this time, are you? One is able to read thoughts like these after living together with someone for a long time. He has always been right, in hindsight. I didn't bring up the subject expecting an answer. Just like the barber in the old tale, I needed a field of reeds in which I could confide about the king's donkey-like ears.

Chomping on the melon, he says flatly, "Forget it."

My husband is the type of person who makes sure that no glass of water is placed too close to the edge of our table. A long time ago I watched a movie starring Julia Roberts. I don't remember the title. Her character's husband can't stand it when the towels aren't hanging in perfect folds on the bathroom rack and the groceries in the kitchen cabinets aren't arranged perfectly. On a stormy night, she stages her own death and disappears from the face of earth. I had read a movie review in the newspaper and gone to see it by myself, though I'm not usually the type who goes to watch movies alone. While watching the film, I found myself weeping. So the details did not stay with me. During the scene in which Julia's character starts crying, I cried along with her. It is probably common to be in a relationship in which you have to choose between the two: disappearing after staging your own death or killing your true self. I don't know whether it's my husband or me who has changed in all our years together. Sometimes I feel my son resembles me, as if we were the wheels of the same bicycle. If someone looks at me and my husband and feels the same way, he may not be wrong, either. This thought makes me blurt out, "Should I just tell our next-door neighbor? That if she's too embarrassed to come forward now, she can hand over the money anonymously?"

"Do you think she can't read the poster? If you feel so sorry, you can put your own money in an envelope and slip it to him anonymously."

He sounds sure that I won't do that. He lifts his hand to adjust the checkered tablecloth that is slightly askew at the corner of the table, corrects the irregular folds, and moves my glass sitting too close to the edge of the table toward the center. If he hadn't done that, I know I'd have been the one to do it.

"Is Hyeon sleeping?"

Do-ran calls, though it is late.

"I don't think so. Hold on."

As I open the door, I see him lying on his bed. He seems to have heard our phone conversation. He says sullenly, "Tell her I'm sleeping."

It looks like arm-twisting can't even get him to take the call. She must have called him on his cell phone several times before trying our home number. I pick up the phone again and say, "He's in bed." She says, "He's not sleeping, right? He's mad at me." There's nothing I can say to her. If my daughter acted this way, I'd find her so much more appealing. I mumble, "Well, you should speak with him tomorrow," and hang up.

"You're mean, young man," I mutter to myself. I know that he's been to Do-ran's place several times and they've spent nights together, too. I also know that kids these days jot down all sorts of stuff in their computer diary.

. . . D accepts her life as is. At least, she doesn't seem to long for a dif-

ferent way of life. This part of her personality fascinated me in the beginning, but it tires me out. These are the times when I feel we're too different. What most makes D a stranger to me is not when I see her where she lives, but the way she goes about her life. Even at times when she can be playful, she clings to her existential seriousness. Mom says that there exists barriers that can be scaled and barriers that one doesn't want to scale; rather than barriers that can be scaled and barriers that can't be scaled. I wonder if she is right after all.

While talking about Do-ran for the first time, Hyeon was worked up and vehemently insisted that he could part with her the very next day if he fell out of love with her, but that he would never part with her because of her poverty. This remark could have stemmed from his attempt to understand, and deny, his own vague confusion.

What is the condition of poverty? Is it having no money or the sense of deficiency over having no money? Or the paucity of desires? Depending on what your standards are, in the same situation you may feel a sense of dire deficiency or a sense of complete sufficiency. To Hyeon, Do-ran's attitude is unfamiliar and confusing. Generally, people have a more persistent prejudice against the things they have not experienced themselves. Though he says it doesn't bother him, Hyeon has decided that Do-ran's illegal shipping container is a terrible place to live in, at least for his girlfriend, and ceaselessly tries to rescue her from it. Beyond the shipping container, her poverty has affected mundane things, and these days the two seem to be locking horns because of that. Several lines in his diary allow me, the person who has raised my son to be the person he is, to read all his emotions. In his diary entry written after a friend's birthday party, I can also picture the day's scene as if I had witnessed it with my own eyes.

. . . About the pink scarf she gave Mom as a birthday gift, I let it

pass because Mom seemed to be pleased, saying that handmade clothes were trendy this year, but I hated what she'd chosen for Seong-sin's birthday. I'd even given her my credit card, asking her to get a nice gift on my behalf. She's free to feel uncomfortable about eating out at Cheongdam-dong, but the way she was dressed that day was ridiculous. I love her but she obstinately refuses to take what little I want to give to her. Her stubbornness drives me nuts. On our way back, I made a comment, trying not to hurt her feelings, but she said, I know, you're the son of an ultra-rich family, and then clamped her mouth shut. That was when I felt we were from different planets.

If he had been dealing with other people, he would have been direct, and said, "How can you buy something like this for that amount of money?" I can see it all. They must have been eating at a swanky fusion restaurant, where a meal costs an arm and a leg, and Do-ran was wearing an uncomfortable expression that only Hyeon could catch. Do-ran was probably dressed exactly the way she usually dressed, even when she was in the company of the girlfriends of Hyeon's friends, and he must have tried to give her some fashion advice like, "You're supposed to have a different attitude when coming to a place like this, you know?" But why is he mad at her now? After hanging up the phone, I enter Hyeon's room and try to get the story out of him.

"Did you two fight?"

"Not at all." He sounds grim, lying with his eyes closed and his right hand on his forehead. Then he bolts up and says, "Mom, I don't think I'll be able to meet another girl like Do-ran. I believe it's the best choice your son has made so far."

"So?"

"But Mom, I don't know why I can accept everything about Do-ran when it's just the two of us, but we keep clashing when we're hanging out with people I know. I don't know why, and it drives me even crazier."

"Complicated, isn't it?"

"Yes, you're right, Mom. Please hand me the remote control."

After I give it to him, he presses the stereo button with the expression of a jilted man, flings himself back on the bed, and shuts his eyes. As the music starts, he mumbles, "I wish technology would stop developing right now." This is what he quips from time to time, as he presses a button on his mobile phone, listens to an MP3 player, or takes out ice cream from the freezer. It is the grownups' prejudice that the new generation wants to be out of the box. Now and then, these pampered kids exhibit surprisingly conservative behavior, even more so than their parents' generation. They want to preserve their life as it is without change. They are happy to reach out and pick up only what they want, just as he addresses his mother in a mixture of the respectful and familiar forms of speech as it suits him. I'm sure he'll also say, "I wish technology would stop right at this point," as he watches TV on his mobile phone, ambling along the street.

At a quick glance, the kids in her age group look all grown up, but when you study their faces closely, something childlike is hidden in their features. I watch Do-ran's lips as she puts down her tea cup. They still look like a child's. Ditto her soft jaw. No trace of the harshness of her life. Still, her entire face, oddly, is etched with the privations of hardship. My son said, "She can't afford to get married now." As he got himself worked up, wondering why she had to start a Ph.D. program while scraping by with her arduous part-time jobs, I quietly stared at his face. I wasn't pleased with him; he wasn't capable of paying for Do-ran's tuition if they got married now, but he made it sound as if the money in his father's bank accounts belonged to him. When Do-ran calmly said, "You're the son of an ultra-rich family," Hyeon couldn't have possibly detected the mixture of distinctly different sentiments, which he could never tell apart, however hard he tried.

I keep looking at Do-ran's lips. Her lovely lips, without any wrinkles. Once upon a time, I too possessed such lips. Those days when I didn't know what bright rays I was radiating, as laughter slipped through my lips, which didn't have a touch of lipstick.

When Cho-pin pleaded with me, I didn't go out to see him at Chopin coffee shop, but we saw each other every week, for both of us taught Sunday school at the same Catholic Church. I was haughty, so much so that I took him for granted, and secretly enjoyed tugging at the strings of his devoted heart and then pushing him away, rather than setting him free. In the summer when we went on a volunteer mission to a countryside chapel together for several days, I clearly saw in Cho-pin's eyes the yearning that troubled him when he looked at me, and I tortured him as much as I could. Wherever we were, I was conscious of his gaze fixed on me. One day, as I passed by Cho-pin, who was so nervous that it looked like his back would buckle if I so much as cocked my finger in his direction, I whispered to him, "How about going out to the lookout shed in the middle of the orchard together? Meet me at the back of the storage hut."

That afternoon the intermittent rain had come to a halt. The day's plan had been for us to go up to the orchard and pick peaches, but the work was put off to another day; we were told that the fruit would be bruised if picked on a rainy day. Taking advantage of this rare gap in our schedule, some took naps and others were doing their piled-up laundry.

I cleaned my mud-splattered rubber shoes, put them on, and ambled along the creek. The swollen stream was sweeping over the weeds along the banks with a force that would easily rip them up, roots and all. As I turned the corner of the storage hut, I saw Cho-pin already there, jumping up and down in place, with his feet together. It looked like he had so much energy that he didn't know what to do with it. When our eyes met, he beamed so brightly that it could have driven away all the rain clouds on earth. Rain wasn't falling, but there was no knowing when it would resume. Neither of us had brought an umbrella, but there was no reason why we shouldn't stand in the rain. It was summer and we were young. My hair was cut short, and I was wearing rubber shoes. On an outing to the market, we had gone out as a group to get T-shirts because our laundered clothes were taking ages to dry. There was only one criterion for selecting T-shirts, which cost 5,000 won for two: Which one was the most ridiculous? Whenever someone picked up a shirt with an indescribably loud design, we all plunged into a frenzy, giggling and pulling, trying to lay claim on it. When a fire-engine-red shirt was torn in half as it was being pulled in different directions, we practically rolled on the ground, laughing until tears seeped out of our eyes. The shirts were of identical design, basic cotton T-shirts colored with crude dyes.

I had chosen a light green one, and Cho-pin must have settled on yellow. Now, in the field, only the yellow and light green T-shirts seemed to be alive and moving in the haze. Pointing at each other's shirts, we merrily burst out laughing. The climb was gentle, but we were soon drenched in sweat. The heavy humidity in the air seemed to cling only to our fluorescent-colored shirts. Raindrops began to scatter. We ran up a sloping path. Whenever I took a step, my rubber shoes squeaked. Only after we had ducked between the stilts below the lookout shed did we begin to catch our breaths. The stench of sweat—whether it came from me or him—was overpowering. "Let's get wet," I said, and emerging into the open, we cooled off, fully exposed to the pouring rain. Cho-pin dashed out to pick two peaches. He washed them in the falling rain and handed one to me.

As I ate the peach, skin and all, my ear canals began to itch. I berated Cho-pin, saying that his sloppy washing of the fruit had caused my itch. When we were done, we flung the pits far into the distance, cupped the rain in our hands and washed them, and standing side by side under the shed, we gazed off at the orchard for a long time. The rain petered out and then stopped altogether. "Take your shirt off and squeeze out the rain," he said. I threw him a dirty look, but turning around, he said, "Let's take them off, wring then out, and put them back on." I heard a squeaking sound as he took his drenched shirt off, followed by the sound of water cascading to the ground. "I will count to ten," he said. The duration between one and two was very long. I hesitated a little before I took off my shirt. Whoa! My bra and stomach were dyed light green. I took a quick look at him. His back, as he was wringing out his shirt, was vivid yellow. Right then, he called out three. I started laughing. "What?" Cho-pin turned around. Shrieking, I smacked him on the shoulder. Looking down at his chest, he murmured, "This is terrible." He then scooped up some dirt from the ground and rubbed it ferociously on his chest. We sprawled on the ground, laughing and laughing as if crazed. I thought I'd never laughed so hard before. That afternoon, I felt as if my entire body were swollen, buoyed by a slight fever, and we didn't even hold hands, but what seized us, clearly, was arousal. After that summer, we were "us" for a long while.

But is a relationship that leads to marriage just a matter of timing? Cho-pin. Was I too young to understand his purity, hidden behind his face riddled with horrible acne scars? Just as I didn't have the faintest idea how seductive my young lips were when I burst out laughing by the shed. Or did I conceal my cunning calculation behind the vague excuse that the timing wasn't right for us? Did I draw the natural conclusion from his circumstances that he had no prospects in his future? He was clearly poor and it seemed unlikely that he would enter a decent university, although he was repeating his preparations for college admission.

When I see Do-ran, I am always reminded of Cho-pin.

"It's not the right season yet, but would you like to have shaved ice with red bean topping?" I ask her.

"Yes. Do you like it too?"

I shake my head. "I really liked it when I was your age, but I don't feel like eating it now, even though it's mid-summer."

I learned of Do-ran's preference for the dessert from my son's diary.

. . . When I was in high school, the kids always had shaved ice with red bean topping at the eatery in front of the school before the evening self-study period began. I envied them so much. I don't know why it tasted so delicious . . . Saying this nonchalantly, D began to dig into her shaved ice. I had never seen anyone who savored the dish as much as she did. I was painfully moved by that sight; she was so adorable. I promised myself, Okay, I will make sure you eat it until the summer fades away, no, even in the middle of winter, until you get sick and tired of it . . .

Hyeon wrote that, but he is unlikely to remember it now. Drinking a hot cappuccino, I gaze at Do-ran as she eats shaved ice topped with red beans. I agree: I've never seen anyone who savors the dish as much as she does. So much so that I am almost tempted to dig my own spoon in for a taste.

"Is it good?" I ask.

"Yes."

Why did I call her, with the excuse of having lunch together? Throughout lunch, I feigned ignorance about the change in the young couple, and Do-ran didn't bring up Hyeon. While reading my son's diary, I might have had the desire to see her before they broke up. It would have been different if I hadn't met her, but I couldn't just nonchalantly ask about Do-ran later, as if I were asking about what had happened to the dried petals stuck between the pages of a book.

"Do-ran, I'm sure that these days some of your friends continue to study even after they're married."

I have an urge to rub her lips, which have turned slightly bluish from the ice.

"That's not exactly the only reason. I have quite a few burdens to carry. My siblings are still young, and more than anything, to me studies are important too at this point."

She said "studies are important too," not "studies are important." Her shoulder, shifting every time she lifts her spoon, incites pity in me, as if it belongs to a donkey burdened with a heavy load. Her comment is not news to me. Hyeon said, "What kind of parents are they? Why did they have children they couldn't take care of themselves, pushing them onto their own daughter? I get annoyed and point out to her, 'Why are your parents so irresponsible? What about your own life?' Then she just responds as if discussing other people's problems, 'You're right. But what's to be done?'"

What Hyeon probably wanted to hear from her was, "Yeah, it's hard on me." He must have felt an odd fear of the girl who didn't reveal, even once, how difficult it was for her. Do-ran has come out today wearing the pants I've bought her. Instead of the skimpy, mustard-colored jacket, she is clad in a sweater with pills on its sleeves. Even when Hyeon squabbled with her because she showed up in a thin pilling sweater to a gathering with his friends, the real issue lay beyond the sweater.

I wonder what it would have been like if I had met Do-ran at another juncture in my life, instead of having the relationship that I have with her now. I can't tell what my feelings are: Do I want Hyeon's relationship with her to come to an end at this point or do I want them to at least get engaged?

"I heard you majored in English literature," Do-ran says.

"Yes."

"Who is your favorite author?"

"It's hard to say. I don't remember being fascinated by any writer while studying. My thesis was on Hemingway, but I think I watched more movies based on his books than I read his fiction."

"For me, it's T.S. Eliot."

It is not clear whether he is her favorite author or if she is writing her thesis on him, but I nod, thinking that she's the kind of person who would choose her favorite writer as the subject of her thesis.

I drop her off at the subway station and, gazing in the side mirror at her retreating image, my heart is ruffled.

As I park, I catch Driver Choi polishing his car with a very fine towel. How much longer will I hear the metallic thud of the side mirror breaking whenever I see him? It is hard to tell what he feels. At one glance, he looks tired and at another he looks at peace. After the accident, he has never stepped away from the car. How did he come up with the money for the side mirror? How come no one but I looked down at the parking lot that morning? Fury surges in me, directed at no particular person, not even at the woman in the light green sweater.

My dinner preparations aren't elaborate. My husband asks me to cook a simple meal, citing his serious belly fat; all he wants is half a bowl of unrefined rice, a plate of vegetables, and bean paste soup. As I get older, I don't even want to bother too much with dinner. I call him on his cell phone. "When will you be home?" I ask. "I'm leaving now," he says grumpily, "but I don't know why the expressway is congested like this on a weekday." He seems to have just left his country club. His pet line is: Why do they bother to expand the roads? If they charged 10,000 won per liter of gas, you'd barely see cars on the road. Now everyone and his mother drives . . . I wonder how such an impatient man can play golf all day long. I ask, "Will you be home for dinner?" He says, "I have a dinner gathering to go to, but I don't know if I can make it to the

Lotte Hotel in an hour. What business do these good-for-noth-ings have, driving around like this? I just came out to play some golf." I interrupt him, "They must all be out to play golf, too." I hurriedly try to hang up before my husband, who only has a head for making money, bursts into his usual tirade that they should triple the green fee. I yank the cord of the electric rice cooker out of the wall socket and turn off the stove. It is far from unpleasant eating microwaveable rice alone; it comes in its own plastic tub and all I have to do is peel off the sheet at the top. What phase will come after the phases of boredom and disenchantment?

So, Do-ran is writing a thesis on T.S. Eliot. I didn't appreci-ate him when I was a student, but as I get older, I find his poems more appealing. Of course, I don't mean that I pull out his books and re-read them. At times phrases of his that I remember flit through my head at an empty hour like this one. His long, long poetry writhes with its chopped-off lines, just like a long snake kept in poisonous liquid, with only its head left intact after the rest of its body has slowly dissolved, beginning with the tail:

> *I myself once saw, with my own eyes, the sibyl of Cumae hang-ing in a cage; and when the boys asked her: "What wouldst thou prophesy, Sibyl?" She replied: "I want to die."*

. . . Now no one asks me what I would prophesy anymore, but I, too, have moments when life seems interminable, just like Sibyl, who, old and wilted, has to live out her days as countless as the specks of dust gripped in her hands.

The girl softly closes the door behind her and brings a sheet of paper to my nose. "This is grapefruit," she says, "It soothes your tired body and soul, and breaks down your body fat." The sweet, acidic fragrance travels to my nose. I open my eyes and close them again, and this time I smell a different scent. "And this is rosemary," she says, "it is a scent that soothes a depressed, over-sensitive mind, feelings caused by too much sunshine." With eyes closed, I nod. The sunlight is not to blame, but I am down and over-sensitive. I want to just lie here, with no thoughts in my head, but I have a hard time relaxing.

"Will you make them a little warmer?"

The stones on my back haven't cooled down. Somehow a chill seems to seep through my back, in this room where the tempera-ture has been adjusted so that it is most pleasant for the naked body. As though I've been jilted, my heart feels sodden and I am cold. "You seem to have a slight cold," the girl says in a concerned voice.

Before he went to his room last night, Hyeon, his eyes down-cast, said, "Do-ran and I have decided to think things over."

I didn't ask why. I didn't feel like hearing his reasons for the breakup again, which were full of excuses, and which I'd read several days in a row on his homepage. In my heart sympathy for Do-ran conflicted with a depressing sense of relief. I silently asked him: Would you say you loved her? You can say that. The love you die for is not the only kind of love. A million kinds of love exist for a million different people.

D is always beaming brightly. I don't know why. My attitude of em-bracing all of her always clashes with her pride. Her poverty is not the problem. I first got mad when she was dressed so shabbily at gatherings and when she made an issue over nothing when we ate out, and then immediately I felt bad for her, and I think these incidents sparked it all. I am angry when I see that poverty is not simply part of D, but that it dominates her whole life, like air. The two of us got excessively touchy over nothing much at all, but in the end it's all my fault.

It is not difficult to say, "It's all my fault." Hyeon, you dislike the fact that she's poor. Don't make a simple matter complicated.

How could I not understand your true feelings, this child of mine whom I've raised since you were a baby, cooing as I potty trained you?"

When I saw Do-ran last, I supposed that it would probably be for the last time, and she must have known it, too. I will never see her again, for all I know. The sense of loss and my guilty conscience will disappear once spring is over. Even the sins I commit these days are so trifling, cowardly, and narrow-minded, as it were. I've reached such an age. I've seen her several times and chatted with her on the phone more times than that. I liked her, and as a matter of fact, for that very reason, I strived hard not to be too drawn to her.

For me, Do-ran is likely to remain like a UFO, which I accidentally captured on the camera I happened to be holding at a boring tourist destination. I saw it and its image remains in my memory stick. It is a being that radiates light, but I can never mention it to anyone in my circle of friends if I want to remain part of it, a being I should keep quiet about because I know that I can expect no one's sympathy. But I am a different person after my encounter with it. The friendly hours I spent with Do-ran and the thud of the side mirror will crumble away some day, just like a flower that was plucked a long time ago. Just as Cho-pin and the heat I experienced with him on that rainy day is now a memory with vegetable qualities, not with animal passion.

One by one, the heated stones are placed along my spine.

Eventually the sensation of warmth will wear off and the stones will cool down slowly.

Cicadas

Tssss, tssss, tssss.

It begins with a low hiss, like air being sucked out of a tiny crack.

Then it is joined by a soft persistent tap, like the sound of dripping water, and then evolves into the metallic drone of cicadas, overwhelming my ear drums. I shut my eyes tight and then open them. So they say I should ignore this sound? They can only say that if they've never experienced it. If there's something you don't want to see, you can shut your eyes tight, but you can't flee from this buzz originating in your ears.

I came across a man suffering from tinnitus, just like me, at the ENT doctor's office during my previous appointment. He started complaining about his pain, but then stopped, hanging his head and shaking it.

He said, "People who haven't experienced it have no idea. Sitting here and watching other patients come and go, I can't describe how much I envy people who have only broken their limbs or torn a ligament. I think, 'If I had cancer, I could have it removed at least.' I can't carve out my ears. And after running all these tests on me, they can only say, 'We don't know what causes it, we can't tell you when you will get better.' To me, the noise sounds as though someone is scratching my nerves with his fingernails."

Now, to avoid the waiting room's depressing atmosphere, as

pervasive as an epidemic, I keep my eyes closed until they call my name. A hesitant voice reaches me amid the ceaseless cicada hissing.

"Is this seat taken?"

As I open my eyes, I first catch a glimpse of a swath of denim skirt under a white T-shirt. There are no other empty seats in the room. I pick up my computer bag from the chair next to me, and the woman bows slightly before she takes the seat.

This is my first visit to the neurology department. What diseases do these people have? Depression, panic disorder, ADHD, autism, delusion, sexual addiction, irrational suspicion that their spouse is cheating, bipolar disorder, propensity for theft, voyeurism . . . You can't tell what their illnesses are just by looking at their faces. The woman sitting next to me doesn't seem to be the type who'd be addicted to sex. Is she suffering from a panic disorder or depression? What disease do people think I'm afflicted with? Who determines the criteria that separates the insane from the sane, anyway?

Last week, the ENT doctor pronounced that everything was normal as he studied my medical chart. This did not mean that the cicadas would no longer buzz in my ears, but that the source of the ringing could not be determined. The doctor explained softly, as if he were trying to spare his vocal cords: "From the tests so far, your ear functions are all normal. There's a mild hearing impairment in your right ear, but it shouldn't be a problem as you go about your daily business. You have no infection or dullness of hearing. In fact, it is very difficult to find the cause of tinnitus. In most cases, it is a symptom of something other than an ear dysfunction."

I asked, "Do you mean that I have to live with it?"

"We will schedule for you some neurological tests next week."

"Neurology for tinnitus?"

"The causes of tinnitus are as varied as the types of ringing in patients' ears. Sometimes it is caused by brain dysfunction and sometimes by psychiatric suppression."

"Do you mean that stress could be the cause?"

"Exactly. There are many cases in which depression manifests itself as a ringing in the ear. To put it simply, some unknown cause prompts the brain to send a wrong signal to your ears. It looks like you'll need to have an EEG and neurotransmitter testing."

"Then you're positive that nothing is wrong with my ears."

"Correct. In cases like this, some patients are completely cured overnight."

I don't hope for a complete cure. I'd be relieved if there were half the number of cicadas living in my ears. There hasn't been the slightest improvement since I started going to the doctors. Now the doctor's office door opens and a nurse calls out a name. The woman sitting next to me stands up. As she passes by me, her scrawny hips wobble. Her gait is so unsteady that I'm nervous, fearing she might fall on my lap at any moment. As soon as she stands up, a middle-aged man leaning against a wall makes a beeline for her chair. Unfortunately, her progress is much slower than his estimation. The tip of his elbow pushes her as he makes his way to the seat, and she loses her balance and pitches forward. The woman falls in a heap on the floor, her face pale. Her purse spills out its contents. Of all places, it falls at my feet. I pick it up and hand it to her, and then scramble to gather what has rolled under my chair. A cosmetics compact emblazoned with a rose, a packet of wet wipes, a few coins, and even a sanitary napkin. Does she even have blood to shed, considering how pale she is? Someone behind me picks up a lipstick and holds it out to me. The woman, now on her feet, looks at me with resignation as I put everything into her purse, and she turns around without saying thank you and inches forward as slowly as a snail. The nurse calls out her name once again. All eyes in the waiting room are on the back of the woman lurching forward.

The man who shoved the woman to the floor is already showing off his medical knowledge to a middle-aged woman sitting on his other side. He intones, "There's no cure for that disease even if you go see one doctor after another. If your senses have already dulled, it won't be long for you, either, lady. In the end, you've got to have your toes or ankles cut off. A guy I know, he had three operations on his leg alone. At first, on his toes, then his ankle, and in the end his leg had to be amputated at the thigh. What you have, that's a horrible disease." The woman, who said she'd come for neurotransmitter testing, looks down at her lap, a desperate grimace on her face. Ascertaining that she is suitably terrified, he brings up the medical equipment he has benefited from. "Doctors make no difference," he says, "You see, if you take drugs, your organs are ruined, that's all. What you need is a fundamental cure." He then details the Japanese electric pressure equipment he's promoting. "All you need to do is sit in a chair," he says, and gives directions to a lab in central Seoul where you can try it out. He is a know-it-all when it comes to diseases. People like him spout a litany of ailments, claiming that they have suffered from the same disease, but they don't exude any sadness or sorrow.

The nurse calls my name twice in quick succession. As I open the door and step into the office, the woman who was sitting next to me backs away from the doorway. She doesn't seem to have smiled once, at least not since she woke up that morning. The hissing of the cicadas, which briefly faded out, is now back in full force as I sit facing the doctor. Sending me to the neurologist seems to have been the right step. If this metallic hiss doesn't disappear, I will end up losing my mind.

"I don't think I can put up with it any longer," I stammer as I explain to the landlord why I have to move. As I spill out minute details, it begins to dawn on me that I must strike him as a loser who is out of tune with the real world. It's no wonder that before I can finish, the old man blows up and blames me for finding fault with his perfectly fine place.

"If you're so picky, you should have gone deep into the mountains in the first place, like to the valley where Baekdam Temple is. Young man, you're such an oddball! How can you expect a neighborhood to have no sounds when people have to go about their daily business?"

I retort, "You should try living here for a day. I can't fall asleep because of the noises coming from upstairs and downstairs. You can even hear your next-door neighbors farting."

"Other tenants have no complaints, and you're the only one who's making a fuss. This is not moving season and I don't know when I can find a new tenant. How can I refund your security deposit now? It's not like I'm sitting on a heap of money that I can give out at any time. If you really can't live there, put the place up for rent with a broker yourself, but you'll have to pay my share of his fees as well." The old man yells and slams down the phone.

When I signed the lease, he told me that he eked out a living by renting out his apartment, but the broker tipped me off that the old man had as many as five units in this building alone. At the time, the old man whined that he didn't have any spare money to play with, and that he should have asked me for a higher security deposit. Hah, with so many units in your possession, I'm sure you're hard up for cash!

Am I the only one who's unusually sensitive to sounds? Are the sounds that don't bother anyone else amplified to such an unbearable decibel when they are joined by the cicadas buzzing in my ears?

I settled on this apartment with a quiet environment in mind.

The description of this neighborhood, an isolated community surrounded by greenery, turned out to be mere fantasy. On moving day, I realized that an eight-lane highway linking a satellite city with Seoul passed behind the complex. Late at night, noises and vibrations from large speeding trucks sent tremors all the way to my gut. At dawn, the mechanical rumbling of street-cleaning vehicles swept away my sleep. That was not all. This apartment was a peculiar place where the noise never abated. Not a moment was quiet. One could describe it as filled with an orchestra of noises.

During the daytime, trucks that sold fish, salt, and fruit took turns descending on the neighborhood, as if they had exchanged timetables among themselves, and ceaselessly played recordings calling on residents to come out and buy their wares. My next-door neighbor paced the hallway at ten o'clock at night with her crying baby on her back, singing lullabies. After she put her baby to sleep, she immediately started a fight with her husband. As their fight died down, the dialogue from historical TV dramas, muffled until then by other noises, blared from all directions. The national anthem playing at the end of the day's TV programs and the flushing of toilets were not the final sounds of the night. I had to sleep to the tune of someone snoring, and at times I was driven to jerk off to female coital moans that drifted into my room, though it was not clear where they came from: upstairs, downstairs, left, or right. All day long, draining water flowed down the pipes behind the sink, joined by other miscellaneous sounds. This din resonated with the hiss of cicadas in my ears. *Tsss, tssss, tssss.* I thought I could no longer endure living here, and that was why I called the landlord.

Now a chopping sound comes from upstairs. Is someone mincing meat at this hour, this early in the morning? Let me be magnanimous, I tell myself and take a few deep breaths. A liquid on the verge of boiling is seething in my ears. The cicadas will soon start crying.

Today, she is already there. She has a paperback open, but she doesn't seem to be focusing on it. I walk around to sit in a chair behind her, and a soft whiff of watermelon hits my nose. I was woken up early this morning by the rattle of the street-cleaning truck and failed to go back to sleep. My eyes are dry, as if dust has been rubbed into them. I close my eyes tight, and the air before my nose trembles slightly and the watermelon scent disperses. I don't open my eyes. I'm sure the woman feels many gazes following her staggering gait, as if she had eyes at the back of her head.

In university hospitals, why do they call in the next patient before the previous one leaves? As I enter, the woman, standing and speaking with the doctor, turns around. She is wearing a black skirt today. I wonder if intolerable noises come from some part of her brain as well. The doctor looks at my chart, goes to the washbasin to wash his hands, and when he returns, asks, "What do you do for a living?"

"I give lectures at universities." Although I spend more time at the publisher where I work part-time than teaching, I feel there's no need to divulge this information.

"What's your area of study?"

Why is he asking me this? *Tsss, tsss, tsss.* The cicadas rush forward from afar.

"German literature."

"Did you study abroad?"

"I returned last year."

"I suppose you are adjusting to life here, as though you've come to a foreign country."

All told, I spent eight years in Germany. If I had known that it would take that long to complete my studies, I wouldn't have started in the first place. Just like the youth in the old tale who went to a country where people ate lotus pips, only after my return did I realize that too much time had passed.

"In some ways, don't you think it's more difficult to readjust to life here than it was to get used to life over there?" the doctor asks.

I stare at him. He already looks drained, so early in the day. It looks like no abnormality has been found from the tests they ran on me last week. What he probably wants to say is: it's all because you're too sensitive and fastidious. But how can I measure the difference in the amount of stress I underwent over there initially and what I am going through here?

Without waiting for my reply, the doctor asks, "Did you start to hear the noises after you returned home?"

"Yes."

"Is there an ongoing problem that you find particularly difficult to deal with?"

When I returned after eight years of study, it didn't occur to me that landing a job at a university would be this difficult. Though my overseas studies were long, I didn't waste any time during that period. I plunged into my studies so wholeheartedly that sometimes I wondered, Do I really have to go to such lengths? If I had intended to use what I learned for some specific purpose, I would not have been able to stick to it so passionately. I thought studying suited me and I was good at it. Upon my return, I discovered that things had changed so much since I'd left. None of my male classmates was working in a field related to our major. A few elegant female classmates, who could pay for hourly helpers at home who cost them more than what they earned as lecturers, were teaching part-time. They were relaxed. Their attitude was, We'll live this way, and if a position opens up somewhere, that'll be great, but if not, that's okay too. To make matters worse, the universities that still offered German studies were far fewer than before. The number of students majoring in German had dropped drastically, with other foreign languages rising to fill the void. Even the universities that were holding out had few students who took courses, so the existing professors were more than enough. No university wanted me.

When J, the publisher, suggested that I come to his office to figure out how to get used to the city rather than feeling anxious, I was thankful beyond description. I hadn't seen him since college, and since then he'd gained a lot of weight. His chubby fingers seemed to convey his sense of satisfaction over what he had achieved. He asked me to do a translation if I found a good book, but German books were rarely considered for publication. All that worked was republishing the classics that had been put out a long time ago. There was no project that could make use of my specialty. It was truly tiring to sit idly in the same space where others were busy working. After business hours, I'd leave the office and stand absently in place, gazing at the cars racing along the street, as if I had no idea where to go. I volunteered to copyedit. Pushing aside the language I'd kept more closely to my heart than my own mother tongue for eight years, I began to copyedit, learning every detail from a young copyeditor. One afternoon, I began to hear cicadas hiss in my ears . . .

The doctor is too busy to listen to all this.

I vaguely nod and answer, "Not difficult . . . how should I put it, I'd say I'm afraid. When I'm in the streets, when I'm with people, even when I'm alone at home, I feel like some aggressive energy is overpowering me."

"Sooner or later you will realize that that's the driving force pushing this society along, like a steam engine. You will feel that it's not as bad as it looks at first glance. Your test results are fine. There's no problem in your brain or neurotransmitters. Take it easy and don't pay too much attention to the noise."

Ah. Tinnitus is not a hymn coming from the other side of the wall. How is it possible not to pay any attention to it? The cicada drone, once started, overflows into the ear canals, the brain, and the entire universe, making me wish I could cut off my ears. I step out to the hallway packed with people waiting their turn. It is noisy, though no one is speaking loudly. As I thread my way through them, I curse all speaking human beings.

The exit from the underground parking lot adjoins the taxi stand at the entrance to the outpatient unit. As I drive out, I notice that several people are waiting for a taxi in front of the woman in the black skirt. She is looking across the road absently, bathed in sunlight, and then she flips her head back, as if someone has called her name, and looks in my direction. Does she recognize me?

There is a sudden roar. Dark spots are beginning to be imprinted on the white sun-bathed road, as if a gigantic dotted piece of fabric is being spread out on the ground. The sound of raindrops hitting the car roof strikes me as almost menacing. Oddly, the sky is bright. I stretch my hand out the window, palm up. Something cold beats it with a force. A mixture of hail and rain. Hail in early summer? There's the sound of popping beans ricocheting from my car roof. The woman seems to look up at the sky, but suddenly she wobbles. Her body, as weightless as a paper doll, topples over. Those around her crane their necks to get a look. A young man in uniform runs toward her.

As I stop my car at the taxi stand, I see only her black skirt in my side mirror. I get out and open the back door and then rush over to her side. The wind lifts up her skirt. I catch a glimpse of slightly twisted legs, as scrawny as plucked bird legs. I pull her skirt down over her trembling legs. I slide my hands behind her back to lift her up, and she is so light that I wonder if she'll remain upright if I take my hands away.

I lay her down in the back seat of my car and shut the door. As I pass through the main gate, I glance back and she is already sitting up. So she was unconscious only for a few minutes. I ask her, "Where are you headed?" She answers in a resigned tone, "Near the Yeonhui-dong Rotary," and looks out to the street, where the rain has already stopped. Strangely, I feel like a shameless voyeur who has taken a peek at someone's secrets. I saw what was inside her purse, and then I looked up her skirt. She maintains an awkward silence until we've almost reached Yeonhui-dong Rotary, and she opens her mouth only to say, "Please drop me off here." She gets out of my car in front of a kindergarten. She says thank you in a tiny voice, and turns around to enter the building. Her back wobbles, making me nervous.

Those who have something to hide habitually rely on pleats and folds in their clothing, but despite their intentions, those only exaggerate their secrets. Her wide, long skirt only emphasizes her irregular leg movements and her staggering gait. As she turns from the door of the brick building, the corners of her mouth turn down ever so slightly, as if she doesn't know which expression to choose, a smile or a grimace. The next moment, that smile disappears as if it never happened.

The woman shows up in a different skirt each time. How many long skirts does she have in her closet?

As I leave the hospital after another appointment, the woman, leaning on a pillar in the lobby, greets me. Her expression today strikes me as the brightest so far, probably the effect of her white skirt. Is she uncomfortable pretending that nothing happened between us?

"About the last time, I apologize. I'd like to treat you to lunch or something . . ."

I don't feel like eating with someone I don't know, but I'm reluctant to refuse her flatly. I decline vaguely, "Um, no, you don't have to . . ." She begins in an unsure voice, "Still . . ." and then trails off. If she had made her offer with a lively voice and sparkling eyes, I could have turned it down with ease of mind. I end up nodding. I think of asking her to wait at the building entrance until I drive out, but I don't know how she will take that, so I go down to the parking lot with her. Before long, I sense from the way her shoulders labor up and down that she is out of breath. I feel uncomfortable.

As I exit the parking lot, the taxi stand comes into view. She doesn't glance in that direction. I notice that the green treetops grow taller and more lush on each of my weekly visits; now the scenery looks completely different. With such a visual sign of the passage of time, a fear grips me, like dizziness. Can I afford to go around leisurely from one doctor to another, dragged by an unidentifiable illness?

I decide not to drive far and head for a row of restaurants nearby. We sit in a restaurant serving pasta, facing its floor-to-ceiling front windows. When she asks for spaghetti vongole, I echo her order. I have nothing to say to her. I suddenly find this situation annoying. Through the windows, the entire hospital building can be seen.

Sipping water, she asks, "What health problems do you have?"

Does she think she has the right to know about me because I've already seen some intimate parts of her? In what mode can two people who've met at the same hospital ward develop their relationship? They won't be able to go through the process in which a man and a woman who know nothing about each other gradually open up and discover things about each other. Is it possible for those who suffer from seemingly invisible neurological diseases to be bound together, their fatal flaws acting as a link?

"There's a ringing in my ears."

"What kind?"

"How can I describe it? It sounds like water dripping or cicadas crying. . . My ears, which are supposed to just listen, create a sound of their own, and then they have to listen to it."

"Is that because you're too sensitive? They say that the universe is filled with numerous sounds that we can't hear. Sounds that are too soft for us to hear, or too loud for us to hear. For instance, the sound of flowers blooming, the sound of cicadas sloughing off their skins, the sound of the earth rotating, the sound of two stars colliding and exploding, and the sound of whales crying. Looks like you hear all those things."

The sound of a flower blooming? This kind of reaction drives me nuts. I simply nod. "You're probably right. I would love it if I could hear flowers bloom, but my ears only catch the sound of stars colliding."

She savors her spaghetti, piling up empty clam shells on one side of her plate. She may have a stronger desire for life than the impression she gives. That has to be the case, since she orders a dish in which she has to pick at the clam meat when she is sharing a meal with a practical stranger for the first time. She is talkative, contrary to my first impression of her; she struck me as the type of person who would hardly acknowledge a stranger's question with an answer. Moving her fork constantly, she talks about herself without any encouragement from me. There is no sign of grief or self-pity. As I listen to her remarks, stripped of sentimental emotions, I feel as if she is relaying someone else's symptoms. When a person suffers from a chronic illness, is it possible to assume such an objective attitude?

"I was a sophomore in a girls' high school. One afternoon, the fragrance of summer grass flooded in from the open windows. It was during the fifth period, and I think it was around summertime. I collapsed during the lesson and it was the first time it happened to me. It was a math class, and from the music room, the song 'O Sole Mio' was drifting in. I wasn't dozing off, but I was falling sideways, with a pen still in my hand. I felt that my arms and legs were twisting in all directions, but they were beyond my control, as though they didn't belong to me. Just like a sudden attack of severe cramps, my legs hurt, as if they'd been slit by a knife, from my thighs to my calves. I collapsed to the floor. Lying there, I wanted to say something to the girl who was sitting next to me, as she was looking down in astonishment, but my tongue and my eyeballs wouldn't move. A home economics teacher ran over from the next classroom and examined me all over. Then she mouthed 'epilepsy' to the math teacher standing by her side. As soon as I read her lips, I fell asleep. How could I fall asleep in that situation? Don't you find it odd?"

She sips water, her mouth seemingly parched. Having asked a question I can't answer, she looks me in the eyes. I imagine her sleeping between the rows of desks, exposed to the many gazes piercing her body. The image of her at the taxi stand floats up.

"You couldn't help it, I suppose."

"Do you think so? I was taken to one doctor after another. They said nothing was wrong with my brain and autonomic nervous system, and I didn't have epilepsy, but I kept fainting at unpredictable intervals. At school I told my friends, 'Doctors say I don't have epilepsy,' and they stared at me and said, 'Yeah?' That was all. Only the doctors said I wasn't having epileptic fits. But they were the ones who weren't part of my actual life."

She has cleaned up the plate in front of her. This type of tale shouldn't stimulate an appetite. One's appetite is mercurial, always easily affected by other emotions. What emotion lurks on the flip side of this abnormal appetite? My plate is still half full, as I don't care for pasta.

"It's getting warm and I don't have much of an appetite," I say. "Unfortunately, the most beautiful season is over."

Today is the first day of June. With the weather as an excuse, I put down my fork. The greenery surrounding the hospital building looks like a green balloon that may float up at any minute.

The woman follows my gaze and mumbles as if to herself, "Do you think May is beautiful? People who can look at the landscape with only their eyes say May is beautiful. Personally, I like June. It gives off a vitality that's almost violent. June is the month when

sensuality melts like golden flakes in ceaselessly flowing river water, and even plants, greedily drinking that water, begin to breathe
hard. If a person is going to have loveless sex, don't you think June
is the right time? If you have to kill someone, do it on a June evening. June is the season when any crime can be forgiven."

This is not something to tell a person whom she barely knows,
whom she's come across only a few times in a hospital corridor.
Loveless sex and murder? Is this the same woman who stood still
after dropping her purse in the corridor, with miserable and help-
less eyes? Is this the same woman who lay weakly on the ground
while wind flipped up her skirt? Her cynical pronouncements
carry an air of obsession. Her utterance strikes me as the sign of
some sort of desperate struggle that doesn't fit her slow speech
and placid expression.

It is only the beginning of summer, but it is hot.

"Thank you for your time," she says, "Next time, I will get you
some earplugs as a gift."

Despite my explanation, she still seems to think that the sound
I can't stand comes from the outside, and not from within me.

"Is that your hobby?" I blurt out, as soon as the door opens. I really am curious.

My neighbor from upstairs seems to find it hard to fathom
my question.

"What do you mean?"

"Pounding on nails."

The man rolls his eyes, his eyeballs staying upward like a sun
rising over the horizon, to indicate that he's never seen a crazier
guy before. I didn't rush upstairs just to say, "I'm sorry to bother
you, but could you please . . ." and then meekly turn around. Seeing the defiant expression on his face, I erupt.

"I'm going crazy. How can you pound on nails all day long?"

The guy's head is slightly cocked to the left. He may want to look down at me to express his contempt, but the top of his head barely reaches my forehead.

"Yeah, that's my hobby. I like woodworking. It's different from driving nails into a wall, can't you tell? No one has complained about the noise before, you know."

"From downstairs, it's no different from driving nails into a wall. My head rings with the sound of your drill and hammer, and I can't read at all."

"No one else complains. You're too sensitive."

"I bet everyone else is just putting up with it. You shouldn't do this as a resident in a communal building."

"Yeah? If you can't stand it, why don't you move out?"

Actually, if he were the type who'd readily apologize and stop his ruckus, he wouldn't wield his hammer day and night in the apartment. I don't feel like wasting any more breath on a person who is beyond reason, so I ask him to refrain from making noise at least in the evening. Before I turn around completely, the door slams shut behind me. I walk downstairs to my apartment and the hammering is still going on. Of course, he can't be deliberately doing it to exasperate me. So I may have the fastidiousness that makes me unable to accept daily life as it is, as the woman I met at the hospital pointed out. Now I begin by blaming myself for every little thing. Sitting at my desk, I concentrate on the phrase I've been reading over and over again. The hammering seems to pause, but it is soon replaced by drilling, the sound of wood being torn; it sticks to my entire body like coal tar. I catch myself imagining that I'm driving a drill into the upstairs guy's thick belly. For some time, the same bars of a Czerny piano exercise have been drifting in as well. Even the water traveling down the pipes cannot sweep away its persistency. The whir of the drill and the din of a knife on a chopping board join the cacophony. I close the book.

Tsss, tsss, tsss.

The volume of the cicadas in my ears is increasing as if to beat out all those sounds. The entire space is filled with sounds. I feel as if I am crouching inside a huge engine. When the cacophony of the cicadas and all the other noises reaches its peak, I pull out a tennis racket from the utility room and start whacking the ceiling with it. The drill comes to an abrupt stop. My fury peaks at the very moment it stops, as though a safety valve has been removed. I relentlessly hit the ceiling with the racket until my entire body shakes uncontrollably. I hate myself for behaving like this. When the racket is finally broken, I am thoroughly drenched in sweat.

Instead of responding to my urging that we should give up the idea if she's not confident, the woman looks up, her expression dismal. She's the one who first suggested it: Shall we try that? She added that she'd been to an amusement park before but had never even been on a merry-go-round. She said, We. So this isn't for our amusement, but for something else. A person who faints while sitting and another person who cannot stand all the sounds coming from inside and outside his ears. Should these two people be riding a roller coaster?

An object which resembles a gigantic black bird whooshes over our heads. Shrieks that sound like the screeching of birds reign down. She does not say anything but walks ahead of me in the line. Our seats are in the second row from the back. A simple instruction is followed by the lowering of safety bars. Right before we set off, a couple sitting in front of us faces each other and they kiss. As the train goes up, clunk, clunk, to the top, the woman and I look down at our own hands clutching the bar. She seems to be taking in a deep breath and slowly exhaling. The train seems to halt at the top before it plunges vertically. After a brief moment when everyone's minds must be blank, frenzied shrieks issue forth. As if they were on the ride to scream at the top of their lungs, all howl differently. Surprisingly, it is less frightening when the train makes a 360-degree turn, but the shrieks grow in intensity as the train twists, hurtles, and drops. I don't know whether the woman is howling or closing her eyes. When we stop at the platform, our bodies lurch forward. The bars are lifted. The couple in front of us kisses again. I am not the only one who's supporting his companion; all the couples are clinging to each other as they go down the stairs with shaking legs, as if carrying the wounded. We scramble out and only then can we face each other.

"Are you all right?" I ask.

"What about you?"

I smile first and she smiles back.

"How about violently shaking our brains and eardrums?" She suggested riding the rollercoaster as a sort of shock therapy, but it does not work in the slightest for either of us. But before we part, we kiss, just like the couple who sat in front of us. It feels so natural; if the ride has any effect, this is it.

"Wow, gravestones!"

As I prepare coffee, the woman, looking down from the veranda, cries out. Gravestones? Does she mean there's a cemetery down there? Carrying coffee on a tray, I step onto the veranda. I had no idea that there were gravestones. I take a good look at the flattened curves and I recognize that they are indeed gravestones, scattered randomly. Severely eroded, they look like heaps of dirt. "How could you not know?" The woman teases me for being oblivious, but it isn't a big deal that I didn't notice them. My hands on the railing, I look down, wondering whether this is really the place where I live. I look back at the living room. I was being driven crazy day after day by the sounds coming from the front of the building, from upstairs, from downstairs, and from the sides of the building, but I had never glanced at the back, which exudes silence as calmly as a sprinkler emitting a spray of water.

"It's absolutely quiet," she says.

"You mean here?"

"Don't you think so?"

"Listen carefully. The noises drive me crazy."

She stands still for a minute, her hands cupped around her ears, and shakes her head. "I don't hear anything."

"Like people who have bad eyesight, there are people who have bad hearing."

"Good ears don't catch unnecessary sounds."

Right. These quiet, desolate gravestones will disappear soon. The building we're standing in must have been built atop bull-dozed gravestones. The early summer sunlight dances, but the graves have the feel of a historic site that is filled with desolation and loneliness. I look down at the scenery without a word, drinking my coffee, and the woman is crying, although I can't tell when she started. I know she is crying without looking at her. Shedding tears quietly, she scratches the metal railing with her nail. The scenery below wouldn't move anyone to tears. She has an odd talent, weeping without making the tiniest sound. I look down at the eroding gravestones. I have never experienced such quiet. The cicadas that used to cry in my ears are silent.

There are relationships that arise out of a sense of fate, rather than love.

Loving someone may be an emotion that arises when you don't know what the other person is like. What is dangerous about two people meeting at the same hospital ward may be the misconception that they know all about each other. For example, when the woman tells me about her sister, I have a feeling of déjà vu. I am already trying to superimpose my life over hers.

"I had a twin sister. How could twins be so different? Only our faces looked similar. I had no interest in studying whereas my sister's hobby was reading encyclopedias. An encyclopedia was always open on her desk. I don't know why that sight annoyed me so much. She was always smiling, and people were tempted to touch her pretty cheeks. When she bowed to people with a bright smile, they would look at her, eyes crinkled in a smile. . . . She was my mirror. The mirror I had to look into every day. The mirror that reflected my pathetic state. As we got older, we became more and more different. So much so that people doubted that we were sisters. During morning assemblies at school, when a red cloth was draped over the lectern for award-giving, the kids whispered, Again? and mentioned my sister's name. While my atrophied legs grew twisted, her legs were straight and lively, like summer trees, and even I found them attractive. On days when I had to hand her the phone because a boy wanted to speak with her, I vented my irrational irritation, but she always smiled like an angel. She loved reading encyclopedias and called me Big Sis, and didn't wear shorts in front of me. Her nice temperament was reflected in her fair cheeks. People thought I was deaf. They said in stage whispers, Did you know that they're twins? I bet they're not identical twins. . . I didn't hate her. I wanted her out of my sight, but . . ."

The sun dips in the sky and the air seems to be filled with golden bubbles, like a saucepan that is coming to a boil. The contours of the grave mounds are more pronounced, bathed in the slanting evening glow.

"When she missed school for several days from a lingering summer cold, I didn't offer her any comforting words. Her fever wouldn't drop and she had a blood test, and ten days after getting the test results, she died. Leukemia. Someone whispered in my ear, 'What you wanted so much has come to pass. How do you feel?' Anyway, have you ever had the experience of your imagination turning into reality?"

"At that age, you could have been blaming yourself for her death."

"The first time I collapsed was a month after my sister's death.

My family thought that I began to have fits because of the sense of loss I felt over my sister's death."

The empty coffee cup is dangling precariously from the woman's finger. I wonder whether I should take it from her but it suddenly falls down. We are too high above the ground for the sound of the smash to reach us. The soles of my feet itch.

I ask, "Do you think that human beings are such intense beings? That if we wish for something ardently, it will come true?"

Without replying, she looks down, her body leaning over the veranda railing. She seems to see her own sense of desolation reflected in the grave mounds. A wind blows from below. Her light green cotton skirt is lifted, revealing the legs that stopped growing a long time ago, pale as scallion stalks.

I don't like to testify to my personal wounds or listen to someone else's confessions. Yet, I spill out what I didn't even tell my doctor, moved by her scallion-stalk legs, helplessly revealed whenever a gust of wind blows. About the pain of tinnitus that those who haven't experienced it cannot begin to imagine, about the hours of preparing dossiers whenever an employment notice was put up, harboring hope, and then returning to yet another despair, about the very, very short woman with whom I departed for Germany but who returned separately. After summing everything up, I realize that my life is actually very simple.

Probably the woman and I are obsessed with proving how different we are, just like adolescent twins, despite the fact that our relationship began at the same outpatient ward.

"After returning here, I feel I've become a useless human being, who has to remake everything from scratch. Even his shadow."

The woman slips her foot out of her shoe and taps it on my shadow on the floor. As if to say I shouldn't be so serious about something like a shadow. Her foot is abnormally tiny, as if it had been bound in the old Chinese custom. I push my foot under hers. The tiny foot has no weight. It isn't just her foot that's weightless.

Later, in bed, lying on top of me, she is so light she seems to be floating in the air.

The raindrops disappear after drawing quick slanting lines on the bus windows. The rainy season has already begun. The bus drives in and out of showers, but always under thick, dark clouds. Fury, sizzling inside me, dies down, turning into a fist-sized ball in the pit of my stomach. In the end it turns into irritation and self-loathing.

I admonish myself: It was foolish of you to harbor hope. I am on my way back home after an interview at a university in a small southern city. A guy I am close to and who was ahead of me in college, teaches at the university, and I talked with him on the phone before applying for the position. I asked, "Is there anyone who's been chosen internally?" He answered, "About that, it's hard to know." When I asked what he would advise me to do, he was vague. "Uh, why don't you put in an application? You have nothing to lose. Keep trying, and luck and timing will eventually land you a position." Luck and timing? He explained, "In a regional private college like this, professors in the department have virtually no say in the hiring process." I wanted to say: It is not difficult to submit an application, but it is aggravating to soothe the sense of humiliation and fury, though I can't tell at whom my fury is directed exactly.

It was an interview in name only. It was a venue to inform me directly that they had no interest in me. Having been in similar situations over and over again, I could catch their attitude toward the candidates who were there only to fill protocol. I kept thinking I shouldn't take it personally, but it was hard to endure.

Throughout the bus ride home, I regret for the first time that I settled on an impractical major a dozen years ago. The realization that nobody wants me makes me miserable.

The bus slows down noticeably after passing through a toll

booth. The raindrops no longer make slanting lines, but fall vertically. The bus is forty minutes behind schedule, but since it is no one's fault, the passengers are absently gazing down at the cars cramming the streets, their expressions revealing disgust over the perpetual traffic jam. The rain has stopped by now. As I step down from the bus, humid heat swirls around me. I walk out of the bus terminal, and all the sounds in the world flood into my ear canals. Faint throbs precede the onslaught of ringing. The din of drilling from an excavator, honking, and other noises—pulverized and floating in the air—are blended together in my ears like concrete being mixed. I miss the woman as though she were water to my parched throat. I believe all these throbs would disappear if she closed all the doors and assured me of quiet. If I put her atrophied foot on mine and gauge its weight, this fierce ringing in my ears would disappear.

Her cell phone is off. Her class should be over by now. I contemplate leaving a voice message, but call the kindergarten.

"Uh, is Teacher O Jin-hui there?"

"Teacher O? She went home early today. Her child is sick."

A child?

"Teacher Oh Jin-hui's child?"

"Yes, she's been sick with a cold and now it has developed into pneumonia."

I hang up after saying thank you, and the veins in my temple feel as though they are about to burst through the skin.

Child? So she's divorced then? That's possible. She doesn't have an obligation to tell me that. I didn't ask, did I? She was probably going to tell me at some point, though it's not an easy subject to bring up.

I stand there for a while, as if I have nowhere to go. I don't feel like going home. I call Y, who has his own business in trendy Nonhyeon-dong. He has called me several times since my return, saying that we should get together, but I always put it off, saying,

"Let's do it later." Now I suggest, "Let's have a drink," and he says to come over to his office right away. It is three subway stops from where I am. As I get out of the subway exit he indicated, I notice his office right in front of me. Y started a business that had nothing to do with his college major, and now he tells me that the entire building belongs to him, not just the first floor where imported furniture is on display. He shows me around, floor by floor, and tells me to hop into his Audi.

He talks about himself until we arrive at the restaurant. I ask how he first came up with the idea of opening a furniture store, and he gives me an unexpected answer: "To tell you the truth, I've made more money on real estate than furniture." He then asks, "What are you doing now?" I tell him that I teach some classes and also pitch in at J's publishing house. He immediately expresses his concerns about J. "Hey, help him out, will you? Every time I see him, he's whining. He didn't listen to me. You know, when he opened that publishing house, I told him, Take out a loan from the bank and buy this building before you start making books. Do you know how much he regrets that he didn't listen to me? Land prices have since soared tenfold in the Hongik University neighborhood. One decisive move is all that counts in life. If he'd heeded my advice, he could've lived comfortably, instead of slaving away to put out books."

Looking out at the road, which shows no sign of cars moving and resembles a parking lot, he says in a self-satisfied tone, "I think it's not too late even now. Seoul is a paradise and a hell when it comes to making money."

Too much time has passed for us to discuss Goethe and Thomas Mann. Y implicitly treats me as if I were a complete hick, who has stared at bare walls in the backwoods for a decade, beyond the reach of newspapers and television, before returning home. He says, "I asked two women I know to join us later. To plant roots here, you should get to know more people and all that, right?" We sit on the floor in a private room of a Japanese restaurant at a table laden with raw fish and other side dishes, too much for the two of us to consume. Y keeps worrying about me. I don't feel a modicum of sincerity in his words.

The women join us at the wine bar, where we go after dinner. One of them, with her short hair, dyed bluish black, framing her face, seems to have a special relationship to Y. Between drinking wine and picking up cheese, Y's hand weasels in and out of her blouse. The woman sitting next to me has no distinctive features. As soon as I turn around, her face is erased from my memory. These women don't look as though they would be helpful in my planting roots here. Y introduces me as a Ph.D. who's returned from Germany after studying there for eight years, but they show no interest at all. Y starts to fool around. He says, "These ladies came from Ilsan. So to share drinks here, you've rushed from Germany and they've rushed from Ilsan." As if this is a great joke, the women burst out laughing. Y's hand has been darting in and out of the woman's blouse, and now the two are sucking on each other's lips. Y told me earlier in the car that his wife, who was our classmate in college, is doing well.

The cicada drone in my ears is getting intense. If I pushed an ear pick in, I'd be able to pull out an endless number of cicadas. The woman sitting next to me asks in a completely incurious tone, "Where in Germany did you live?" And before I can answer, she recounts an unrelated story. A few years ago, she went on a trip to Europe and bought Henckels knives. It was soon after the terrorist attack, and the knives were detected at the airport she was passing through, and it created a huge scene. What can I say to a woman who is reminded of only Henckels when she hears about Germany? I sit quietly and Y suddenly addresses me in a voice full of suppressed anger, "Hey, they came all the way from Ilsan. Hold her in your arms or something, okay?" Instead of holding her in my arms, I lift my wine glass. Eros comes from a wild emotion, the desire to embrace someone, not from the instruction that I hold someone in my arms. Observing the three people drinking ceaselessly as they exchange dull, uninteresting remarks, I feel that what they possess is a talent, too. The women start badmouthing their husbands, as naturally as though they were discussing television soap operas. I would think minimum etiquette dictates that they should tell lies, like the fact that their husbands died two years ago or that they are going to be overseas for a long time. Have relationships evolved so much while I was out of the country that a woman lets a man fondle her breasts while merrily talking about her husband?

The woman from the hospital has actually taught me how to create tranquility in my daily life. When I shut the veranda door behind me and stare down at the graves, thrusting my body as far as it can go over the railing, the noises that used to harass me, the noises that ceaselessly came from inside and outside of me, die down gently.

Earlier in the day, I met my friend teaching at the college in the south, where I had applied for a position. He had come to Seoul and suggested that we get together, but sitting face to face, he remained silent. I asked as if in passing, "How did it go?" He would only say, "The decision has been made." There was no need for me to ask what the decision entailed. We sat quietly for a while. If I had laughed, I would have looked silly, and if I had cried, I would have come off as maudlin. Being told face to face that no one wanted me was more difficult than I anticipated.

I come home, go to the veranda holding a cup of coffee with lots of ice cubes, and close my eyes, leaning my back on the railing. I think of her and remember how chatty she is. I didn't realize it when I was with her, but standing at the veranda, only her jabbering comes to mind.

"If you have to hear sounds no one else can hear, listen for other sounds, not the cicadas. How about the crying of a white-whiskered whale swimming in the ocean, or the sound of a flower opening? Because you're scratching your mind too much, you hear the metallic noise in your ears."

"What does a crying whale sound like?"

"Oh, woo, oh, woo, oh, woo, woo, woo . . ."

"Isn't that a wolf?"

"Is it?" She opened her eyes wide, as if she'd had no idea.

That expression comes to me when I'm alone. Now, come to think of it, she has burrowed herself deep inside me in such a short period of time. I haven't contacted her since the day I called her at the kindergarten. When she called, I hung up with some vague excuse, feeling that I was a narrow-minded, mean-spirited guy.

How generous people can be to strangers! Between us, there is already a dense entanglement that makes it impossible for me to ignore the fact that she didn't mention her child. Crunching on the ice, I look down at the graves. The phone rings. "Are you home? Why did you miss you doctor's appointment today?" I slowly say I had some urgent business to take care of. I don't like the way I sound. She says, "I'll come over." I answer tightly, "Okay." I can't keep talking with her on the phone.

"I thought I wouldn't feel like going out again once I arrived, so I bought some food." Saying this, she puts down a plastic shopping bag on the table. She then fans herself with her hand. Her cheeks are flushed, hot from the walk. "Plums are already out in the market," she mumbles as she spreads out what she has brought. My twin! When she stands still, without walking, she is dolefully beautiful.

She lifts the lid of a lunch box, revealing neat rows of sushi rolls. I sit at the table, and she hands me a pair of chopsticks. Only after she puts a roll covered with fish roe into her mouth and eats it with relish does she try to gauge my feelings.

"Has something happened?"

"Not really." My voice comes out choppy, giving her an important hint.

"What is it this time? Did your upstairs neighbor make a casket or something?" She stretches out her hand over the table and playfully rubs the furrows between my eyes.

Leaning backward to avoid her hand, I blurt out, "You have a child?"

Do I believe I have the right to ask this much? What I want to make clear is this: *What I want to point out is not the fact that you have a child, but that you didn't tell me.* My rationalization goes: *Though I have never been married, I'm not in a position to make an issue of your divorce. I told you about my previous relationship, but you didn't mention your husband, which is unfair.* The woman throws a quick look at my eyes, chopsticks still resting on her lips, fixes her gaze at a point on the table, and carefully chews what is in her mouth and swallows.

Then she looks into my eyes. "I have a child and a husband, too."

Something in my ear pops. The same Czerny phrase is being repeated from somewhere nearby. Not long ago, a Japanese man strangled a high-school girl who was learning to play the piano and lived upstairs from him.

"I married young. To a man who kissed my twisted leg and vowed that he loved me. I hurried things along, not because I loved him but because I thought no other man would ever want to marry someone like me. I realized this only after we were married. He had more interest in what my family would give him. He constantly demanded things from them, and I could no longer stand it. I couldn't let my whole family sink into a bottomless pit because of me. I stopped delivering his demands to my family . . . He thought he had made a bad business transaction by marrying me. He phoned another woman in my presence and chatted with her affectionately, and he was horribly violent with me, yelling that I was a cripple. From our relationship, I learned a few things pretty well. How I come across to other people objectively, how many faces a person has, and the fact that what never changes is only this miserable, pathetic life. I'm the one who's clinging to our marriage. I believe no other man is willing to be a father to my daughter. If I don't expect too much, it's bearable, more or less. It's rather late to be telling you all this, but this is me. I have a husband, I have a daughter, and I'm a woman who limps around and will sleep with any man."

"Why do you live like that?" My voice is hoarse.

The whites of the woman's eyes, calmly gazing at me, are bluish. "Then how should I live?"

The crying sound of the next door neighbor's baby makes its way into her even voice. The chopping sounds from upstairs cut the crying into tiny pieces. She opens her purse and takes out a familiar bag of prescribed drugs.

"A long time ago, I gave up the expectation that my fate would change just because I changed small things. I needed some other drug than the one I had to take a handful of three times a day. The me who's getting old tediously. The me who at night dreams of maggots crawling out of rotten things. The me who has to limp around. I needed another drug."

She doesn't even blink. If only she had given me a pleasant lie, if only she'd said she'd wanted to become the object of someone's desire, then I would have pretended to understand it all.

"That day, at the hospital," I accuse, "you collapsed intentionally. You staged it after seeing my face through my car window. Did I look that easy of a target?"

She lets a faint smile slip.

She stands up and walks around to my side of the table. "Look at me."

I glare at the lunch box with two of the rolls missing. I hear a hook snap open and her skirt drop to the floor.

"This is me. I weigh only thirty-five kilograms. Thirty-four years old. A kindergarten contract teacher. I take medication, but it doesn't prevent me from fainting. Look, when I take everything off like this and walk, really . . . look, look at me!"

I stubbornly stare at the table, but she takes backward steps and urges me to look at her.

"If I had told you, what would have changed? Okay. I'll tell you the truth. That it wasn't difficult to pretend to faint, when necessary. That in order to endure the devil, I needed another man. That I didn't sleep with you because I loved you. That I don't feel apologetic because I don't love you. What else do you want to know?"

The cicadas rage insanely. Sharply, as if rubbing against one another's metal wings. The cacophony at its peak rends my nerves.

I can't stand it, this sound.

I only block my ears, I only grip the cicada that is within my reach, but something pulses under my palms. The weight of the handful in my grip is as light as a paper doll. I feel nauseated. The woman's face doesn't register a look of shock or pain. As though she has no idea what expression to wear, her lips droop slightly. The pulsing weakens in my palms, and the scallion-stalk legs flutter. Outside the veranda, a June evening has descended like a thick curtain. My fingers are interlaced in sticky dampness. The woman who has shrunk into a tiny heap jumps into my ear and starts crying.

Tsss, tssss, tsss.

Signal Red

I had forgotten.

That K had said, I wish my heart would stop as I push a shopping cart, and I would die right then and there; if I could close my eyes surrounded by abundant goods lining either side of a shopping aisle, it'd be the happiest death for me.

On another occasion, he had said, My only hobby is to shop on a rainy day, slowly pushing a cart through a brightly lit department store. He added, I love only the material side of life, and personal relationships seem to begin only to be broken in the end. I gave him high marks for his frankness, if not his preferences. As a person who had studied stage art and worked as an art director, he might reasonably dream of his last moments in which he would collapse slowly, grabbing his heart behind the stage he had created, amid wild applause. When he told me that, the large cart he was pushing was crammed with groceries, but he kept tossing in one thing after another, throwing sidelong glances at the display shelves on either side.

I still remember that among the goods he had thrown in his cart was a bag of apples. With my fists buried in my pockets, I walked along, for I didn't want to interfere in his favorite activity, but something odd happened, prompting me to spring to action. Unable to ignore the apples he had just selected from a huge heap, I picked out several greenish ones from the clear plastic bag.

"These don't taste good. They are hard to bite into, too. You've got to choose red, shiny ones. You're not going to use these as a stage prop or something anyway."

He picked up another greenish apple and said with a vague smile, "I see things differently from you."

"In what way?"

"Uh, I'm not you, so how would I know? Except that it's different."

At the time, I interpreted his word "different" in my own way. Earlier, on the stage strewn with wood pieces and nails, he had said, "Throw out your fixed notions first. Don't cling to visible forms and colors. What people look for on a stage is not everyday life." Remembering his words, I wondered, What is his unique criteria for choosing apples?

"I am blind to the color red," he said in his car on the way home after shopping.

Only then did it occur to me that he probably hadn't been talking about an abstract concept.

I kept blinking for a while and then managed to ask, "Do you mean that you're color blind?"

He frowned slightly. "Well, I don't know whether my symptoms mean that I'm color blind."

Looking at his profile as he braked in precise alignment with the white line before the traffic light, I asked, "How does that red light appear to you?"

"Do you think I can describe it?"

He was right. I'd thought I knew what color blindness was, but my biological knowledge could tell me nothing about the world K was seeing. A flurry of confusing questions popped into my head, but I didn't ask any of them. I thought he wouldn't be able to answer them, and no matter how he explained, I wouldn't get it. Just as I couldn't begin to describe how objects captured by my highly myopic eyes looked to those who had perfect eyesight.

That day I also learned that K didn't have a driver's license, but he had never been in an accident, and so no police officer had ever asked him for his license.

In any event, neither his color blindness nor his passion for shopping was a disease that affected one's longevity.

Yet, as soon as I heard from the assistant director that K had died, a scene flashed through my head, as if watching a play, in which K, pushing a cart at the store we'd gone to, was slowly collapsing. Floating up vividly in my mind, as if it had only been yesterday, was his cheerful voice when he said, I wish I would die as I push a cart, right then and there; his self-indulgence that sounded as if he were mocking death, because his remark struck me as unreal; and his resolute eyes, unblinking like those of a young bird that did not know what death meant. Was it really the material side that he had preferred? Only after I broke up with him did I imagine that he fled to the store's aisles, among the silent goods in mountainous heaps, when he felt suffocated in his tangled relationships. All these thoughts occurred simultaneously and clamored for attention in my head, but not a word escaped from my lips.

Unable to stand my silence, the assistant director's voice came from the other end of the line. "He jumped from his apartment, but they say there was no apparent reason for his suicide."

She must have called me, believing that I was linked to his death in one way or another, but I simply said, "Oh, I see."

There aren't many people who can determine the course of their own lives, he once said. What words could I add to the life of such an eccentric? I hung up and looked out the window. It was a cloudy afternoon in March, neither winter nor spring, with scant sunlight.

Who approached the other person first? If you think that the two of you did so "at the same time," it is likely that you were the first to make a move.

Before I met him, I had heard of K but he hadn't heard of me.

A person whose name is not a brand in itself needs an affiliation. In this field, lulls between jobs tire you out. It is always precarious to make a living with irregular work, joining this crew and then that one.

These idle periods made me question my talent and feel timid. K's company was highly regarded. The harsh system in which reputation begets assignments is more pronounced in cultural areas. He had started out in theater, but made money in films, and his work on musical stages earned him his reputation. His theater sets and colors were unique, showcasing his interpretations of characters. The protagonists' internal worlds came to life, as if electrified by the stage. Naturally, people lined up to work with him in one capacity or another.

When there was a public notice that he would hire more staff after accepting an offer to manage the stage for a performance that had been all the rage in Europe, a hoard of applicants flocked to the audition. After the screening of written applications, a technical test was offered. I grumbled, "What is this? Do they think it's a college entrance exam?" When I reported to the audition site, I recognized most hopefuls by their faces, those who were in the same shoes as I.

There were two instructions on the test: First, to read the text below and sketch a stage set. Second, to express the set's backdrop with only colors, and without any props.

Below the second direction was an additional instruction: Use only shades of red. Instead of painting, divide the stage into sections and number them. Specify the name of the color at the bottom.

I thought, I've heard of perfect pitch, but never of perfect color vision, and how do they expect us to achieve effects with just the names of colors? What an outlandish instruction!

The given text was the introductory part of the "Twilight of the Gods" in *The Ring Cycle*. Why this heavy-handed pedantry when selecting crew members for a musical stage? And a color test? Most crews use achromatic colors and lighting for effects. This is safer, given production costs and the director's unknown preferences. While handing in my work, I noticed that other candidates' sketches were heavily influenced by the visiting Russian opera troupe's staging the previous autumn. There was an outpouring of acclaim and criticism for that particular treatment, which made use of gigantic statues, reminiscent of the eroded monoliths on Easter Island. I had fallen in love with it, but the impression that staging gave was intense, lingering in a lot of people's memories. For this particular test, I thought I had no choice but to go in a completely different direction. Glancing at other sketches showing mammoth structures as I handed in my sketch, however, I worried that mine was too timid.

I got a call the very next day. I reported to the theater, where a carpentry job was in full swing. I mentioned K's name to one of the staff on the stage strewn with nails and wooden boards, and he pointed to the stairs leading backstage. Leaning on the stairs, a tall, strikingly slender man was examining a stack of papers. I went over and introduced myself to him, but his expression said he had no idea why I was there. In his hand was the sketch I'd submitted. I pointed to it, and only then did he nod, saying, "Ah. What was your major? What performances were you involved in? I see you studied at Pratt for two years. What's your ambition?" He was using the form of speech to address a total stranger. Not only that, he was asking for information that I'd already written on my resume. Ambition? Are you making fun of me? By then, however, I was used to unpleasant questions. I answered all his queries with sincerity and a polite expression.

"Do you know why you've been chosen by any chance?" He asked out of the blue.

I blinked and he kindly informed me. "What I want is timidity. I can't stand the dimwits trying to decorate a stage with some philosophy they don't understand."

Hammers and drills were making a ruckus. Dust wasn't visible in the dim light of the hall, but my throat began to hurt. He yelled, "Assistant Director, will you come over here?" One of the people working with their backs toward us turned around. From her back, I'd had no idea that she was a woman. A woman with an attractive round forehead, whose hair was cut short with bangs that barely covered half of her forehead. He instructed her, "This newcomer's resume looks impressive, but keep an eye on her, okay?" It was impossible to feel favorably toward a woman who didn't even smile, as a formality if nothing else, when being introduced. She stared at me as I bowed to her, spat out only her name, and nodded so slightly that it was hard to tell whether she was lowering her head or lifting it. She then returned to her work.

My first impression of the entire crew was that they were one cold bunch; no team spirit seemed to exist. It's okay, I won't be with you guys after this production, I consoled myself. Probably because I had such low expectations, however, it turned out that they were easy to work with. When they grew tired, they vented their irritation, criticized each other, or exploded in fury. I thought they'd never talk to each other afterward, but that would be it. A female staffer had a spat with a know-it-all carpenter, and wept loudly for an hour. I could see where she was coming from, but it was a far from pretty sight.

Ditto with that assistant director woman. With some resignation, I called her Team Director Cho. She made a face; her taut forehead crinkled and her jaw dropped. "You know, I hate being called Team Director. Just call me Assistant Director, okay?"

Faced with the imminent opening, we had to stay up several nights in a row, taking uncomfortable catnaps in a corner. An unbridled interest in others, or being too friendly or too attentive, would have been most difficult to deal with as we worked in such a confined space day and night. I saw that their attitude was driven by economics: Decorum dictates that if you take care of me, I am obliged to return the equivalent attention to you, and if you talk with a smile, I cannot answer sullenly. My head said so, but at one point a surge of tears accompanied hurt feelings. Driving a nail into a wooden wall to hang a picture was nothing much, so when I picked up a nail and a hammer, I assumed it would be over in a second or two. But the plywood wall was thin and there was a tiny gap between the picture and the wall. When I hit the nail, it kept sliding sideways. Holding the nail in my left fist and pressing it hard into the wall, I took aim and swung the hammer with all my might. The nail, as if to mock me, slid off. The hammer struck a corner of my thumbnail and a yelp escaped from my mouth. Blood streamed out, nicked by the head of the nail. K, who had been speaking with the production manager below the stage, rushed up and grabbed me by the hand. He calmly studied my thumb where blood was gushing forth, a great departure from the urgency he'd shown when he had grabbed my hand. It was as if he'd never seen blood before. The assistant director ran over and pulled out her handkerchief. She addressed K curtly, "All blood is the same color, you know." He took her handkerchief and covered my thumb with it. Wrapping my thumb with his hand, he applied steady pressure on it. It hurt more than when the hammer had struck my thumb. I let out a shriek. The assistant director scolded him, "What are you doing, squeezing that hard? Press it gently, just enough to staunch the blood." She retrieved my hand from K's grip. She then took the hammer from my right hand, and commented, "You didn't injure the bone. You can't even scream if you've hurt your bones."

K descended the stage, and the assistant director spread out her palms before my eyes. Calluses and scars covered her hands in thickened masses. She whispered so only I could hear. I thought she was offering some comforting words.

"I've never cried out, not even once, and my hands have become like this. If you want to keep working in this field, forget that you're a woman, that's the first thing you should do."

My chest burned as if I had been harshly scolded for being unsuitably coquettish. I thought, Hey, what's this? But that was all. Looking at her back as she walked away, I was convinced that she couldn't just be a colleague of K's. Did she show such suppressed hysterical feelings toward me because she instinctively sensed the attraction between K and I, which I wasn't even aware of at the time? He treated me like a child, though I was only a few years younger than he. Once, he told me, "You'll fall again if you run around like this," and squatted down to tie my sneaker laces, which had come undone. Even though he had never seen me fall. After an evening meal with our entire group, he stopped in the middle of the street to button my coat, commenting that I would be cold if I didn't button up, even though it wasn't a cold day at all. When I wasn't happy with the shade of a conventional felt cloth and went out to Dongdaemun Arcade to get a similar color in cotton fabric, he praised my good taste a bit too excessively.

If someone had been watching me closely, he would have noticed that I was following K around pretending to feel cold, and compelling him to button me up. I read the shade of the assistant director's heart from her single comment that I should forget that I was a woman. It was not because I was unusually sensitive. Rather, it was like phone lines getting crossed, allowing you to overhear someone else's conversation; we were on the same wavelength regarding the same object.

The stage work for the musical began with production meetings. The basic concept came from the original production, but

K wanted to add his own color to the stage, where every single nail would have to be removed after the production was over. Ceaseless discussion ensued over materials, sizes, and ratios of space and then these ideas were thrown out, and new ideas were introduced. If I missed a meeting, I would be confronted with a completely different draft the next day. The staff grumbled behind K's back, "Why do we have to work so hard? I bet the production company won't be thrilled if we deviate too much from the original." Despite everything, K plunged himself passionately into the job as if he were creating a stage set from scratch. The crew's mood during these meetings could be generally summed up as: *Let's play it safe, instead of insisting on new things when an enormous amount of production resources is being poured into this as it is. You can take a risk only when you have nothing to lose.*

During one such meeting, K pointedly asked, "Assistant Director, is there anything you want to contribute?"

She had been sitting with a scowl, advertising how unhappy she was, and now she let loose her observations:

"This is just ridiculous. This is between us, but only the music is salvageable in this musical. No one dares to say anything, as they're overwhelmed by the reputation of the original work, but the story boils down to disgusting phallicism. All it does is to brazenly reveal the shameless male unconsciousness. An ugly guy thinks there's a woman out there who will choose him on the basis of the beauty of his soul. A guy who doesn't possess anything hopes that he won't be judged by it. Isn't that what this work is all about? Men have such impossible dreams. They hide their ugly interiority underneath their dreadful appearance, they have no money, not even a warm heart, but they openly spout that they can forgive bad-tempered women but never ugly ones. Isn't that true? Look at Esmeralda, for instance. Even if she's pretty, her legs shouldn't be perfect, at least, or she should have a bad temper. If it were a story about a hunchbacked woman who falls in love with a handsome, golden-hearted man, I'd come up with all sorts of ideas. But this is impossible. It's basically saying, I'm a hunchback, but please notice the beauty inside my hump. Laughable! Guys can barely hide their interiority, which is even uglier than a hump, under a thin layer of skin and they don't even know it when that skin is torn and what is inside oozes out."

After pouring this out breathlessly, she lit a cigarette and shot K a final taunt. "To tell you the truth, I'd rather buy the original soundtrack."

The mood dampened. She was being difficult toward K, and the rest of the crew sat, eyes downcast, their expression revealing that they knew why she was behaving the way she did. Only K, with a clueless face, threw around more ideas.

"What comes to your mind first when you hear the word Notre Dame?" he asked.

"Of course Notre Dame Cathedral," someone joked.

K snapped at him. "We're already talking about that. So let's find something totally different and approach it from that angle."

K turned to me, of all people, as I was sitting beside him. "You've done some backpacking, right? What was the most memorable thing about it?"

"Ah, well, I found the church smaller than I'd imagined, and . . ." I stammered at this unexpected attention. The first image that floated into my head was the lips of a young black woman selling orange juice at the back of the church. I was exhausted in the sweltering heat and her lips struck me as more refreshing than the orange juice she was selling. If I had digressed by recounting this impression, though, K would have lost his temper right away.

"Not that. I mean images. What about the stained glass? What feelings did it give you?"

All eyes were on me.

"Director, sir, last month when you went to Paris, didn't you visit Notre Dame Cathedral? What did you think?" The assistant director's voice hid a thorn, sowing dread in the listeners.

After the incident with her, demanding that I should forget that I was a woman, I had naturally been harboring a bit of resentment against her, an understandable reaction from any normal human being, I'd say. The impression I had of the stained glass on the church ceiling? Conscious of her gaze on me, I gave an exaggerated, detailed account, looking K in the eyes.

"Uh, well, I'd say it was like a high-end prostitute's smile seen through a coarse black lace fan. Through the slits between the thousands of glass pieces, red and black, the volume of sunlight shifted, moment by moment. The color composition changed, just like in a turning kaleidoscope. I'd say that the colors whispered to me. Or shall I put it this way? I seemed to hear languid laughter redolent of the scent of ambergris. . ."

Was it possible to give a logical explanation of the impression that stained glass gives? I was trailing off, at a loss for how to link it with the project at hand, and only then did I notice that K had pushed his face close to mine.

"A red smile seen through black lace? Let me see what that's like. Smile that way."

I turned crimson and mumbled, "I'm not sure . . ."

Actually, I'd never said "a red smile." The moment he said, Smile that way, the rest of the staff turned into dust and faded away, and only K and I were bound together in a circle, as if sitting under a light shining down from a high ceiling. I'd missed the moment he drew closer to me, but the assistant director hadn't. Her eyes flashed below her round forehead.

A taboo acts like bellows for passion. The assistant director didn't know it. Without her, it would have taken longer for K and me to get closer.

At least we took one step toward each other.

How many shades can you call red?

Vermillion, rose red, ruby, magenta, burgundy, raspberry red, geranium, red violet, bordeaux, scarlet, cadmium red, cardinal red, crimson . . . and signal red, the standard of all the shades of red. To expand the list a bit, we get burnt umber and burnt sienna, but naming every visible shade of red will only extend the spectrum of red to the endless unnamable. Just as when you define an object or a person with one term, you lose all other properties.

When K seemed to be focusing on the color red, I would say in an effort to make him feel better, "Trying to give names to all visible colors is like trying to grasp a rainbow with your hand. Human eyes can discern more than 10 million colors. Trying to classify them under just a few names is tyranny, don't you think? The evening glow changes every day, and the autumn foliage of blood-red maple leaves differs every year, depending on temperature changes between day and night and the volume of sunlight they get. The colors of a bonfire by the water differs from one in the woods, and the sun rises in different colors every morning." Actually, he'd never been completely dispirited about his inability to distinguish red, so all my comforting words were futile. Confronting the color he couldn't see, he stared at it, not anxiously, but with a thirsty expression.

While working with him, I had not realized that he had trouble distinguishing the color red until he selected the apples at the basement food hall and confessed that he was blind to red.

Yet, he insisted that he was not color blind, but just blind to one color, and that he didn't have hereditary color blindness because he hadn't been born with the problem. What was the difference between being blind to a color and color blindness?

"Did you hurt your eyes?" I asked.

"Yeah."

I put my eyes close to his and looked into them. "They look fine."

"You always look at the surface of things, just like this."

"Do you really think so?"

"You didn't know that?"

"Okay, I admit. I've rarely met anyone who doesn't, anyway. But how did you hurt your eyes?"

This time, K looked into my eyes.

"When I wanted to poke my own eyes, when I really wanted to do it, my eyes voluntarily rejected the color red . . . Do you want to hear the story?"

I didn't say yes. If someone says, Go ahead and hit me, the one with a clenched fist hesitates. K had confessed that he was blind to a color, and if it was the result of some accident, he would pour out his story, as irrepressibly as an outburst of tears, whenever it might be, to whomever it might be.

"My stepmother was a shaman."

K started his tale as he stabbed at a large, greenish apple with a knife and started to peel it.

"The women who lived with my father for several years or for a very short time were all pretty. I had no trouble calling them Mother. It was because I had no memory of my birth mother, and also because they treated me extremely well, unlike stepmothers in fairy tales. I don't know whether they didn't have their own children because it was my father's intention or whether it was their own choice. Other than that my father didn't give them children, though he wasn't a bad husband. He was always affectionate and attentive. He never beat them and they never experienced monetary hardship. Still, the women generally left before three years were out. Looking back, I think it was all a matter of timing.

She was the woman who joined us when I was a high school senior. My father, a sailor, used to open small shops for his women, probably because he felt sorry that they had to wait for him for months on end if he went on a long haul. The shops he opened for them were shoe stores or haberdasheries that would keep them occupied with a stream of customers. That was what my father thought, but the women seemed to have other difficulties of their own. They always left when I was at school. Then I would be on my own for a while until I found a new woman at home after school.

I learned that she was a shaman only during my summer vacation, because until then I left for school at dawn and came home late at night. She was the most diligent of all the women who'd lived with us. She got up at the crack of dawn, cleaned the house inside and out, and served me a good breakfast, whether my father was around or not. After breakfast, she cleaned the kitchen so thoroughly that you could eat off the kitchen floor. Then, sitting at her dressing table, she would start making herself up. The woman sitting before the mirror, with her bedroom door ajar, was not the same one who'd served me breakfast. Before the dressing table, she first whitened her face until it glowed a bluish hue . . ."

Neither of us touched the apple, which had been peeled and sliced into eight pieces. K continued with his story as he chopped the apple skin into small bits.

"Her makeup ritual always ended with her lips. She stared at the mirror with such intensity that one would have thought that spirits had descended on her face as she meticulously painted her lips with vivid red lipstick, the same color as the seals that shamans stamp on paper amulets. For the final touch, she would gently fold together her upper and lower lips, perfectly transforming her face into a palm-sized paper amulet. The moment her folded lips bloomed into gorgeous flower petals, I suddenly felt like I had to pee . . . After I entered college in Seoul, I found a room of my own. The first year I didn't go home even during school vacations. When my father arrived at the port, he came to Seoul first, took a look around my room, and gave me a large sum of pocket money before he headed home.

The summer after I joined the army to fulfill my compulsory military service, I went to my father's place as soon as I was given the first furlough. It was simply because I had nowhere else to stay. As is the case with most youths that age, my friends desperately tried to get away from their parents, but within me there was a fundamental sense of deficiency, the way an orphan would feel. I missed the home that seemed to belong to a stream of unfamiliar women, rather than my father. I had volunteered for the Unconventional Warfare Task Force, and the military discipline was ferocious. And so, during my first furlough, I went home. The woman welcomed me affectionately, saying that my father had been home for two weeks in May and wasn't likely to be back until the end of summer. She cooked a wild chicken with a handful of garlic and ginseng, and brought it to me on a tray. When she tore off a chicken leg and handed it to me, my heart melted.

An unseasonably late rainy spell came. Behind the curtains of rain all day long, all I did was eat and sleep for several days. When the fatigue and virulence, balled up hard like a stone, were gone, more fatigue billowed up. One afternoon I woke up from a nap and looked outside, and saw that the rain had stopped. The sunlight cast on a small puddle of water sparkled, refracting the light like tiny chips of tin. I momentarily wondered whether it was morning or afternoon. Just as I addressed her without calling her Mother, she addressed me without calling me by name. I heard a throat-clearing sound and looked back and saw her lips, red as amulet seals, moving. She said that she was on her way out for a fortnight's prayer retreat, and the road might have been destroyed in the heavy rain, and she would appreciate it if I could help her carry her things. It was the first time she had asked me to do anything for her since she'd joined us. She had two bundles, whatever was in them, and they were too heavy for her to carry by herself. I searched for a cap that would conceal my military crew cut and followed her out.

As we got out of the taxi and entered a mountain path, my ears rang with the sound of water cascading everywhere, down the valleys and slopes. From the foot of the mountain it was hard to distinguish a footpath from a watercourse. Besides, it was hotter in the mountains than I'd imagined. The air enveloped me heavily as if it would turn into water and drip off if I so much as spoke loudly. The woman's footsteps, though slow, were light. The sunlight blazed on the tree tops. Dragging my gaze away from her waist, which glided ahead of me ever so slightly, I looked up at the fractured blue sky. A shrill cicada drone filled the woods, as if it emanated from the sunlight itself. When we found ourselves at a destroyed part of the path, she'd gather her skirt with one hand and sashay on, balancing herself with another hand stretched out, just like a circus performer. I was the one who was gasping for breath.

It was an oddly persistent heat. After climbing two hills, her traditional *hanbok* dress was drenched in sweat, though she had walked ever so lightly as if floating inches above the ground. The contours of her body were graceful and slender. She seemed much younger than I'd assumed. I felt suffocated, probably succumbing to the intense heat. After another hill, an open space appeared, created by three or four huge rocks lying side by side, just like the site of a dolmen. Trails of candle wax covered the ground here and there. She rummaged through a bundle and took out a towel. Handing it to me, she told me to go down and wash up in the spring below. Below the rocks, a spring was gushing out, the water sloshing in a pool. The water was so icy that when I put my hand in it, palm down, it drove away the heat from my entire body. As I was taking off my sweat-drenched shirt, I noticed that she'd followed me down. She said, Bend down. Then she scooped up a bowl of water and poured it over my back and rubbed it with her hands. When her palm touched my waist and pushed deep into my sides, a sudden dizziness seized me. Drying my back with a towel, she said, Go on up first. At that moment, why did an image of her naked body, which I'd never seen, dance before my eyes? When I climbed up to the rocks, I saw the offerings she'd laid out: fruit, dried fish, rice, candles, and plastic-wrapped, fluorescent-colored cookies and paper flowers.

After bathing, she came up in a new *hanbok*. A whiff of something slightly pungent but sweet drifted in my direction, like the odor from a cat that has just torn and gobbled up a carcass. My eyes met hers across the offerings that had been laid out. With her lips parting slightly like a flower blooming in the morning, she asked me . . ."

The apple had turned slightly brown, the exposed surfaces having lost moisture. No more peels were left to cut up into tiny pieces. Now, K started chopping the apple pieces on the plate.

"'. . . You want to do it?'

Surprisingly, my body accurately grasped the meaning of that cryptic sentence. From my throat, came a stranger's voice.

'Yes. . .'

The woman's body was cold yet hot. And deadly sweet. Just like ice cream fried in thick oil. I dug into the mass that was cold, sweet, warm, and yet repellant, as if I'd be done with it once and for all. *Mother*. Why did that word drift out of my throat at the climax?

The woman got up and knotted up her blouse ties smartly, and looking down at the scattered rice grains and squashed paper flowers on the ground, spoke in an unruffled voice. 'Today, let's just go down. It's become unclean for the gods . . .' Until the day

I reported back to my unit, we performed the fortnight prayer every day, all day long, and since that was not enough, all night long.

On my way back to my unit, I blinked several times before the red traffic light. The red in the light looked like a runny, burnt sienna. The color that's obtained by burning the iron-rich clay from the Sienna region. The muddy, cloudy color that you could only see after squeezing it out of a paint tube. The color that was like old rusty water. I looked around, wondering whether the light was broken. Coincidentally, a fire engine ran the red light and passed before me. The same color as the traffic light! The moment that the red color signal disappeared from my vision, somewhere inside my head, a speck from the red amulet seal stuck, just like a rain-sodden flower petal."

K gently put down the knife between a mound of fruit flesh and a mound of peels, and added, as if he had recounted the long story to say just this:

"So, the moment that the stain of the red amulet seal stuck to my brain, all shades of red were lost to my eyes."

"Tell me," K would often say, cradling my cheeks with his hands as he lay on top of me.

"How does that color appear to you?"

The Banpo Bridge could be seen from the open window.

The sun was setting, a time when the evening glow burned in the most primitive colors above the smog enveloping the bridge. Just like the first time I'd met him, the whites of his eyes were pinkish. At such moments, I was seized by a sense of hopelessness. Just as if I were facing a native in an isolated place on the Indochinese Peninsula, there was no language with which we could communicate. I simply kept tucking his short hair behind his ears.

"Tell me."

K said that the only red color he remembered was signal red. That red of the amulet seal covered his eyeballs when he closed his eyes but disappeared when he opened them. He asked persistently even as he said that he couldn't see it.

"Tell me. How does it appear to you?"

Pink violet, burgundy, crimson, magenta . . . When my lips recited a litany of the colors anyone who studied design could give, he shut his eyes tight and opened them, just like someone who couldn't see at all.

Was it simply a visible color that K wanted to know? Or was it the color that filled his own depths?

People live with the misunderstanding that they know all about themselves, but human life may be designed in such a way that people live out their lives without fully knowing themselves. Just as people can float in outer space but cannot touch the core of the earth. I, too, realized that my eyes were "brown," not "black" only when I was applying for a driver's license in the States, where I went to study at the age of twenty-six. A green-eyed woman sitting at the counter compared the application form I'd filled out with my face, and enunciated clearly, "Your eyes are not black. They're dark brown." Her green eyes—which revealed disbelief that an adult didn't know the color of her own eyes—were of a color that couldn't be pinpointed in one word, being a mixture of green, black, and transparent dots. Until then, I'd believed that I had black eyes. So when it comes to internal colors, what can one say?

Observing K's obsessive yearning, as he tried to tease out the color from his fading memory, making the blood vessels in his eyes pop, I might have already guessed that instead of trying to get away from the memories, he was actually afraid of losing them. Chasing a fire truck is said to be fun, but can it be compared with watching a fight that is breaking out right before your eyes? It is fun to watch a fight that begins with two men springing out of their respective cars, which have screeched to a stop, tearing off their jackets. It is also fun to watch a late-night fight with people suddenly getting tangled up in an alley lined with bars. But what is most fun of all is a fight between two women over a man. They are not fighting for love. They fight because of a hunger inside them. They fight because they hate the man who doesn't have eyes only for them, because they feel sorry for themselves, having failed to gain a person's heart, and because they feel sorry for their own attachment, which makes them unable to toss their love out like a stale piece of bread. In most cases, the person who appears to win in such a fight is the one who has already been defeated. The person who possesses love puts up with the opponent's attack in a relaxed manner. The person who accepts the violent storm with the attitude, "Okay, I know why you're doing this to me," is the one who has won, and the person who appears to be winning, either with force or with words, is merely lashing out at her opponent.

Or so I thought, that day at least.

Things eased up after the dress rehearsal. We watched it in a relaxed mood, like the Creator who has just forged the universe. After we put the final touches on the opening stage, we were told that there would be a small after-party at a beer hall nearby. I went to a department store for the first time in a long while and bought a dress and a pair of sandals. Summer was approaching and I didn't want to look like hired help at the party. But more than anything, I wanted to look pretty for K.

Decked out in a white dress with a round neckline and sandals, I pushed open the beer hall door and heard a flurry of comments. *Hey, you didn't know that today's dress code was casual? You stand out too much. You look pretty, really.* A table was laden with beer, wine, dried snacks, and summer fruit. Someone pressed an opened beer bottle into my hand. The cold sensation was followed by a flooding sense of happiness.

K's staging had been praised unanimously in various reviews. They said that the new aspects K had brought to the staging within the framework of the original symbolically portrayed the characters' interiority. Some lauded that the lighting, so delicate and attentive to detail, lifted local performing arts to another level and was worth seeing in itself. Clipped reviews were piled up on one side of the table. A woman who was affiliated with the publicity department of a production planning company was talking to K. Her hair dyed bluish black, she was dressed in black Prada, from her dress to her shoes to her purse. Those in the performing arts consider black their uniform. Someone commented that she seemed to have come to talk to K about the next production, to make sure that he would be available; it was pretty apparent that K would be in charge of it as well. Black Prada paid for the party, attracting a lot of attention to herself. She must have come just to do that. A man, after waiting his turn, sidled up to K. Seeing that others were in their work clothes, mostly black at that, I felt my back stiffen, as I stood in a white dress holding a beer bottle. K and the man he had been talking to approached the table where I was standing. K introduced me to him, giving him my name.

The man said, "I appreciate your great idea. I was actually worried about the original set that had only rocks. I really love the feeling of the sunlight that pours down from the mosaic glass pieces."

It sounded like K had told him that the idea was my contribution. The assistant director, who hadn't even glanced at me when I arrived at the party, ambled over, with three wine glasses precariously held between her fingers, handed one to each of us, and poured wine. First for the man, then for K, and then for me. While pouring wine into my glass, she smiled and started talking to the man and suddenly flipped her wrist. The wine gushed over my glass and then onto my dress. As if I'd peed standing up, the red wine dripped down onto my light blue sandals. Someone patted my skirt with a napkin.

"Oh, I'm so sorry!" The assistant director was blatantly play-acting, as if she hadn't done it deliberately, as if she'd rather break her wrist in repentance.

". . . it's okay."

Bluish stains were left on the white fabric. The dress wouldn't be wearable even after it was dry-cleaned. It was too white, and it would be impossible to hide the faintest of stains. It would have been better if she had told me that dressing too excessively was not in good form.

In the face of this immediate, lowbrow attack, hostility billowed up inside me. As if I couldn't care less about the dress, I looked at K.

"Can you drive me home? I need to change."

K searched his pocket, held out a key, and walked toward the stairs. Walking behind him, I felt the assistant director's gaze boring into my back. I thought I'd won by letting her defeat me in this tooth-and-claw battle, but things weren't so simple.

The next day at work, the assistant director called me out to the hallway, saying, "Let's have coffee." She didn't bring up the subject of my dress. She pulled out two cups of coffee from the vending machine and handed one over to me, asking whether I would participate in the next production. Shaking my head, I said, "I don't know yet." This was the victor's generosity. There was no reason I wouldn't join. She took something out of her pocket and placed it on my palm.

"I'm done with it."

A key on a round metal ring. Did she mean that she was going to quit the company? Did she mean that she was going to give up K? Or both? She didn't explain. On the plastic tag of the key, K's initials were embossed. I didn't ask her why she was giving it to me, but I also didn't tell her that there was no reason for me to get it from her. More than anything else, it didn't make any sense to give a key to someone without telling the owner. In a blood-spattered battlefield, however, no logic existed.

"You heard that K can't discern the color red, right?" she said. I didn't answer.

"Of course he said that he'd done it with his stepmom until his eyes went blind, right?"

Neither affirming nor denying, I glared at her.

"And that you look like her, right?"

Her tone precisely conveyed this message: That's the story he goes around telling everyone. He must have said the same thing to you . . . It looks like you are the only one who doesn't know, so . . .

Putting the key in my purse, I said, "I do remember that he said I reminded him of the woman's smiling face, glimpsed from the open door."

She couldn't have imagined that I'd readily put it in my purse, just like that, right before her eyes.

"Do you think he wants to break free from that?" she asked.

I didn't get what she was driving at. What did she mean by "from that"?

In the low tones of someone who was afflicted with a summer cold, she said quietly, "Some diseases can't be cured because people cling to them and won't let them go."

I was not susceptible to feelings of loneliness. On the contrary, my great fear was of having no space to savor my solitude if I had to live with someone. Still, the loneliness that bloomed when the two of us were together was odd; it was like a shadow, or a mirror of obsession.

Can one use the word "sexless" between new lovers? It wasn't that we didn't make love. Rather, he wasn't particularly interested in it. At times, when I noticed his little finger delicately raised when holding a coffee cup, I wondered whether he was a latent homosexual. It wasn't that he had any physical issues. Whenever I slept with him, at the moment our bodies came apart, at the moment my back touched the sheets, why was I seized by some bizarre sense of loneliness? If it had to be explained in words, sex with him was closer to sex between plants. If one were to analyze it further, it could be called spiritual sex. After I broke up with him, I counted the hearts I had drawn in my journal and they were so few in number that I could count them all on both hands. Even when we lay on top of each other, belly to belly, not once did I feel a film of sticky sweat. Nor did I feel the kind of heat that would burn my hands when I stroked him. Like a couple who had lived for years together, he seemed more comfortable when we went to a big-box store together, wheeled groceries in an overflowing cart, chatted while snacking, or watched a video.

So what was it that made me uneasy? There were moments when I caught a glimpse of an existence, whooshing away like ash, just like the feeling you have when you turn around at a faint movement behind you. The implication of that shadow made me sigh, with the feeling that no matter how long I was with K, I'd never be able to completely know him.

There are moments when a woman hopes that a man will give his entire self to her, when she hopes to confirm that she possesses a strong magnetic power inside her. If emotional disarmament, which renders one defenseless like a baby, does not happen when there are just the two of you, can that be love? On my way home after having been with K, I would find myself thinking these thoughts.

A person's fate is probably like the starlight coming from afar, something very unstable that is affected even by the day's weather.

At the end of summer, a college friend of mine got married. The wedding ceremony, held at a five-star hotel in Gangnam, was over around seven in the evening, but I waited around to wave goodbye at the honeymoon car decorated in light yellow crepe paper, and joined other friends for a round of drinks at a bar. It was almost eleven when it was all over. Left all alone in the dark street, I felt a pang in the corner of my heart, wondering how long I could insist that I was lucky to be unattached. People were still in short-sleeved shirts, but it wasn't warm any more. I had come out with a summer handbag. If the weather had been a bit cooler, I would have carried a different purse. I opened the outside zipper. The key was still there. Because I'd never taken it out. Under the dim light, K's initials weren't visible. His apartment was not too far away. With the key clutched in my palm, I thought I'd stop by and take a look at his sleeping face.

I got out of the taxi and looked up at his apartment. He probably hadn't come home yet. His window was unlit. The key slid into the lock smoothly, silently. As I gently pulled the door open, the scent of overripe bananas hit my nose. K didn't eat bananas. I stood in the doorway until my eyes got used to the darkness. Next to the small living room, where a desk stood, was a tiny bathroom that had only a showerhead attached to the wall, and next to the bathroom was a cement partition. The bed was beyond that partition. The layout was so simple that I could have walked to the bed from the doorway with my eyes shut. But the darkness was much thinner than when one closed one's eyes. In the thin darkness, my hearing bloomed fully, like a night flower, taking in the sounds of the apartment. I heard breathing.

It came fast, and it wasn't made by someone sleeping, and it wasn't coming from one person either. The breathing, the sound of bedsprings creaking, and the stifled moans came simultaneously. They were joined by groans and moans, like the expression of sweet pain when you bit on your tongue by accident instead of the candy in your mouth, trailing and lingering faintly. The sounds of two people making love. Instead of running away, I stole toward the bed. I couldn't see the face of the woman who was on top of K, but her head wasn't that of the assistant director. Instead of the assistant director's short hair, K was clutching the hair draped on the woman's shoulders. The slippery sweat between the two was evaporating, exuding the smell of overripe bananas. Without having to touch his forehead, I could tell that it was feverish with intense heat.

I turned around and walked out. The lovers' breathing followed me doggedly as I walked to the door and turned the doorknob, holding my breath. I shut the door quietly for the lovers who couldn't hear anything but their own breathing. I didn't have the presence of mind to lock the door. I ran all the way to the subway station without stopping, as if I were being chased.

Only when I stood under the dusky, bluish light inside the station, where tired faces were scattered like ghosts, did I wonder why I'd run. Without much interest, the sallow faces looked at me while I was panting. When I saw a train charging forward, with red lights on its forehead, I threw the key I'd been clutching all along onto the rails.

Something about love makes one wish to weigh it ceaselessly. The assistant director and I, looking at each other, had flailed about precariously as if we were standing on either side of a balance, but both of us had our eyes on the wrong opponent. When I spotted the stranger's head in the dim darkness, my balance was broken with a thud.

The last time I saw him, K said he couldn't leave his mother. Yes, he said "mother."

"That has nothing to do with me." As I said this calmly, K looked at me with his bloodshot eyes, as if red rusty water had welled up inside. I wanted to tell him, Your eyes are amulet-seal red.

He said, "There aren't many people who can determine the course of their own lives. Sometimes, a cliff exists right after the climax of desire. I mean a fatal desire that people experience while they are alive. Knowing that they will fall, they take a step forward at the cliff edge. With their eyes wide open. Are they stupid? But I realize that there is always a moment that makes them take a step forward in full knowledge that they will step into air. I know . . . that people call it taboo."

Instead of saying he was sorry, that was all he said. Instead of retorting that he was crazy, I felt small. If I had accused him of being crazy, I would have shuddered at myself, who was too cool-headed to ever go crazy.

K, who carefully braked every time at the signal-red traffic light; K, who was frowning, as if tired, at a scene in a Zhang Yi-mou film in which swathes of red cloth flapped in a vast field; K's vague smile as he put both red apples and green apples into the same plastic bag; K, who felt as if sand had been rubbed into his eyes, without realizing how reddish the whites of his eyes were; and more than anything, K, who, whenever he encountered the color red, would ask constantly how it appeared to me. Even after I stopped seeing him, sometimes—actually, at least once a day—I thought of him.

It would have been better if the assistant director hadn't phoned me on that wan afternoon. I had lost the person to whom I wanted to say, I hope to be either a woman who robs someone of the color red in an instant or the woman who magically restores the lost color for him.

Night, Be Divided!

A foghorn bellows and the sound disperses, blending into morning mist. The sound turns into fishy moisture and seeps into my skin. Every time I inhale, my stomach turns.

The gigantic passenger ship I am onboard, practically a hotel on the sea, makes a slow turn, the scenery of the Gothenburg coast unfolding like a panoramic photo before its windows. The scene is a replica of the northern German port Kiel from which we departed the night before, momentarily disorienting me with the illusion that we've returned to the same port: similar mammoth cargo ships, intercontinental passenger ships, small fishing boats rocking in the waves, warehouses in achromatic colors, even the hue of the air is the same.

Unlike the other travelers, I don't have much luggage. The dock, deserted early in the morning, is gradually getting busier with the passengers streaming out of my ship. We have only crossed a strait overnight, but the temperature feels dramatically lower on my skin. I scramble to unwrap the sweater draped over my shoulders and put it on. My neck, exposed under the sweater, still feels the chill. It would be nice to drink some hot tea.

Leaving the dock, where passengers are crowded with the cars coming out of the ship's parking deck, I scan around me, just in case. P hasn't come yet. We are supposed to meet at the cafeteria in the shopping mall at the entrance to the dock, so I will wait there. The entrance to the mall is open but the shops are closed.

At the end of the hallway, I can see a café, aglow with orange light emanating from its interior. It must be just opening for business judging by the way it is being readied, with the doors leading to the terrace wide open and a young man in a long apron bustling about, arranging chairs. Despite the warm interior glow, the chair I choose is cold and hard.

Restaurants near train stations or ports are all similar, whether they are in Gothenburg, Shanghai, or Suncheon. You feel as if you are floating a little above ground, like sitting in the restaurant car of a levitating train. There is no warmth or coziness in these restaurants, for they are just places where you fill your stomach and move on, places that sadly remind you of the animal side of your existence. No dish on the menu gives you a sense of satiety, and the atmosphere seems to put pressure on you, implying that you should hurry up, fill your queasy stomach, and leave as soon as you are done.

The sandwich, brought by a waitress with no trace of make-up, is stiff and cold. It tastes like sand and makes me gulp down coffee even though my body doesn't need to be awakened. As though still onboard the boat, I can't shake off the sensation of slow swaying.

The source of this sensation, the floor wobbling as if an earthquake has taken place far away, must be my own heart, nothing else.

P insisted that he would come to meet me.

Although I said, "You must be busy," I thought it was natural that he would come meet me. Had it not been for P, I wouldn't have entertained the idea of coming to Oslo after a screening event in Hamburg. To tell the truth, I agreed to go to Hamburg with the thought of visiting P. When was the last time I saw him? Nine years ago? Ten years ago?

So it has been almost ten years since I plunged into moviemaking, abandoning my career and hearing people call me crazy. There have been many difficult patches, but I don't think I have been unlucky. After my fifth film, critics crowned me with the title "auteur." It's not clear exactly when it started, but when a new movie of mine is released, the media feature it in boxed articles, whether the reviews are favorable or scathing. In film festivals I attend, it isn't rare to see my fans citing my filmography in one breath, their eyes revealing awe as though they were in the presence of a god. I've grown to feel rather proud. Even though my domestic audience will never surpass a certain number, this doesn't reflect my capabilities, and commercial viability isn't the goal I have been pursuing from the outset, anyway.

My reputation in Europe is pretty good. On a sleepless night, excited after an invitation to a film festival in southern Europe, I thought of P. Surely it was exaggerated, but before my departure for Hamburg a domestic paper printed a special feature saying, Director So-and-So, who is causing ripples in Europe, will visit European film circles. The moment I received an invitation to the screening in Hamburg, I knew the real purpose of my trip was to see P.

I spent my youth watching God's special favors being showered on P. We weren't exactly like Mozart and Salieri. Unlike Mozart—who, despite his talent, experienced misfortune in his lifetime—P is enjoying the glories of life here and now. While packing for this trip, I included news clippings about me, solely for P's eyes.

I get up to ask for a coffee refill, and a young Scandinavian woman cheerfully smiles and says, "You arrived on the ship, didn't you?" She pours freshly brewed coffee up to the brim of my cup. Her hair is even lighter than blond. Is her pubic hair the same color? This useless thought flits through my head. This has nothing to do with lust. The anxiety percolating in my heart can also be blamed on the two cups of strong coffee I've drunk in quick succession, or so I want to believe.

I catch sight of P hurrying down the corridor toward the café. I bolt up without realizing it. Looking into each other's eyes, we grab each other's hand, then hug. Neither he nor I say anything trivial, like, It's been ages. We leave, each carrying a bag of mine. The August sunlight is brilliant, but the air is still nippy. "Where's your car?" I ask, looking around. He opens the door of a Citroën parked right in front of us, which looks like half of a badly dried gourd placed upside down.

"Hah, you haven't changed one bit. What's this? Avant-garde graffiti?" I make a joke.

P cracks his standard confident smile. Is this guy, who could afford a Porsche, and if he desires, a Porsche in every color, driving a subcompact reminiscent of an art installation, with paint peeling here and there? Is this a facile mockery of life from the guy who has everything? Yet, he has gone too far. The floor under the passenger seat sports some holes, big enough for coins to fall through, allowing one to catch glimpses of the road beneath.

"How was the screening?" he asks.

Where do I begin? I have been trying to find a thread to start the conversation, but he asks about what happened the day before. This must be the right way to begin. In order to talk about the ten years that have passed, going backward like this may be best for finding a shortcut, quickly and accurately.

"Um. It was crowded. They regarded an artist from a far-flung corner of the world so seriously, and it made me wonder whether we Koreans would treat an artist from the third world that well."

"They would never go beyond that though. The longer I live abroad, the more I feel it. That's it. I mean, they would never accept us wholeheartedly."

"Do you think so?"

"I think being a movie director is a pretty okay occupation. You can delude yourself into thinking that you're a god while making a movie."

Classic P. He hasn't changed at all. His words jolt me out of the elated bubble I was encased in for several days in Hamburg. I am curious about what P is up to now. How far has he run ahead since he disappeared from my sight?

"Are you very busy?"

"The same as always." P furrows his brow slightly, as if he were a little bored with his constant accomplishments.

Before we leave town, he stops his car and, telling me to wait, goes into a market. There are so few people around that calling it a city street is a stretch. With P out of view, I feel as if I am part of a gigantic landscape. Is the population of this big city really fewer than half a million? People here surely must be glad to come across other people in the street. Before long, P comes out with two plastic shopping bags, sagging almost to the point of breaking, and stows them away in the trunk of his car.

A short driver later, P says, "Sweden ends here."

Passing an abandoned outpost, we enter Norway. P says that to get to his house we will have to drive for about an hour and a half north. Why did he, a well-known surgeon in Los Angeles, move here, and why did he stop seeing patients and start working in a lab? He didn't explain any of this during our phone conversation.

"What are you doing these days?" I ask.

"Me? I'm . . . working in the field of immunology, and when my academic paper comes out, it's going to be groundbreaking." His tone is deadpan, as if he is sick and tired by now of his groundbreaking accomplishments.

"Immunology? Then it's closer to biochemistry. Aren't you an action type of guy? I imagine you'd find a lab confining. Are you working on something like a cure for lupus or for a new virus?"

"Not such boring stuff. Listen, it's about immunity of the soul."

Immunity of the soul? We studied at the same medical school, and I can still practice as a family doctor, but the term is unfamiliar. Has the territory of medicine expanded this much in ten years? Or is he talking about the realm of psychiatry? P doesn't go on to elaborate right away; he lifts a Volvic water bottle from the cup holder and takes a sip. A waft of a volatile solvent pinches my nose. The water is pale amber.

He goes on, "Perhaps I can call it immunity against memories? Immunity is the memory your body possesses of a disease you once had. Just as you will never contract measles and chicken pox again if you've had them once, my research concerns whether we can medicate people to dismantle memory mechanisms in a certain part of the brain."

"I get the idea, but is it feasible? What is the specific memory you're talking about?"

"It's . . . love."

I refrain from asking whether he is kidding. Come to think of it, when I was in medical school, if someone had said that new organs could be made from stem cells, he would have been treated as a mental case.

"Will that be possible?"

"Everything comes down to the issue of imagination. I believe it's possible."

Soon after our reunion, P is once again sucking me into his world. Listening to him, I think he can probably do it. As far as imagination goes, no one is in his league.

In the operating room, where even a smidgen of imagination seemed unnecessary, this guy displayed amazing powers of imagination. He had an uncanny instinct; when a patient with an abdominal incision was suddenly seized by a high fever, he would combine two or three procedures among many to deal with the infection. In the most tense moments, he grew calm and seemed to enjoy the moments of tension which were as sharp as a scalpel blade. His suturing skills were impeccable; you could say that if his patients desired, he would have been able to embroider a daisy or a rose on any internal organ. He was the only resident veteran surgeons entrusted to finish up after them in the operating theater. P once quipped that he didn't understand why no one wanted plastic surgery on their stomachs, when everyone said the real beauty came from within. I gave him a nickname—the Korean Quilt—a nod to the title of a movie that was showing at the time.

Now, driving, he drones on. "In a nutshell, it works like this. Two people share a tablet, and its effect is that they can only love each other, not anyone else. The drug affects brain waves with what even Cupid's arrow couldn't give: simultaneity, equal amounts of love, and consistency. The drug can make people love each other as long as the half-life period of a radioactive isotope, if that's what they wanted. What do you think is the cause of tragedy in love? Ultimately, it's non-simultaneity. A person is still warm, but his partner is as cold as a pot which has been taken off the stove a long time ago. People cite Aspirin, Penicillin, and Viagra as three major drugs created by mankind, but my drug will be more sensational than all the three drugs combined. We can call it the final installment of happy pills, such as Viagra and Botox, that began to comfort human beings in the 20th century."

P's profile is serious.

He continues, "So this works in a different dimension from something like Viagra, which works on physical properties, like a change in blood flow. I believe that this drug, which works on a certain area in the brain and simultaneously regulates the body and the mind, will lead us to groundbreaking new medicine, combining science and soul in a mutually complementary manner. The name of the project is Lovepia."

Lovepia?

This doesn't sound like P. The word, a crudely coined amalgam of love and utopia, as anyone can recognize right away, has all the subtlety of a condom in a convenience store.

"The drug is simple to take. Two people divide a two-color oval tablet into two and take a piece each. It's the foamy kind. It will be completely dissolved in ten seconds. It has no side effects and is not habit-forming. Not to mention diabetic, hypertension, and cancer patients can take it without any conflicts with their prescribed drugs. Terminal cancer patients will be able to live out their last days on earth, basking in the splendid rays of love, day after day, with their hearts aglow. As a bonus, it will have a stronger painkilling effect than morphine. Its absorption mechanism will be similar to alcohol, so it will take an amazingly short time to take effect. It will begin to kick in as it is being absorbed in the esophagus, and particularly sensitive people will feel the effect as soon as they inhale the gas being produced in the foaming process."

"What do you mean?"

"Everything about your partner will look lovely. The gleam in her doe-like eyes; her breasts which in reality are the size of chewed gum, will be so adorable that you can't resist biting them whenever you lay eyes on them. Her nipples will probably bleed because of your urge. Corns on her soles will appear so beautiful that you'll be begging her to tread your face with her feet. If she begins to have gray hair, you, someone who knows nothing about art, will see in those strands the aesthetics of black-and-white minimalism. When you lick her sweat, you will feel sorry for people who, mere slaves of sweetness, are missing out on the ecstasy of that salty taste. The cheery sound she makes when she passes gas will be the most pleasing music to your ears, and the fermented scent from the nutrients of the five food groups will give you the added philosophical insight that humans must eat to survive."

"Who will buy the drug?"

"People who have suffered from love with different half-life cycles will react enthusiastically to this drug. They're the ones who've experienced that the love that had once been passionate, uncontrollable, and seemingly everlasting, and the pledge of dedication that they'd rather die than live without their partners, has faded away and turned cold in a single stroke."

The car seems to be heading directly north. With the temperature dropping gradually, the scenery has changed into a landscape of moss-covered fields. The air is utterly transparent, looking solid as if it were made of glass. P's remarks are as outlandish and fantastic as the passing scenery.

I ask, "Do you think the loss of love is a disease?"

"Well, doctors call what they can cure a disease and what they can't cure inherent human traits. They don't call loneliness, jealousy, and sorrow diseases. Before the advent of sleeping pills, people just couldn't sleep. Insomnia wasn't an illness. With the emergence of Prozac, depression became a more common ailment. When my drug is perfected, the extinction of passion will become a disease."

He seems thirsty after his impassioned talk. He picks up the Volvic bottle and takes a few sips.

How far has this project progressed? It isn't something I can believe easily, but then again I can't afford to doubt it, either, because I've watched all of P's dreams come true. There seems to be no such thing as impossibility in his life. People who enjoy God's special favors tend to attract intense jealousy from those around them, but P also has the talent of making them accept the grace God has bestowed on him as a matter of course.

I was in the same section as him when we were seniors in high school, but I had known of him because he was a walking legend at our school. As I entered the senior-year classroom and saw P sitting there, my first thought was that I'd never be at the top of my section that year. I never saw him poring over reference books during breaks. There was a rumor that he was from a dirt-poor family, but there wasn't a shadow of poverty around him no matter how closely I looked. A hopelessly wrinkled old T-shirt was incredibly fashionable and vintage when he put it on. When top college applicants say during a press interview that they received perfect scores by relying only on school lessons and enjoying a good night's sleep every day, people brush their remarks aside as an exaggeration or a downright lie. After observing P, however, I realized that such people actually do exist in the world.

When I stole a look at P's profile in class, I'd simultaneously feel a sense of deprivation and fascination. I spent the summer vacation sitting at my desk until eczema raged in my groin, but I still came in second in the first mock entrance exam in the second semester. Both P and I applied to medical school, and P passed the exam with the top score, while I made the cut as well. Who knew what my rank was in the entering class, given that only the top applicant's name was made public? Getting into medical school was an outcome beyond my expectations, probably a fruit of my strenuous efforts to beat P, if just once.

There was a myth that to work in the university hospital of our alma mater, you had to be lucky all around: You had to have a certain family pedigree, wealth, ability, and heavenly intervention. Yet, no one doubted that P would be offered a spot there. What P did during his presentation was controversial, however. The atmosphere of presentations was so tense that most of us couldn't eat for days, and if unexpected questions were thrown in our direction, seemingly to put us in our place, we'd sweat so much that we'd be drenched down to our underwear, even in the middle of winter. When P's turn came, he sauntered up, dressed in a collarless T-shirt and a wrinkled pair of pants. He was empty-handed. Watching him stand there with no prepared material in hand, sweat began to seep out of my forehead. He was outrageous, no matter how you looked at it, but his talk was concise and to the point. More than anything, his presentation revealed outstanding creativity, not the garden-variety version the rest of us had cobbled together. Aside from his style of presentation, no one could have denied the fact that it was a medical paper written in the most beautiful language. He was clearly arrogant and that arrogance was dazzling. I still remember how small I felt while witnessing his performance.

Rumor had it that the day's evaluations displayed a wide discrepancy among the professors. A professor fiercely opposed to giving P a position cited his insolence, and to underscore his opposition, he enclosed a resignation letter with his evaluation sheet. P didn't make the cut, either because he had stoked fury by blaspheming academic tradition, just as our friends had analyzed, or because another candidate who was shooting for the position wrestled him out in the final round. P left for the United States. I failed to detect regret or resentment in his words and actions. In a place without him, I asked myself: Is being a doctor what you really want? Will this profession make you happy?

Was P my rival? No. The etymology of the word rival is said to come from someone running on the opposite side of a stream. The person who makes you throw a sidelong glance, who pushes you to forge ahead as you drag your faltering legs, even if your heart is about to explode. But I had never run side by side with P. I was always huffing and puffing behind him. When he disappeared into the distance on the other side of the river, I was immediately lost. I hadn't expected that the frustration I would feel after he was gone would be bigger than the frustration I'd felt when he was in sight. P was my GPS, a rainbow I could see but couldn't get closer to. I still have a recurring dream. On the other side of a misty riverside, I see a young man running, his profile cold and neat, beyond the bluish mist. He never looks back at me.

After he left for the United States, news about him reached Korea practically in real time. We weren't greatly surprised to hear that he had joined a top-notch medical school in California, that he had firmly established himself there, that he had bought a mansion where the edges of his garden were licked by the waves of the Pacific, and that soon after, he had become the head of the surgical department. He would do all of that, we agreed. I was doggy paddling in the pool which he'd left, which was too small for him to play in. After his departure, my obsession with him ballooned viscerally.

I could not let him go.

I gave up the doctor's life. Instead of looking at the inside of the human body, I chose to aim my camera at the soul's internality. I thought: P, if you want to run along the breezy riverside, I will run in the field where there is no path. The invisible river kept flowing between P and me, though we had been apart for so long. I hoped I could show him something I'd done that he couldn't do. Before I'd heard that P had packed up for some unknown reason and left for Scandinavia, I was always aware of his coordinates, if not his every move. No one knew much about his life afterward, but when our classmates got together, nobody disagreed that P would re-emerge with something big, astonishing the world.

Lovepia? How far have you run? How far ahead have you flown, you, who are sitting so close to me that if I reached out, I could touch your face?

"We're almost home."

The car, seemingly heading north forever, turns off the main road and into the fields. It is so sparsely populated that a house seems to make up an entire village.

I wonder how M has changed.

But then, the appearance of people in their thirties changes the slowest of all the decades of their lives despite the internal turbulences they go through. When I added Oslo to my itinerary, was I only thinking of seeing P? After we pass a pasture, where horses with shiny dark brown manes graze, and climb a slope, a red-roofed house comes into view. A simple compact building, a typical farmhouse. P parks his car in the open lot that is protected only by an overhead covering, and we get out. A large, wheat-colored dog saunters up and rubs himself against P's legs, without even a bark.

The garden lies in absolute waste, and it doesn't seem to have received a human touch in ages. New vines stretch over the tangles of last year's yellowed vines. Purple flowers, the size of fingernails, bloom at each vine node. In a corner is a pile of logs, overcome with a reddish hue as if rusted. Overgrown tree branches cast shadows over the house and, except for a narrow path leading to the front door, yellow wildflowers carpet the lawn in the absence of trampling human feet. Every breath I take in sends refreshing air to my respiratory path. The air is brilliantly transparent. Several apple trees standing at the edges bear tiny red fruit, reminiscent of decorative Christmas lights. The surreal touches of this picture render me speechless. A desolate but utterly beautiful yard.

That's the way it strikes me, at least.

This is the way I've always accepted what belongs to P. In his aura, everything acquires an awe-inspiring dignity, with beautiful things as they are and ugly things as they are. Just like a religious woodcarving whose unrefined craft underscores great suffering.

P removes my bags and, shutting the car trunk, throws me a quick glance. "Don't tell my wife."

"What?"

"What I told you on the way. It's a top-secret project being carried out by a multinational pharmaceutical company and a handful of researchers who work without borders. Besides, it's a long-term research project."

"Okay."

Though I readily agree, I wonder whom M can talk to about the project, living in the middle of nowhere like this. As we talk in the desolate yard, the door opens and M's face peeks out. Something in me stirs as though my frozen body were suddenly transported to the edge of a blazing fire.

"It's been a long time."

"Yes, really, it's been so long."

Is this all we can say to each other, as if no one is aware that we haven't seen each other for a long time? Standing there, we talk about which route I took from Seoul, how hot it has been in Seoul lately, and what my itinerary will be in Oslo. When I mention the polluted air and constant traffic congestion in Seoul, the corners of M's eyes crinkle with longing, and she lets out something like a lament, "I miss that thick, smoky air. I wish I could breathe it just once." We laugh uproariously, as though we have heard the funniest joke for the first time in a long while. M hasn't changed and yet has changed a lot. I can see what hasn't changed, but can't pinpoint the changes. Absolute silence floods into the short intervals between our exchanges.

The interior of the house is extremely simple. Just like a log cabin bed-and-breakfast, the small kitchen holds only a long wooden table. The table is already set for a meal. As if I came all this way just to eat with them, the first thing we do is sit at the table. The meal is simplicity itself; bean paste stew, broiled eggplants, seasoned cucumbers, and salad.

"So, you live in a place like this," I remark to P. "It's paradise." Looking out the windows, I exaggerate this way, a bit taken aback by the meal, which is much too simple to serve a guest. While M is scooping rice into our bowls, P goes out and comes back with a bottle of wine.

Looking at him, M comments as if in passing, "Drinking in the daytime?"

"A friend came from far away . . . and he brought it."

I can't correct him. Well, what was I thinking, coming empty-handed?

The bean-paste stew, boiled with only sliced fish cake and po-tatoes, is delicious. M keeps apologizing, "It's hard to get Korean ingredients here." P drinks wine, scarcely touching his food. After the meal, as M is going into another room, she says to P, "Can I have a minute with you?" P closes the door behind him. M's voice is slightly high-pitched and her speech is rapid, though I can't make out her words. I don't hear P's voice. What is wrong? They don't come out for a long time. They can't be fighting in the presence of a friend whom they haven't seen for ten years, can they? I knock on the door and without waiting for a reply push it open. "Hey, what are you guys up to?" I ask in a joking tone. M turns her head toward me and says without a trace of a smile, "Will you please wait outside for a minute? This is between us." Embarrassed, I shut the door and stand at the window looking outside. When the two come out, their expressions are natural as if nothing has happened.

M says she'll show me to my bedroom and climbs the nar-row stairway in front of me. The room has a single bed under the slanting ceiling, resembling an attic. The bedding on it seems brand new. The room seems to not have been occupied for a long time, the strong odor of an old grain storeroom permeating the air. I wonder whether I am imposing.

"I could have stayed in Oslo."

"That would have been unnecessary. My husband is lonesome and we have an extra room."

"Stop using that respectful form of speech."

She stares at me. She hasn't changed at all. Yet, this is not the M I knew, the M with whom we went out together as a group to watch movies and share sweet beans over shaved ice. I thought I had so many things to tell her, but here I am, asking her to ad-dress me in the familiar form.

"What's the name of this village?"

"Onsøy Kårbolig."

"Onsøy Kårbolig. It's as beautiful as paradise."

M blurts out, "Paradise? I miss Seoul. I want to go back."

Earlier in the yard, I laughed at her comment that she missed the polluted air, but this repeated remark sounds like a code. A code tossed into the air, with the hope that someone will decode it. But we've lived far away from each other for too long. I put down my bags and look out the window. Would it have been better if I had stayed at a hotel in Oslo? A body of water, seen through wooden shutters, looks cold blue.

"There's a lake down there."

M sighs softly. "It's a fjord. Take a walk to it if you have time. People here swim there, but the water's too cold for me."

After M leaves, I change into more comfortable clothes and go downstairs. P pushes a plate of red apples toward me, saying that he's just picked them in the yard.

"Eat the skin and all. Did you bring your film with you? Let's watch it together. I don't think I can make it to your screening tomorrow because of my work at the institute. My wife can go with you instead."

"Okay." I answer nonchalantly, but to be frank, I am deeply disappointed. I thought I would go to the screening tomorrow with P. I wanted to show him my work in a venue that was perfectly equipped. I hoped to show him how I was doing, how I was basking in applause and glory, though my share of acclaim wasn't much compared to his.

I insert a video of behind-the-scenes footage first. It begins with swaying images as if the cameraman were laughing hard. The chaotic scenes at a shoot. Me wearing shorts. Me wearing a cap. Me giving directions to the staff and dashing off somewhere. Me smiling, lifting a glass of foamy beer up high after the final scene was shot. This is the same video, so why does it seem different from when I watched it in Korea? My smiling face looks unfamiliar to me, and my voice all the more so. I am dismayed by my high-pitched voice, shouting out in an unstable, impatient tone.

There are moments when one wishes to look like a peacock at noon, if not for everyone in the world, then just for one person.

M says that she will watch it at the screening and that she is going out to run errands. She explains that she needs to go grocery shopping. I am put off by P. Since it would take her more than an hour to reach the nearest market, it is going to be almost a three-hour trip for her. Why was it so hard for him to get groceries on our way home? Sitting on the sofa, I watch the gourd-shaped Citroën crawling along the path between the wheat fields until it disappears. P stands up and brings a bottle of wine and two glasses. The effects of the wine I drank during lunch haven't quite worn off. Just like me, it appears that P finds it hard to fill the gap of years between us.

He pours my glass to the brim and clinks it with his. Clang! It resonates a little too loudly. I assumed it was wine, but it turns out to be something stronger. After a sip, I frown, but P gulps it down.

"Calvados. Did you read Remarque's *Arch of Triumph*?"

"No."

"You should have. Well, in that novel, a character named Ravic drinks this liquor all the time. Apple brandy from Normandy."

P pours himself another glass as if he has no choice but to drink it because of that character, and says, "For Ravic!" Then he downs it. I detect a faint whiff of overripe apples. It is too strong to drink just like that, I mumble to myself.

P says, "I don't like movies. They show only the surface of life. I will watch your movie and if I believe you're capable of making a good film, I'll write you a screenplay. The script is half the movie, isn't it?"

He isn't kidding. I still remember the title and content of the story he wrote as a high school senior. It was pornographic. I was his first reader and the only one who didn't have to pay for the pleasure of reading it. Our all-male classmates had to give him two pastries and a carton of milk to get their hands on the contraband text in his free-flowing handwriting. It was a great hit. So much so that he had to make a waiting list for his readers.

During a lesson one afternoon, a classmate who was engrossed in the story hadn't been aware that the teacher was standing next to him, silently reading it along with him, until the guy sitting by his side poked him. *Mr. Horse and the Newly Harvested Barley* . . . As the teacher read the title, having closed the notebook to look at the cover, the guys who'd been dozing grew alert and watched what was going on, wiping spit from their mouths with the backs of their hands. Turning the cover, the teacher called out P's name. Why had P been so proud of his authorship, jotting down his name there for the world to see? P stood up and the teacher slowly approached him. In the tone he used when he reviewed what he'd taught during the previous lesson, he asked, "What is 'newly harvested barley'?" P answered, "Something that looks exactly like the female organ, sir." The teacher snickered. That smile was unguarded just like the satisfied grin of an old teacher who'd found a genius in one of his students, as if the years he'd spent choking on dusty chalkboard air had not been futile. We anticipated that the teacher would let him off the hook. The arms of the teachers always exhibited symptoms of chronic muscle weakness in the presence of our top student. "And Mr. Horse?" The teacher asked. P answered, "The male version of the protagonist in the movie *Horse-Riding Lady*." The students giggled. We called that long-faced Korean literature teacher Mr. Horse. "I see," he said. He then slowly bent down to grab one of his slippers. Later, P testified that Mr. Horse had smacked his cheek as if tolling a church bell during Korea's enlightenment. It was a blasphemous description, but the best figure of speech judging from the blow's speed and intensity. Only when I looked at P's cheek did I learn that the sole of the teacher's slipper had a diamond pattern. Despite such adversity, P went on to write two more stories, eventually completing a trilogy. The readers' response was passionate. Our classmates willingly traded their day's snack for his fiction: Wherever did they read that passage in the holy Qur'an that goes, *If thou hast two loaves of bread, sell one and buy roses.* Some readers grumbled that the climax came too late in his stories, but P wasn't swayed by his readers' criticism. He'd retort, "Hey, the part before you actually do it is always the best." We'd dubbed the genre of his stories "cheerful porno."

In his writing, P was already exhibiting a good command of gynecological knowledge. For example, he used the term "clitoris" and narrated foreplay techniques in a biologically accurate yet poetic style. We weren't free of the suspicion that he'd lifted some passages from pornographic novels, but what was surprising was a certain level of style he maintained throughout, considering how graphic his novel was. Some of our classmates claimed that when they masturbated, it worked better while reading the descriptions in P's stories than looking at a photo of some naked woman. Years later, whenever I was with a woman, I searched for the intense dream-like feeling I'd experienced in his fiction, but reality always fell short of the world he'd depicted.

Looking back, just like a thirteen-year-old girl who doesn't know how beautiful she is, his fiction had a certain dazzle and couldn't be categorized as simply pornography. It was art, showing why life was ultimately beautiful, though contained in a disturbing vehicle. His sentences were shot through with an irrepressible energy for life, like a bubbling fountain. If my memory is correct, his series grew more disturbing, transcending mere smut to achieve an absolute aestheticism steeped in sorrow. Afterward, no pornography, in print or film, so vividly penetrated my fantasies, and I've yet to see an account that describes the animal side of human beings as sorrowfully and beautifully as his rendition. In some sense, my films were the offspring of a desire to surpass his achievements. Does P still remember the contents of his stories? Even so, he wouldn't remember them in as much detail as I do.

With his eyes on the screen, P starts talking. The film's dialogue is interrupted by his comments.

"Is that Seoul? If I returned now, I'd be more of an outsider there than I am here."

"Only the places that changed are like that. Some places are exactly the same as twenty years ago."

"Tell me about yourself. What have you been doing with your life?"

"This film tells my whole story."

P's eyes, fixed on the screen, are drifting, and I wish that he would concentrate on it. I've put too much passion and energy into the film for it to be watched so casually. I didn't neglect even the characters' shadows, and while filming it, I kept a notebook to jot down everything, including the angles of the characters' gaze. I thought, You may be the Korean Quilt, but you could never make a movie like this.

Now P starts talking about himself in a distracted way. "Is that right? What do you think of my project? A paper about my new drug will be published in a top medical journal two years down the road, at the latest. It will shake the world, just like the news that humankind stepped on the moon or that somewhere on earth the countdown for the birth of a cloned baby has started."

"Won't it be a Pandora's Box?" My voice sounds a bit unpleasant.

P doesn't seem to mind. "Science will go beyond the dimension of nucleic acids and proteins. A living human being is an odd specimen, a combination of nucleic acids, memories, proteins, and desires, though he is reduced to a handful of ash when cremated. They say it's impossible. But I can do it. I will be remembered forever as a medical scientist who made it possible to manage memories and desires."

As he incessantly talks about his research, the credits are already rolling on the screen.

"About the last scene. What if you had done it this way?" Now, when he opens his mouth, a strong whiff of liquor hits me. "I mean the face of the weeping woman. Instead of showing her, wouldn't it have been better if you had captured a dark corner of the room and the stairway, and let her call out his name? Sorrow could have resonated more vividly from the woman's expression beyond the camera, don't you think? While showing some lifeless objects that have no emotions. Wilted flowers in a vase might have worked better. The last scene seems to be limiting itself rather than fully revealing sorrow, regret, and the strong fury that makes her almost go crazy. Your scenes are too heavyhanded. Isn't that right, Mr. Sentimental?"

His voice is neither high nor low. He doesn't stammer or slur his speech. I feel as if I've been hit on the back of my head with an empty liquor bottle wrapped in a napkin. Why didn't I think of that? I thought I was keeping all possibilities open. Revising the synopsis constantly, I made many mock films, at the risk that I would look foolish to my crew. This is the sequence I chose, firmly believing that no better effect could be drawn out. Why hadn't my imagination thought of the possibilities he'd mentioned?

P comments, "Movies are merely shadows of life. Shadows are shadows because you can't grab them. Instead of trying so hard to tell something, depict what you cannot tell and let reality speak for itself. You're too kind. Too slow. Just like a drowned body that floats up to the surface as it's rotting. . . . Being kind means being obvious and being obvious means boring."

M is still not back. I get up, saying that I'd like to go to bed, with the excuse of jet lag. As I walk up the stairs, P calls out to me. I look down at him.

Squinting, P asks, "When he was a boy, do you know what Hans Christian Andersen wanted to grow up to be?"

Without saying yes or no, I stare at him.

"His dream was to be scouted by the Chinese emperor and live in the golden palace and sing there." For the first time that day, P frowns slightly. What is it that he wants to say? He adds, "A dream shouldn't come true."

I briefly look into his eyes without a word before resuming the climb. The color of the fjord has changed to gray. It does not grow any darker outside. In the dim light that produces no shadows, the yellow wildflowers look more vivid than before. If the stalks were cut, they might float up instantly. I didn't come all this way just to show P my film. I certainly wanted to show him that my work is being screened in Oslo, to show him that I am getting the attention of the critics and the media, and to share with him the newspaper clippings that praise my movies.

But P said he was not planning to come to the screening. He said that only my agenda speaks volumes in my film. That only my obsession is distinct. That it is kind, obvious, and boring. P who presented his paper with utter arrogance; P who was said to reign as a god with the nickname Oriental Express over the patients in an LA hospital that catered to the rich and famous; P who settled in Onsøy Kårbolig, the tiniest dot on the Scandinavian Peninsula, a true paradise, and vows that he will invent a new drug that controls memories and desires. For him, there is no night, just like the scenery here. I stand at the window for a long time, gazing out at the air that never turns dark, the wildflowers that exude gorgeous colors, and the fjord that looks like a frozen river. At the end of the field, a dot appears.

A harried bug is flying toward me.

M is coming back. Why are they driving that car? Is it a joke that mischievous P is trying to play on his glamorous life? The most valuable of P's possessions is approaching, encased in the most trivial of P's possessions. I feel like crying at the sight. A drug that regulates memories and desires?

The night does not grow dark.

In the morning, P says preemptively again, "I would have loved to come along." So what can I say to him? In the new pharmaceutical field where coming in second is no different from being last, research must be more arduous and require more patience than embroidering a daisy on a heart.

How far did M go to get groceries yesterday? Laid on the breakfast table are spicy potato soup with a generous sprinkling of onions, broiled salmon, and freshly made cabbage kimchi, with red pepper grains so few and far between that you can almost count every speckle. This allows a glimpse into the hardship of living in an isolated hamlet in a foreign country, quite different from northern Germany, where I spotted many Asian supermarkets. I kick myself for not bringing a few boxes of ramen, if nothing else. M wasn't wearing makeup yesterday but this morning her face is lightly made up. Before getting into the car, M corners P and says something that I can't catch. P nods perfunctorily. When M starts the engine, the Citroën makes a noise as loud as that of an ancient truck. I wave to P and buckle up. The screening is scheduled for the afternoon. It was P who suggested that we leave early to visit the Viking Ship Museum or the Munch Museum.

The road is a never-ending series of gentle hills, and spread on either side is a carpet of various ferns. I believe that in my heart, no passion for M remains. Not because too much time has passed, but because she is P's wife now.

At certain junctures in my life, M would come to mind out of the blue. It was her bare arms that I remembered, not her face. Several inches of her arms below a white high school uniform blouse, which used to choke me up whenever I caught sight of them; no other word could describe her arms than "white," though different from the white of her uniform. At the time the object of my desire was not her lips, not her breasts. How much

I yearned to brush my hand over her bare arm poking out of her short-sleeved uniform! When I imagined my palm touching it, I flushed and couldn't breathe. Those arms are now very close to my hands. I notice freckles, big and small, dotting the back of her hands and arms all the way to the elbows. It is possible that I didn't notice them back then. The rays of sunlight, fluttering in like butterflies, descend on her arms. The freckles waver and dance like butterfly eyes. From the very beginning, exactly like this, everything about her was a mixture of fantasy and reality. The arms that I used to recall as having the skin of an angel, not human skin—pearly, glowing, and emanating light—no longer disturb my breathing. Only a distant, dull solitude wells up in the pit of my stomach.

M and I were active members of our school's co-ed literary club only for a few months in the second semester of our freshman year of high school. By our sophomore year, pressure to study for the following year's college entrance examinations made it impossible for us to get together more than a few times a semester, and the club became more of a social gathering. M must have known that I had fallen for her. I believed that the urgency of feelings could be conveyed without words. I could feel that she was favorably inclined toward me. I was to blame for our not getting closer. I had a fear that I might lose my voice in front of her. This was a bigger, boundless fear than the fear that I might drop a glass of water in her presence. I was frightened that my voice wouldn't come out if I spoke to M, though I had no problems addressing a group. When I was about to speak, as soon as my eyes fell on her arms, my breathing became irregular. During our senior year, when P, who wasn't even a member of our club, came to a meeting with M, I experienced anxiety, anger, and resignation, all rolled into one. From M's facial expression, I could tell that she was in love.

When P left for the States, M went with him. A year later I

went to New York to attend film school. We were on opposite coasts of the United States, but even when I went on a location shoot near where they lived, I didn't look P up. It was because of M. She couldn't have been unaware of my feelings toward her.

She must be feeling uncomfortable about the silence we have maintained until we reach Oslo, for when the city streets come into view, she cheerfully asks, "Where should we go first? The folk museum? The Viking Ship Museum is worth visiting, too."

"Let's just go see Munch."

She resets her course right away; it looks like she knows her way around. The gallery, situated on a gently sloping lawn, is a striking structure with a minimalist façade. While M buys tickets, I wait in front of the glass-paneled wall bearing an embossed explanation that the gallery was built with donations from Japan. For the first time since my arrival in the country, I see a crowd, murmuring amongst themselves. Inside, a group of people stands before "Puberty," which I have seen often in reproduction. Exposed to the strangers' eyes, the slender female figure looks anxious. The naked girl is trying to hide her body by draping her long arms over herself. Her arms are too thin to conceal her body's budding sensuality. If she parted her tightly pressed knees a little, the pungent smell of her first period might waft up and she might burst into tears.

M murmurs, "I think it is Munch's self-portrait."

"You think so?"

"I imagine that he wore the same expression, the guy who suffered from depression and was obsessed with death all his life."

Encountering the originals of what I've seen in art books always leaves me with a feeling of betrayal. Standing before *The Mona Lisa* or Millet's *The Gleaners*, I felt that they were smaller in real life, and that the wonder of seeing the originals, not the reproductions, fell far short of my expectations; a dim sense of emptiness would envelope me once my desire to see the originals had been fulfilled. As I experience these familiar emotions again, why do I see P's face?

"What's the difference between a reproduction and an original? Except for the price, of course," I ask, not because I am particularly curious. I have no expertise in, or special affection for, paintings in general.

As she stands blinking, unable to give me a ready answer, I am reminded of the several inches of her bare arms sticking out of her uniform.

Eventually, she ventures, "Layers of brush strokes, like layers of one's heart, can't be captured in a reproduction, however well it is done, I'd say. You can't see shadows in reproductions."

"Oh, I see. But where is *The Scream*?" I look around, searching for it.

"There's a lot of *The Scream*."

That sounds grim. *A lot of* The Scream?

Only when we reach the last exhibition space do I understand what M means. In the room with white-painted walls, which doesn't even have a wooden chair for viewers to rest their feet, is a space reserved for *The Scream*. This is what I remember of the painting: at first, you see the distorted face of a person, whose sexuality is indeterminable, and the fearful eyes, as if meeting death face-on, the round mouth that appears as if it will never shut. The bloody sky is depicted as a swirl, not in colors, just like the sound waves of a scream, and two men in the background are walking leisurely, as if they don't hear a thing. If you look closely, a small boat and a church are floating in the folds of dark blue water.

The room, as big as a large classroom, is filled with different versions of *The Scream*. Monochrome wood-block prints, colored wood-block prints, paintings in slightly different shades of colors, pencil sketches, big screams, unfinished screams, screams in achromatic colors, red screams, black screams, indistinct screams, palm-sized screams, screams that could rupture eardrums . . . For a brief moment, I feel like opening my mouth and blocking my ears, just like the person in the painting. This room seems to be filled with high-pitched screams, too sharp for human ears to catch.

M says, "Sometimes I come here for no reason. I assumed that this guy, Munch, killed himself early in his life after looking at his own paintings, but he lived into his eighties."

"Were you disappointed?"

M smiles faintly. "I'd say I was consoled. Living that long despite the fear of tuberculosis, which was the illness that took his family, the fear of his fanatic father, his constant psychiatric episodes . . . Thinking that the harsh reality anchored him, it comforts me."

Her voice is low and sad. What is it that she wants to say?

She goes on, "A consolation that someone on my behalf, or someone other than me, is screaming in silence."

M, do you really need to be comforted? Your man knows no impossibility in life, you have a house in Onsøy Kårbolig, a virtual paradise, and you live in natural beauty that strikes me as some kind of music. You've accumulated wealth at a young age. What more do you need?

"Which is the real *Scream*?"

M lets out a short laugh. I smile.

"People generally give credit to completed paintings, but there's no fake *Scream* here. I like this particular pencil sketch a lot. That one over there was in our high school textbook, I think." She points to a delicate drawing.

Afterward, she leads me to an outdoor café at the tip of a gulf, its round outline thrusting into the land. After seating me, she brings over some steamed shrimp and two glasses of draft beer. The shrimp is very cold. The midday waves lick the breakwater and seem to hesitate for a beat before ebbing away. A seagull with glistening wings flies over us and tries to get our shrimp.

"I didn't know seagulls were this big."

"That's because you're seeing it close-up."

The shrimps' salty juice seeps into the tiny creases in my hands, stinging them. As the alcohol courses through my body, my heart wavers slightly like the fishing vessels anchored along the breakwater.

I ask M what I couldn't ask P. "Why did a top surgeon switch to immunology so suddenly?"

"Hmmm." M lightly bites her lower lip, looking away to the sea. She shakes her head and says, "I don't know exactly why. I thought he needed something he could throw his entire self into. Shall I put it this way? There were times he wanted to walk, but he was always forced to fly."

That was him all right. So did he find life boring because everything was possible? Did he mean that it was better that Hans Christian Andersen's dream of becoming a singer for the Chinese emperor hadn't come true?

M is not forthcoming.

"So, how's his research coming along?"

M answers reluctantly, "I guess it was a project he chose knowing that it looked impossible to others."

P asked me not to discuss his research with M, but her answer gives me the impression that she isn't completely in the dark.

"Is his research institute located in Oslo?"

Instead of answering, she picks up her purse and springs to her feet. "Looks like we're running late."

After we leave the screening, we find the city in an uproar. We learn that a theft has taken place in the museum we visited earlier. The thieves took *The Scream* and *Madonna* at gunpoint in broad daylight. They quickly removed the paintings and walked out leisurely, leaving behind witnesses, who were literally screaming. Why did they make off with those famous paintings, which they probably couldn't sell? But then again, without desire and stupidity, the world would be like a black-and-white silent movie without a climax.

It is after dinner, but telling time is no easy matter here. As soon as we get on the freeway, M drives as if she's being chased. When she presses the accelerator to the floor of the car, the engine whirs with a sharp metallic buzz.

Tapping the hole-ridden floor with my foot, I ask, "What kind of eccentricity is this? Are you guys nostalgic for poverty?"

"Who would have nostalgia for poverty? He doesn't bring home a penny, pouring everything we have into his research, and there's no knowing when it will be over." M's voice is drowned out by the sharp noise of the engine. "We're in survival mode these days. Not knowing when our savings will run out entirely."

With her sudden revelation, I am rendered speechless and stare at the holes in the floor. M exhales very, very slowly. She seems to be already regretting what she has blurted out.

I say, "That's how it is in big science. A battle against patience and research funding. But an astonishing result will come at some point. I believe he can make it happen."

M and I keep our mouths shut until we reach home.

The windows are brightly lit; P must be back.

The yard that struck me as the pinnacle of desolate beauty has lost its glow overnight. I look with pain at the shrubs surrounding the yard, where dried-up vines are tangled up layer upon layer, left undisturbed for years. This aching isn't for P, but for M. Before getting out of the car, M asks me not to say anything to P during my stay. Even if she hadn't asked, I'd have no reason to meddle in his affairs. When the car door opens, the chill raises goose bumps on my arms. As we enter the house, steam is rising from the electric rice cooker and the spicy tuna stew smells delicious.

"Ah, you cooked dinner!" M's voice is quite bright. This cheeriness sounds like a warning to me: You're an outsider. You will stay briefly and leave, and that's it, don't encroach on our territory.

At any rate, it is easier play-acting peace than unhappiness, for both the actors and the audience.

A fire crackles and dances in the fireplace. It seems unseasonable to have a fire going, but without burning logs, we would be cold. A reddish dancing fire can warm one's heart with its color alone. The room reeks of alcohol; P was probably drinking beer while watching television. As M sets the table, P comes out with a bottle of wine. M shakes her head at him.

P is unfazed by her gesture. He quips, "It won't do not to drink wine when a friend has come to see us from abroad."

During dinner, the wine in M's glass and mine doesn't go down much, but P finishes up the rest of the bottle. He goes out and comes back with beer and whisky.

"Now that we have an audience, let me make a boilermaker. How was the screening?"

M answers on my behalf, "It went well. There were many people in the audience and the organizers were happy about the responses we got."

P asks me as if he hasn't heard her, "Did you like Oslo?"

I down the boilermaker P made. There seems to be no other way out but to drink it up for his sake. Still, I can't compete with him when it comes to speed. I dislike P, who is giving M such a hard time.

"The city wasn't as pretty as the name implied."

"Did you go to the Munch Museum? Two paintings were stolen there, right?"

He must have heard it on the news.

"I'll tell you a secret." P's face is quite serious. "I stole them. Do you think I didn't? When my wife goes there, she gets depressed for three days at least. My pretty wife. That woman who's an angel with no wings. So that's why I stole them. It was no big deal. All I had to do was cut the wires and walk away with them. I can show them to you, if you want."

He is too drunk for me to ask whether he really believes the paintings make his wife depressed. Instead, I say, "Yeah? Let me see them."

I shouldn't have.

P opens his mouth wide, makes his eyes bulge, and covers his ears with his hands. With his neck stretched out as if shouting. Looking at his open mouth, I feel as if a scream that only I can't hear is filling the room. M feigns indifference as she washes the dishes. I feel like tears will spring into my eyes at any minute, just like a small boy who happens to see the backstage of a fascinating play.

"And *Madonna* is my wife. She is. She's exactly the same when she takes off her clothes. When I make her come, that's exactly the expression she wears."

P lies down on the sofa and starts laughing, his eyes closed. M, standing at the sink, hangs her head, with the water still running.

Pointing at the dying fire in the fireplace, P mumbles on. "It gets cold before August is over. Honey, throw in more logs. Soon three-dog nights will arrive. Somewhere in the North Pole, people sleep hugging dogs when it gets terribly cold. If it gets somewhat cold, one dog. If a little colder, two dogs. If very cold, three dogs . . . If it's colder than that, they offer their wife to their guests. You came, and I have nothing to give you. Nothing but my wife. Believe me, she's exactly the same. When she reaches orgasm, she wears the same expression. What I can give . . . is only Madonna."

I bolt up and smack him on the cheek. He stares at me with a perplexed expression, as if he isn't feeling the pain, and I land a punch on his chest. If M didn't let out a low scream, telling me to stop in a teary voice, I would have beat him up until I saw blood.

Your back that beckoned me while you ceaselessly ran on the other side of the river. Gazing at your back, I could give up vacations, spend my youth without once dipping my feet in seawater, and stay up all night energized by a mug of coffee. I readily accepted humility and humiliation as if they were vitamins and willingly swallowed them. My life to date could be a mere shadow of your life. I wanted to catch up with you, I wanted to run by your side, and I wanted to step on you and run ahead of you, if just once.

As if I am the one who's lost everything, and not P, as if he's made everything I've achieved futile, I collapse into my chair like a sand castle that's been trampled upon. "I say, it's true!" His voice is utterly innocent. Slumped on the sofa, making his mouth into a circle, and blocking his ears with his hands, he keeps babbling incoherently.

"She's Madonna. When she opens her eyes, her eyes have a yellowish cast. That woman, she's an angel to me. You can't make love with an angel."

Knocking back the remaining whisky, P stretches out on the sofa. Looking at me, he smiles. That smile: the corners of his eyes crinkle and spider-web wrinkles emanate, as every cell of his seems to smile. I have observed him from up close for many years, but I have never seen him radiating such happiness before.

As I pack, I hear M coming up the stairs. I called a taxi company and they said it would take fifty minutes to get here. Even if P won't remember a thing when he wakes up in the morning, I don't want to see his face again. M opens my door without knocking and comes in. I look out the window, unable to face her.

She says, "I'm sorry. He, he started drinking at some point. At the prime of his life. Why he started drinking, he doesn't know and I don't know . . . Later, he'd go into the operating theater under the influence. He operated on patients when he was unfit to even drive a car. Still, he never had a malpractice incident. But what he was doing couldn't be tolerated. At first, the hospital ignored it. Because the patients asked for him. In the end, instead of firing him, they sent him to the pathology department. He drank constantly but published outstanding papers. Whenever his hands started trembling, his assistant would pour whisky in a paper cup and give it to him. Right before he was fired, he handed in a resignation letter. I thought he was telling me the truth when he said he was going to join François Jacob's research institute. Only when we arrived here did I learn that it wasn't true. He claimed that he would do it on his own and when research results came out, they would come begging at his door and plead with him to join them. He opened a private research center, but it was too expensive for an individual to set up and manage. Some capable researchers joined him. In the beginning. But they quit one after another. Funding was a problem but I guess the bigger reason was their doubt of the research results. We poured everything we had into it. It looked like he was faced with an inevitable downfall, but he kept up the big talk. Now, he . . . he isn't doing anything. I take away bottles and he hides them and drinks behind my back. That's our project these days."

"Alcoholism is a disease. Why don't you get him treated?"

M shakes her head. "You know him. Who can control him? Yesterday, he bought liquor when he was driving you here, right? Last night when he fell asleep, I ransacked the house like a crazy woman. I couldn't find them, wherever he hid them. He's hiding the bottles and I'm finding and pouring out liquor. This is a battle that began in the States. When he was working at the hospital, he wore a custom-made jacket, carrying portable bottles in the pockets on either side. He buys liquor behind my back, buries bottles here and there in the yard, and drinks from them with a straw. In places where I would never find them. When I steal a look behind the curtains and see him lying flat on the ground like a dog, his face buried in the dirt sucking on liquor, I freak out.

It's worse than if he were cheating on me or if he loved another woman. He is no longer apologetic and he doesn't feel the guilt."

Standing by her side, I sense that M is quietly weeping.

She goes on. "When I can't stand it any longer, I drive out to the room with *The Scream*, and stand there for a while. Where can I cry here, and in whose presence? I bottle it up and I always cry in the car on the way home. Crying my heart out, but braking at every red light. Tears gather on my chin and drop onto my lap and it gets soaked with warm tears, but I carefully look left and then right to make sure that no one is crossing the street, just like that. Trying not to die, just like that, I drive down that road to go home."

I put my hand on M's wrist. Her arms no longer suffocate me, and they no longer glow. Those arms she would lift to block her ears from the scream bursting out of her mouth. The never-darkening evening hours are surreal, like a space where time does not exist. It has only been two days, but I already miss the darkness. The sky doesn't turn dark red or swirl around; it's just pale, like the complexion of a Scandinavian girl without makeup.

"What made P an alcoholic? He doesn't lack anything."

M shakes her head. If a person could pinpoint a reason for his drinking, he wouldn't become an addict.

M's voice sounds as if it's coming from underwater. "You don't realize how beautiful night is, do you? During white nights, you can't sleep if you don't keep your shutters closed. If there's no night, if you work without sleeping, you'd think you'd be incredibly successful, but it doesn't work that way. To him, his life seemed like an endless white night. He must have chosen memories and desires because he knows all too well that they're in the realm of God. I think he wants to search for his shadow."

A taxi comes into sight, with the headlights on, along the path between the wheat fields. M tells me over and over that she'll drive me to Oslo if I really have to go, but I can no longer put up with her voice, which is straining with the effort not to reveal a smidgen of sorrow.

"I'm sorry. I thought I could keep it from you for three days." M smiles faintly as she shuts the taxi door for me. Her dark eyes are disoriented, like someone who has lost her way in broad daylight.

I know that I will never see M again. Hotel Oslo Plaza, I call out my destination, and burrow myself deep into the seat. I don't look back. If I caught sight of M, standing as if she would seep into the indistinctness of a white night in the desolate yard, I might do something that I won't be able to handle later. I don't look back, confining under my eyelids the desire to see a small, yellow moon on her disoriented eyeballs, the desire to take off her clothes in search of Madonna.

The car makes its way toward the road's vanishing point, as if searching for the night that has disappeared.

I fall asleep at dawn and wake up around eleven. I go down to the restaurant to have breakfast.

The lecture at the University of Oslo will conclude my official program for this trip. I have prepared an English text, so all I have to do is read it. I have practiced reading it at least a hundred times. Whenever I practiced, the imaginary audience in front of me consisted of only one person—P. So today, I will be reading it to an empty auditorium. I am going to use an interpreter for the Q&A session, so I am not stressed about my delivery.

I leave the hotel, hail a cab, and direct the driver to take me to the Munch Museum. The driver says that there was a theft yesterday and that I won't be able to see two important paintings. He seems to be asking me whether I still want to go. I don't tell him that I will check on their absence. I imagined that surveillance would be tight around the museum but unexpectedly nothing much has changed. As I enter the building, I notice that it is teeming with people, so navigating through them is no easy feat.

Most spectators are standing on the other side of the cordons, staring at the empty spaces on the wall where the paintings used to hang. I, too, stand among them and gaze at the empty spots for a long time.

The empty wall silently swallows the numerous faces in front of it, just like a rusty bronze mirror.

During the lecture, the students are serious in their attitude and questions. They are fired up but I am cold. Answering their questions, I find myself gradually sinking into a feeling that I find unbearable.

It's a skeletal movie, whose bones you can see through. Obvious and kind. Fascination comes from the flesh, not from the skeleton. The flesh that can't be captured by X-rays. Make a film no one can analyze. If you try to explain, the light disappears. Don't misjudge yourself, thinking that you're a step above Emir Kusturika, and that other people don't get it. Or, that what you've made is another masterpiece like Silence of the Lambs, *but that other people don't understand it.*

The words P babbled in his drunken state stick densely to my film, just like Spanish Needles.

Only when I am done with the final question do the tension and fatigue of the week wash over me. As I return to the hotel, rashes begin to sprout on my tongue and a headache assaults me. I want to have a good long rest. After packing, I think of going down to the bar for a drink, but instead take a melatonin pill and go to bed. I am dead tired but sleep is elusive. The drug kicks into effect only an hour or so later.

The telephone rings, cutting through a dreamless sleep. When I pick it up, someone says my name in clear English. My name pronounced by a stranger's voice sounds like three staccato cries. The call is from the bar. "The bar will be closed soon, and your friend is looking for you. He hasn't brought his credit card and he says you will take care of his check." Then he enunciates P's name just like three staccato shrieks.

"I don't know him."

The bartender says that he is a Korean like me and that he is very drunk.

"I don't know him. Please don't wake me up again."

My voice is deliberate and cold. Reluctant to deny him the third time before morning comes, I put the receiver down on the night table. I decide to wipe the three days in Norway from my life.

I shouldn't have come to Oslo. P was a beacon inside me. I know that if he disappears, I will die as an indistinct form, just like the shadow of a fire. I said I didn't know P because I didn't want to lose him.

Sleep has fled to the other side of the universe. I get up and fling open the shutters. The trees outside have no shadows, just like the spirits of dead people. The night doesn't grow dark. I, too, am afraid of that clear night. O white night, be divided! Something, not sorrow, not deep regret, turns into water and floods my eyes. Only then does the night begin to twist in waves and swirl around. The white swath of the night is split vertically, and between the cracks, a wet, dark reddish mass gushes out ceaselessly. Blocking my ears with my palms to prevent my voice from reaching me, I mumble:

It has been a long time since I last saw P.

JUNG MI-KYUNG is one of the most distinguished writers of modern Korean literature. She attended Ewha Womans University, and was the recipient of the prestigious Yi Sang Literary Award in 2006. She is the author of the novel *The Strange Sorrow of Wonderland*.

YU YOUNG-NAN lives in Seoul. She has translated numerous Korean novels into English, including Park Wan-suh's *Who Ate Up All the Shinga?* and Yom Sang-seop's *Three Generations*.

The Library of Korean Literature

The Library of Korean Literature, published by Dalkey Archive Press in collaboration with the Literature Translation Institute of Korea, presents modern classics of Korean literature in translation, featuring the best Korean authors from the late modern period through to the present day. The Library aims to introduce the intellectual and aesthetic diversity of contemporary Korean writing to English-language readers. The Library of Korean Literature is unprecedented in its scope, with Dalkey Archive Press publishing 25 Korean novels and short story collections in a single year.

The series is published in cooperation with the Literature Translation Institute of Korea, a center that promotes the cultural translation and worldwide dissemination of Korean language and culture.

MICHAL AJVAZ, *The Golden Age.*
  The Other City.
PIERRE ALBERT-BIROT, *Grabinoulor.*
YUZ ALESHKOVSKY, *Kangaroo.*
FELIPE ALFAU, *Chromos.*
  Locos.
IVAN ÂNGELO, *The Celebration.*
  The Tower of Glass.
ANTÓNIO LOBO ANTUNES, *Knowledge of*
  Hell.
  The Splendor of Portugal.
ALAIN ARIAS-MISSON, *Theatre of Incest.*
JOHN ASHBERY AND JAMES SCHUYLER,
  A Nest of Ninnies.
ROBERT ASHLEY, *Perfect Lives.*
GABRIELA AVIGUR-ROTEM, *Heatwave*
  and Crazy Birds.
DJUNA BARNES, *Ladies Almanack.*
  Ryder.
JOHN BARTH, *LETTERS.*
  Sabbatical.
DONALD BARTHELME, *The King.*
  Paradise.
SVETISLAV BASARA, *Chinese Letter.*
MIQUEL BAUÇÀ, *The Siege in the Room.*
RENÉ BELLETTO, *Dying.*
MAREK BIEŃCZYK, *Transparency.*
ANDREI BITOV, *Pushkin House.*
ANDREJ BLATNIK, *You Do Understand.*
LOUIS PAUL BOON, *Chapel Road.*
  My Little War.
  Summer in Termuren.
ROGER BOYLAN, *Killoyle.*
IGNÁCIO DE LOYOLA BRANDÃO,
  Anonymous Celebrity.
  Zero.
BONNIE BREMSER, *Troia: Mexican Memoirs.*
CHRISTINE BROOKE-ROSE, *Amalgamemnon.*
BRIGID BROPHY, *In Transit.*
GERALD L. BRUNS, *Modern Poetry and*
  the Idea of Language.
GABRIELLE BURTON, *Heartbreak Hotel.*
MICHEL BUTOR, *Degrees.*
  Mobile.
G. CABRERA INFANTE, *Infante's Inferno.*
  Three Trapped Tigers.
JULIETA CAMPOS,
  The Fear of Losing Eurydice.
ANNE CARSON, *Eros the Bittersweet.*
ORLY CASTEL-BLOOM, *Dolly City.*
LOUIS-FERDINAND CÉLINE, *Castle to Castle.*
  Conversations with Professor Y.
  London Bridge.
  Normance.
  North.
  Rigadoon.
MARIE CHAIX, *The Laurels of Lake*
  Constance.
HUGO CHARTERIS, *The Tide Is Right.*
ERIC CHEVILLARD, *Demolishing Nisard.*

MARC CHOLODENKO, *Mordechai Schamz.*
JOSHUA COHEN, *Witz.*
EMILY HOLMES COLEMAN, *The Shutter*
  of Snow.
ROBERT COOVER, *A Night at the Movies.*
STANLEY CRAWFORD, *Log of the S.S. The*
  Mrs Unguentine.
  Some Instructions to My Wife.
RENÉ CREVEL, *Putting My Foot in It.*
RALPH CUSACK, *Cadenza.*
NICHOLAS DELBANCO, *The Count of*
  Concord.
  Sherbrookes.
NIGEL DENNIS, *Cards of Identity.*
PETER DIMOCK, *A Short Rhetoric for*
  Leaving the Family.
ARIEL DORFMAN, *Konfidenz.*
COLEMAN DOWELL,
  Island People.
  Too Much Flesh and Jabez.
ARKADII DRAGOMOSHCHENKO, *Dust.*
RIKKI DUCORNET, *The Complete*
  Butcher's Tales.
  The Fountains of Neptune.
  The Jade Cabinet.
  Phosphor in Dreamland.
WILLIAM EASTLAKE, *The Bamboo Bed.*
  Castle Keep.
  Lyric of the Circle Heart.
JEAN ECHENOZ, *Chopin's Move.*
STANLEY ELKIN, *A Bad Man.*
  Criers and Kibitzers, Kibitzers
  and Criers.
  The Dick Gibson Show.
  The Franchiser.
  The Living End.
  Mrs. Ted Bliss.
FRANÇOIS EMMANUEL, *Invitation to a*
  Voyage.
SALVADOR ESPRIU, *Ariadne in the*
  Grotesque Labyrinth.
LESLIE A. FIEDLER, *Love and Death in*
  the American Novel.
JUAN FILLOY, *Op Oloop.*
ANDY FITCH, *Pop Poetics.*
GUSTAVE FLAUBERT, *Bouvard and Pécuchet.*
KASS FLEISHER, *Talking out of School.*
FORD MADOX FORD,
  The March of Literature.
JON FOSSE, *Aliss at the Fire.*
  Melancholy.
MAX FRISCH, *I'm Not Stiller.*
  Man in the Holocene.
CARLOS FUENTES, *Christopher Unborn.*
  Distant Relations.
  Terra Nostra.
  Where the Air Is Clear.
TAKEHIKO FUKUNAGA, *Flowers of Grass.*
WILLIAM GADDIS, *J R.*
  The Recognitions.

JOSEPH MCELROY,
  Night Soul and Other Stories.
ABDELWAHAB MEDDEB, *Talismano.*
GERHARD MEIER, *Isle of the Dead.*
HERMAN MELVILLE, *The Confidence-Man.*
AMANDA MICHALOPOULOU, *I'd Like.*
STEVEN MILLHAUSER, *The Barnum Museum.*
  In the Penny Arcade.
RALPH J. MILLS, JR., *Essays on Poetry.*
MOMUS, *The Book of Jokes.*
CHRISTINE MONTALBETTI, *The Origin of Man.*
  Western.
OLIVE MOORE, *Spleen.*
NICHOLAS MOSLEY, *Accident.*
  Assassins.
  Catastrophe Practice.
  Experience and Religion.
  A Garden of Trees.
  Hopeful Monsters.
  Imago Bird.
  Impossible Object.
  Inventing God.
  Judith.
  Look at the Dark.
  Natalie Natalia.
  Serpent.
  Time at War.
WARREN MOTTE,
  *Fables of the Novel: French Fiction
    since 1990.*
  *Fiction Now: The French Novel in
    the 21st Century.*
  *Oulipo: A Primer of Potential
    Literature.*
GERALD MURNANE, *Barley Patch.*
  Inland.
YVES NAVARRE, *Our Share of Time.*
  Sweet Tooth.
DOROTHY NELSON, *In Night's City.*
  Tar and Feathers.
ESHKOL NEVO, *Homesick.*
WILFRIDO D. NOLLEDO, *But for the Lovers.*
FLANN O'BRIEN, *At Swim-Two-Birds.*
  The Best of Myles.
  The Dalkey Archive.
  The Hard Life.
  The Poor Mouth.
  The Third Policeman.
CLAUDE OLLIER, *The Mise-en-Scène.*
  Wert and the Life Without End.
GIOVANNI ORELLI, *Walaschek's Dream.*
PATRIK OUŘEDNÍK, *Europeana.*
  The Opportune Moment, 1855.
BORIS PAHOR, *Necropolis.*
FERNANDO DEL PASO, *News from the
    Empire.*
  Palinuro of Mexico.
ROBERT PINGET, *The Inquisitory.*
  Mahu or The Material.
  Trio.
MANUEL PUIG, *Betrayed by Rita Hayworth.*

The Buenos Aires Affair.
Heartbreak Tango.
RAYMOND QUENEAU, *The Last Days.*
  Odile.
  Pierrot Mon Ami.
  Saint Glinglin.
ANN QUIN, *Berg.*
  Passages.
  Three.
  Tripticks.
ISHMAEL REED, *The Free-Lance Pallbearers.*
  The Last Days of Louisiana Red.
  Ishmael Reed: The Plays.
  Juice!
  Reckless Eyeballing.
  The Terrible Threes.
  The Terrible Twos.
  Yellow Back Radio Broke-Down.
JASIA REICHARDT, *15 Journeys Warsaw
    to London.*
NOËLLE REVAZ, *With the Animals.*
JOÃO UBALDO RIBEIRO, *House of the
    Fortunate Buddhas.*
JEAN RICARDOU, *Place Names.*
RAINER MARIA RILKE, *The Notebooks of
    Malte Laurids Brigge.*
JULIÁN RÍOS, *The House of Ulysses.*
  Larva: A Midsummer Night's Babel.
  Poundemonium.
  Procession of Shadows.
AUGUSTO ROA BASTOS, *I the Supreme.*
DANIËL ROBBERECHTS, *Arriving in Avignon.*
JEAN ROLIN, *The Explosion of the
    Radiator Hose.*
OLIVIER ROLIN, *Hotel Crystal.*
ALIX CLEO ROUBAUD, *Alix's Journal.*
JACQUES ROUBAUD, *The Form of a
    City Changes Faster, Alas, Than
    the Human Heart.*
  The Great Fire of London.
  Hortense in Exile.
  Hortense Is Abducted.
  The Loop.
  Mathematics:
  The Plurality of Worlds of Lewis.
  The Princess Hoppy.
  Some Thing Black.
RAYMOND ROUSSEL, *Impressions of Africa.*
VEDRANA RUDAN, *Night.*
STIG SÆTERBAKKEN, *Siamese.*
  Self Control.
LYDIE SALVAYRE, *The Company of Ghosts.*
  The Lecture.
  The Power of Flies.
LUIS RAFAEL SÁNCHEZ,
  Macho Camacho's Beat.
SEVERO SARDUY, *Cobra & Maitreya.*
NATHALIE SARRAUTE,
  Do You Hear Them?
  Martereau.
  The Planetarium.

FOR A FULL LIST OF PUBLICATIONS, VISIT:
www.dalkeyarchive.com